ADVANCE PRAISE FOR STUMBLING TOWARD GRACE

These stories are like a diamond, and Scalia's prose is a fine cut. Her debut sparkles with the energy of its characters -- all of them radiate their hopes, their tragedies, their humanity on the page. Reading this collection is like being given a close, multi-faceted look right into the heart of a city and its people."

— Susan Muaddi Darraj

Rosalia Scalia is Baltimore's Flannery O'Connor. She inhabits her disparate characters, warts and all. Not an easy task considering the bigots, religious fanatics, hoarders, alcoholics, drug users, and damaged lives presented here. And yet, like the fictional Father Brown, she refrains from judgments, allowing each a generous shot at redemption.

—Richard Peabody,
editor/publisher, *Gargoyle Magazine*

D1490474

STUMBLING TOWARD GRACE

To Callie
All the best!

Rosalia Scalia

ROSALIA SCALIA

For information contact:

Unsolicited Press

Portland, Oregon

www.unsolicitedpress.com

orders@unsolicitedpress.com

619-354-8005

Cover Design: Kathryn Gerhardt

Editor: Analieze Cervantes; Robin Ann Lee

ISBN: 978-1-950730-82-7

For my parents, the late Joseph A, and Philomena Scalia

And for Richard, Erin, and Antoinette, their partners and children

ACKNOWLEDGMENTS

Amarillo Bay – "Stumbling Toward Grace"

Taproot Literary Review – "Picking *Cicoria*"

Portland Review – "The One Who's Left"

Loch Raven Review – "In a Starry Night"

Notre Dame Review –"Hiding in Boxes"

South Asian Ensemble – "Nine Twelve: We Love America"

Quercus Review – "Saved"

Willow Review – "You'll Do Fine"

Pebble Lake Review and *City Sages Baltimore* – "Sister Rafaele Heals the Sick"

Pennsylvania English – "Unchartered Steps"

Ragazine and *Baltimore City Paper Fiction/Poetry* edition – "Mother's Dresser"

Spout Magazine – "On Becoming a Professional Pet Hair   Stylist"

Epiphany – "A Lesson in Colors Parts 1 & 2"

Talking River – "Fingerprints on the Flowers"

Mad River Review – "Lazarus Died Twice"

TABLE OF CONTENTS

STUMBLING TOWARD GRACE

IT WAS DURING a particularly nasty ice storm in the winter of 2009 that brought Baltimore to a standstill when Adolph Ott realized, at age eighty-seven, that he missed his daughter, Polly, more deeply than he wanted to admit to anyone. For a brief moment as he trudged through the snow and sleet, walking in the tracks left by the salt trucks, he imagined her walking with him, steadying him under his elbow so he wouldn't fall. She visited him on Sundays with her family. Then remembering her family and considering what they must look like, he shook the image from his mind. He'd never been the kind of man who leaned on a woman, no matter the circumstance, and Polly had made her choice. She'd married that Black man against his wishes, without his approval or blessing.

Not wanting to fall, Adolph trod carefully, avoiding shiny surfaces that could be ice. Walking the six blocks to the church took longer than usual in the snow, even with his rubber skidded boots, but he slowly moved forward, leaning on the sides of parked cars to steady himself. The snow's coldness bit through his gloves, and his fingers felt numb. The effort winded him. He avoided sidewalks that his neighbors had not yet cleared, and although Father Mark assured him that the furnace would be fine and urged him to stay home until things melted more, Adolph knew the furnace needed him. He considered it his furnace, and he took pride in keeping it as fine-tuned as a Stradivarius. For twenty-two years, ever since he retired, he maintained the church's heating and air-conditioning systems. Thanks to his precision and keen dedication to detail, St. Elizabeth's Church hadn't experienced a day without either heat or air-conditioning.

Two blocks from his Monteford Avenue house and three blocks from the church, he heard a gang of children. They shouted and squealed with laughter. Their voices were strong and vibrant, echoing along the narrow streets and breaking the silence imposed by the storm. Then he spotted them bundled in bright jackets, hats, and gloves. Carrying shovels, brooms, and pickaxes, while pulling a large bag of salt in a wooden wagon, seven or eight kids knocked on every door along Monteford, asking residents if they wanted their sidewalks cleared for a price. Enterprising bunch! With their faces obscured by colorful scarves and hats, the kids appeared giddy from the snow day.

When he noticed they were black, his mood soured. Probably cruising houses to rob them later! "Go on back home!" he shouted at them. "Nobody wants you here!"

They faced him. Their smiles were gone from their faces.

"Go on! Go back home! Nobody wants you here!" he repeated.

"Speak for yourself, old man!" a gravelly voice shouted at him from behind one of the storm doors. Adolph knew it belonged to Mookie, a jigaboo-loving troll if he ever knew one.

"You'd know these neighborhood kids if you weren't so damn cantankerous and ornery all the time."

"If you get robbed, you'll know why. Don't say I didn't warn you!" he yelled back.

The kids stared at him. The whites of their eyes matched the icy snow covering the streets. "We want to know if you want your sidewalk cleared," said the oldest-looking child, who couldn't be more than ten. "We're providing a service," one of the bigger ones said. He flashed Adolph a wide gap-toothed smile; his teeth were larger than this face.

"Spit in the air, and it falls in your eyes, Adolph," Mookie shouted while she handed them each a dollar. "When you all finish clearing my sidewalk and steps, I'll double that," she told the kids. "Now, how many are you? Seven? You all like hot chocolate? When you're all done, come on in for hot chocolate."

The kids shouted at once, a cacophony singing, "Hot chocolate! Hot chocolate!"

Annoyed, Adolph stopped and watched Mookie with the little jigaboos. One or two of them were already working to clear the icy snow with a pick. A few others smiled; their white teeth shined like high beams.

"You all be careful, now," she said, smiling back at them like an idiot.

Her stupidity infuriated him. What did she know anyway? Nothing but a bar-owning woman her whole life, used to interacting with riffraff. He thrust his foot forward into the icy snow and moved on, step by careful step. He hoped that Mookie's foolishness would come back to haunt her just so he could say, "I told you so." He shook his head. "Mookie, you're a damn fool!" he shouted.

"Maybe so, Adolph, but you ain't exactly bucking for sainthood, no matter how much time you spend up at the church," Mookie called back. "Maybe these could be your grands for all you know." She laughed as she closed her door.

Adolph paused, looked closely at the children. He examined their faces for a family resemblance and decided that Mookie enjoyed tormenting him. As if he didn't already struggle with enough torment.

But Mookie invoked Polly and her family, something he didn't consider a coincidence, and it forced him to wonder about Polly's kids as he walked on toward the church. What were they like? He couldn't help being curious.

In the belly of the church's basement, in the stifling heat behind the giant furnace, exhaustion plagued him, frustrated him, and defeated him like prey. With his shirtsleeves rolled halfway up his arms, he sat on the metal chair that he had kept for himself and rested.

He hated the fatigue. For fifteen years, he'd secretly battled a disease that did not exist when he was young, a disease with its funny, ironic name—HIV/AIDS—which came from a streetwalker named

KandyKane. He'd visited her regularly for more than a year, when he was seventy-five, until she no longer appeared on Lexington Street. Was the virus she gave him a punishment or a penance? He couldn't decide, but he'd first sought KandyKane's young, taut body and supple skin in a fit of loneliness and lust. He'd liked her youthful beauty and liked her doing things to him that neither Estelle, his wife, nor Rose, his girlfriend after Estelle had died, would dream of doing to his body in exchange for a clutchful of bills, no questions asked.

"You sure KandyKane was a woman?" Doc Palmer had asked, holding the paper with the positive test results.

"What? 'Course she was a woman!" Adolph, shocked and embarrassed, had shouted. "I ain't a fairy!" Adolph had trembled, and the question had caused him to doubt himself. Only a fool couldn't tell the difference between a man and a woman.

In the furnace room, determined to air the pipes, Adolph pushed himself off the chair and leaned against the cold, brick wall, mustering the energy to drag the large, gray toolbox closer to him. He managed to pull the box a few steps and then, overwhelmed by the effort, decided to simply grab the tools he needed. He got a screwdriver and a can of lubricant, and then found the pressure gauges on the pipes to release any air. He removed the large, green manifold and began lubricating the motor and belts. He'd done it thousands of times; the task was second nature.

His mind wandered to Estelle. It disturbed him that he had trouble picturing her face now. He saw her dimpled smile, her large, black eyes, and her nose but never together, and he feared he was forgetting what his wife had looked like. He had no problem visualizing Rose's face— whom he'd liked but not loved the way he'd loved Estelle—and he missed the things KandyKane had done to him. Rose, her husband Henry, Estelle, and Adolph had circulated together before they all died one by one. After Henry and Estelle died, he and Rose took up together, but then she joined others, leaving him behind and off balance.

Adolph attempted to balance the heating system before checking the pilot light, which was not burning a full two inches. He preferred it to be two inches exactly. On his knees, he tightened the thermocouple nut and then turned the gas valve slightly to adjust the flame. He stood and reached for the access panel leaning against the brick wall. Fighting fatigue and dizziness, he pulled the large, metal panel toward him. He lifted it as he'd done many times before, but this time it slipped from his fingers and landed on his foot. Pain radiated from his foot, outward like ripples in a pond, extending up his calves and into his thighs. The pain robbed him of his breath.

"JesusChristAlmightyGoddamn it to Hell," he cursed, letting go of the panel, which fell to the floor with a clang. He staggered to the chair. His left foot throbbed; his head ached. There, alone in the heart of the church basement, he wept, stifling his sobs in the crook of his arm. He rubbed his foot, knowing not to remove his shoe, which would speed the process if it was going to swell. He worried about the injury, its impact on his body, knowing it would usher in a boatload of difficulties because of the virus.

The virus had slowly sucked life out of him. He swallowed what Doc Palmer called his "drug cocktail"—a handful of red and white pills—daily without fail to keep him healthy enough. If it wasn't the virus, something else would kill him. Adolph, ready to die, refused to fear it, refused to pretend it wouldn't happen to him like so many of his friends at the St. Elizabeth Senior Center. He'd survived the Second World War, all kinds of mishaps at the steel plant, and at construction sites, where his coworkers had teased him about having a lucky horseshoe up his ass. He'd outlived Estelle, who died when they were both seventy-one, after nearly fifty years together, and they both had outlived their son, a twenty-year-old boy stolen from them by Vietnam and bad politics. Greg's memorial army picture still hung on his living room wall, a reminder of his and Estelle's sacrifice, which was a piss-poor substitute for the living and breathing son they'd entrusted to the army against their wishes. Damned war draft lottery.

Despite that, Adolph kept the news about the virus to himself. It wasn't anyone's business anyway. And now, insulated from the icy cold of the storm in the hot belly of a church, he wiped his face on his shirtsleeves, wondering if those poor saps from work would still envy the so-called horseshoe up his ass. Pain pulsated in his left foot. Grateful he was alone in the church basement, he pushed himself off the chair, limped toward the access panel, and slipped it easily into place. If only people fit together so well. After thirty years of silence between them, he would telephone Polly. Soon, to set things right before he ran out of time.

He grabbed his coat and boots from the hooks behind the furnace room door and limped up the stairs to the church. His left foot dragged a little.

Adolph didn't pray. Keeping the church comfortable for everyone in it was his prayer. He nodded at the altar, as he always did, because that was what he was taught to do. He sat on the last bench and pulled on his boots. The constriction of the boot hurt his left foot. He sucked in his breath but put on his coat, scarf, and gloves for the walk home.

Keeping in the grooves carved into the snow by traffic, he limped homeward, each step stinging. The pain in his left foot forced him to stop every ten steps, and he leaned against snow covered parked cars. A red pickup truck with a snowplow attached to the front slowed near him.

"Hey, Grandpa, you okay?" the driver asked through the window.

Adolph sucked in his breath before turning to see the driver, a young Black man wearing a navy-blue hat, a bright yellow scarf, and a blue, nylon snow jacket. He nodded but didn't speak.

"You don't look okay. How far you going?" The man stepped out of his truck and placed his hands under Adolph's elbow to hold him steady, the same position he had imagined his daughter doing. "Let me drive you home."

"That's okay. I'm fine," he managed to croak.

"You don't look fine to me, Pops. You look like you're in a world of hurt."

Adolph waved the man away and stepped forward with his right foot, slightly dragging the left one. It'd be a rainy day in hell before he'd accept help from a jig-a-boo.

The driver watched him take four painful steps without holding his elbow, and Adolph nearly slipped into the street. The man caught him before he fell.

"I may not be the sharpest tool in the shed, but it don't take no mental giant to see you're having trouble, Gramps." The man held up his palm to Adolph. "Let me help you, man. It's dangerous for you to be dragging along through the snow in the middle of the street."

Adolph allowed the man to guide him into the pickup. Inside the warm cab, he leaned down to rub his foot, which felt swollen.

"Where to?" the man asked.

"Montford near Fairpark," Adolph said. "Three blocks north."

The man nodded. "So, what you are doing outside in the snow?"

"Went to check on the church furnace," Adolph said. "What are you doing outside in the snow?"

"Four-wheel drive and a snowplow. Made for snow. Actually, I got to pick up some nurses near here and drive them over to the hospital on Greene Street. I'm Marvin," he said, stretching out his hand to shake.

Adolph ignored the man's hand. His left foot still throbbed in his boot. "Thank you for the ride," he said.

"You alone?" Marvin asked.

Adolph raised his eyebrow but didn't answer because he feared Marvin would come back and rob him if he knew he lived alone.

Marvin handed him a card. "In case you need something. My wife's aunt lives up near here. We can check in when we're in the area."

Adolph looked at the card with the university logo which read, "Marvin Gainer, Development Officer." "What the hell is a Development Officer?"

"A fancy-pants word for fundraiser," Marvin said. "The office is closed because of the snow, so I'm helping transport the clinical staff. They don't get off work like us office jockeys."

Adolph's face flushed with gratitude for the ride. His foot definitely ached, but it ached less when he kept his weight off it. Somebody who raised money for a university wouldn't seem like the kind of guy who'd rob him. It would have taken him hours to reach home had Marvin not insisted. He slipped the card into his pocket. Marvin crossed Fairpark and continued up Montford.

"Right here's fine," he said when Marvin reached the middle of the block. He unbuckled his seat belt and unlocked the door, but to his astonishment, Marvin threw the gear in park, flicked on the blinkers, and made his way around the truck to the passenger side. He helped Adolph climb out of the truck, steadied him as he limped toward the curb, helped him up, and held onto him tightly when he reached the top of his stoop.

"You okay by yourself now?" he asked and flashed a smile. "If you decide you need a ride to Greene Street to get that foot looked at, give me a holler. And try not to get out too much in this weather," he said as he rushed back toward his truck.

Adolph knew he'd never have helped Marvin if the situation had been reversed. He'd have driven by without a thought.

Before Adolph fished his keys from his coat pocket, Marvin had already shut his driver's-side door and pulled forward. Adolph couldn't wait to take the boot off his throbbing foot, but he stood on the stoop's top step, watching the red taillights of Marvin's truck until they disappeared around the corner.

* * *

In Adolph's living room, the television's blaring voices and loud commercials collided with the radio he kept on in the kitchen. The noise gave him a small comfort against the haunting echoes, muffling them. He heard the *ticktock* of the grandfather clock, chronicling the slow passage of time and keeping rhythm like a metronome. Its reverberation vaulting everywhere in the house as if it was stalking him, along with all the other sounds that haunted him. His own footsteps echoed, following him from the living room and into the kitchen, the slap of his slippers against his feet. His left foot, colored purple by the giant bruise across his instep, had swollen, and he knew that he'd better get to a doctor sooner rather than later. He made a mental note to call Doc Palmer. In the meantime, he'd ice it, so he emptied an ice tray into a plastic bag and sat on the sofa with his foot raised, the makeshift ice pack atop his instep.

He cleared his throat; every noise multiplied and amplified, creating a din that enveloped him. It made the house feel larger and emptier than it ever had been. The ice bag chilled his foot and his leg, and he wondered if he should call Doc Palmer for an appointment.

Too antsy to continue sitting, he heaved himself off the sofa and toddled to the kitchen. He set the newspaper down on the kitchen chair, the rustling sound crackled, and he said, "Hello, hello" to test the echo. Sure enough, the sound of his own feeble voice pinged, jumped off the walls, and ponged into his ears as if pealing his solitude. He fixed himself a grilled cheese sandwich. Afterward, he set the pan and the spatula in the sink. Without a plate or a napkin, he shuffled back to the living room, dragging his left foot a bit, which failed to stop the sound of his flapping slippers echoing behind him.

He remembered when he and Estelle had to run Polly over to the university hospital, when she was four years old, after she'd fallen down the stairs and cracked her head open at the bottom of it. Her curly, black hair streaked red with blood and the subsequent need for eight stitches. Adolph sank into the sofa, raised his leg onto the cocktail table again, replaced the ice pack, and ate his sandwich in front of the blaring television, careful not to drop any crumbs on his clothes or the furniture.

He racked his brain over what he could possibly say when he called Polly, but he couldn't think of a single thing. "What the hell do you know?" he shouted at the blaring TV, hurling his slipper at the screen. It fell to the floor with a thud, adding yet another clatter to the haunting echoes.

Later, Adolph returned to the kitchen to rifle through the shelf where Estelle had kept her personal phone book. He'd kept it all these years, kept everything the same, though he never looked inside her book. Flipping through the pages, he reveled at the sight of Estelle's handwriting. He'd forgotten her loopy numbers, her Catholic school penmanship, and her neat cursive. He perused the list, names of many people now dead—next to their telephone numbers, the fours and fives with loops, the sevens with slashes through their stems. He'd forgotten them too until he saw their names in her book. He touched the names, but he longed to touch Estelle again. He searched under "P" for Polly but didn't find anything. He searched under "D" for daughter and "C" for child as he struggled to remember Polly's married name. He must have blocked it from his memory; the thought of her married to that Black man still sickened him.

Both legs hurt from standing, and his foot continued to smart. He tucked the book into his waistband, held onto the shelf briefly to steady himself, and slowly stepped toward the kitchen table, where he sank into the nearest chair. Determined to find Polly's number, he sat at the table and examined each page, beginning with A and ending with Z without success. "Damn it, Estelle!" he said aloud. He flipped the back cover up and down, struggling to recall Polly's married name. It simply escaped him. He set the book upright and knocked it down, irritated that Estelle must have hidden her number elsewhere. Then he noticed a set of curious entries on the second to last page, written sideways near the book's spine in the tiniest letters. POH and two numbers. Underneath came EMH, followed by a number, and then POHW and

KHW, also with numbers. Who or what the hell is POH, he wondered, and EHM?

He started from the bottom with KHW and dialed, letting the extra long phone cord lies across the table. A woman's voice said, "Henderson and McCready Law Offices."

"Wrong number," Adolph said and hung up. Was Estelle trying to divorce him before she died? Why had she written the phone number to a law office in a hidden place? He pushed the button to get the dial tone and tried a second number, the one listed next to POHW.

"M. Henderson, here," a woman said.

Too surprised to speak, he grunted. Polly's unmistakable voice, sounding eerily like Estelle's, caressed his ear. It must have been a private line. Just after Estelle's funeral, when he had been furious and searched everywhere for evidence that Estelle had kept in touch with Polly and her family, he couldn't find a shred of it. He hadn't thought to look at the second to last page under notes in Estelle's phone book, a reminder of her stubbornness and wiliness. It was now something for which he was grateful for. Silence dominated the phone line, but Polly, again another surprise, kept the line open, and Adolph listened to her breathe.

"I know it's you, Dad. Caller ID," she said softly, almost a whisper.

His heart pounded. He hadn't thought about what he wanted to say. He hadn't considered Caller ID either. He didn't have it on his phone. He imagined her as a little girl with her hair in thick, onyx-colored sausage curls. Her head had been bent to the right; the knees of her pants were torn like that of a little boy, beaming a facsimile of Estelle's dimpled smile.

"Dad?"

"It's me. It's me," he said, repeating himself out of nervousness.

"It's been a long time," Polly said.

"Yes," he agreed. "A long time." He paused. Another silence. " I...I...I would like to see you, if that's okay," he said. He rubbed his forehead with his wrist and listened to her breathing as if he couldn't get enough of her sound.

Another long silence. "All right."

"You'll come to the house?" he asked.

She sounded lovely, alive. She sounded like Estelle, and if he didn't know that Estelle had been dead for so long, he'd have been tricked into thinking she was alive again. Her voice sounded so soft, an echo of Estelle's, and it thrilled and saddened him at the same time. He tried to picture what Polly looked like now, thinking she'd grown plump with age, probably gray-haired like her mother. Or maybe she looked terrible like a ruined wreck because of that husband of hers who perhaps was unable to provide, pummeling her like a boxer. Maybe she divorced and never told him. His mind raced, wanting to fill in the blanks and fearing for the worst.

"How about that new coffee shop just two blocks from your house? I think it's called Morning Edition. Can you walk there?" she asked. "When works for you?"

He paused. Any other time, he'd be able to easily walk there. Except now his injured foot prevented him from walking, especially on the slippery streets.

"I hurt my foot," he said.

Another long silence. "I'll send a cab. When?"

"When's good for you?" he asked. He fidgeted with the long, white telephone cord, squeezing the rings together into a tight ball and letting them go.

"Tomorrow?" she asked.

So soon! Adolph allowed himself to feel a little excited. It surprised him that she hadn't banged the phone down on him, and now she was suggesting tomorrow.

"What time?" Polly asked.

"Before lunch. Ten o'clock," he said. Then he realized she might be working. "Is this where you work? Can you get off your shift?"

"Not a problem. See you then?" she said, sounding brisk. Another long silence before Polly hung up.

He wondered why she waited, and he listened to the click but cradled the receiver in his hand, close to his ear, for a few minutes, as if he could recall the sound of her inhaling and exhaling, before he finally set the phone down. Tomorrow, he'd finally see her and tell her what? He didn't know. He let out his own breath, unaware he'd been holding it.

* * *

In the new coffee shop near his house, one that he'd never been in before, Adolph occupied a small, round table by the window and paged through a tabloid. Too nervous to read it, he flipped through the pages for something to do, something to keep his hands busy while he waited. He sipped coffee, annoyed that it had cost so much, annoyed that the store had the gall to charge a right arm for a damn cup of coffee.

He also didn't know so many varieties of coffee and tea existed. Fancy bags of whole and ground coffee beans, and teas in multicolored boxes, lined the shelves next to brightly colored boxes of things he couldn't identify like "flavored chai," which were next to things he could identify like small teapots. Did people actually buy this crap? After he flipped through the entire paper, he turned it over and started again, but this time, he gazed at the pastries behind the counter, things with odd names: poppy lemon bars, cardamom and fennel cookies, and sesame somethings. Whatever happened to plain old apple pie? Or French apple pie with raisins and icing? Pie à la mode with ice cream.

He considered getting something to eat, but he didn't want to risk becoming sick, vomiting, or dry heaving in front of Polly. His foot, still swollen and painful, throbbed and didn't fit into any of his shoes. The slipper on his left foot embarrassed him, and the snow outside had wet his sock. He peered at the dressy brown shoe on his right foot, irritated that his swollen foot precluded its mate, and he wondered if the mismatched shoes made him appear senile.

He couldn't remember being this nervous, not even when he'd asked Estelle to marry him when they were both twenty years old, after she'd waited for him to come home from the war. How Polly had known of this coffee shop baffled him.

The last time he'd seen her was at Estelle's funeral, fifteen years ago, when she brought that nigger husband of hers and their mongrel brood—three children—taking up an entire front-row at the church. Adolph had turned his back to them, pretending Polly was a stranger. He hadn't told them about the services. He didn't want them in church or at the luncheon that followed, and he made sure they weren't invited to the restaurant afterwards. They weren't welcome since Polly was an embarrassment with that husband of hers and those mixed-breed kids in front of all his and Estelle's friends. But Polly and her family, red-eyed and weeping, had sat in the pew holding hands. Her husband's arm was around her; his brown fingers kneading and patting her waist. It had hit him then, a sucker punch to his belly: against his wishes, Estelle must have seen them regularly. These children knew, loved her, and wept for their grandmother. What else had Estelle hidden from him? He couldn't confront the dead Estelle for defying him. And she'd left behind no clues, and him felt unsettled.

Taking another sip of his now tepid drink, he gazed out the picture window at a woman approaching the shop. Tall, wearing a red hat, a black coat, and red gloves, she marched directly toward the counter without looking around for anyone. She pulled off her gloves, folded them together, stuffed them into her coat pocket, and waited in line. He stared at the back of her head, straining to see if dark, curly hair sat under the red hat.

"Dad?"

He looked away from the tall woman to see an unmistakably thinner, younger, and taller version of Estelle standing beside the table. The resemblance startled him, the ghost of his wife appearing suddenly before him. Polly's curly hair was still black, covering her shoulders. A few laugh lines were around her eyes and glowing skin. She wore expensive clothes. Not like Estelle. Automatically, he rose. Flustered, he extended his hand to shake hers but pulled it back. One doesn't shake hands with one's own child. "Thanks for coming, Polly," he said. Certain she intended to stand him up, he felt relieved as he gestured to the empty chair. "Sit."

"You're looking good," he said, meaning it. She didn't appear impoverished. She looked younger than he'd expected and as polished as a TV news woman.

"You're thinner than I remember," she said. Her wide eyes seemed careful not to show her utter shock at his gaunt appearance. "A lot thinner."

But Adolph knew the visible ravages of the virus. "Coffee?" he asked.

"No, thanks," she said. "Iced tea." She straightened herself in the chair and moved it closer to the table.

"It's winter," he said. "With snow on the ground."

Polly shrugged.

Conscious of his unmatched shoes, Adolph joined the line and ordered another coffee for himself and a medium iced tea for his daughter. He waited for the drinks by the stack of paper cups perched on the counter as he'd been directed. Polly pulled a twenty-dollar bill from her wallet and placed it on the table. Adolph pushed it back toward her when he set the tea in front of her. He watched her use three pink fake sugar packets.

A tense silence hung over them. What to say after thirty years? He cleared his throat; he had so many things to tell her, but he didn't know how to begin. He stared at her instead, noticing how translucent her skin looked. She glowed.

"So what happened to your foot?" she said.

"Accident. Dropped the access panel to the church furnace on it," he said.

"Maybe it's fractured?" she said.

He shrugged, wanting to avoid the host of problems that would be sure to ensure. "I don't know about that, but I don't like wearing two different shoes. At least they're both brown," he said, staring at his feet.

"You wanted to see me. What's up?"

Adolph nodded. "How've you been?" he asked, starting with the basics. How much she reminded him of Estelle startled him. Seeing Polly regularly, he'd never forget Estelle's face.

She smiled, and her dimples transfixed him. "I forgot how much you looked like your mother," he said. "It's like you're almost her."

"I miss her too," she said. Polly played with the empty pink packets, lining them up in a neat row by her cup. She dug around in her purse and then set a photograph on the table. In it, a dimpled Estelle with a wide smile hugged three brown children close to her. Their thin arms wrapped around her too. Drawn to the image of her, Adolph picked it up and held it closer for a better view. She radiated joy; she was in love with these children. After she'd returned from her all-day Wednesday bingo trips with Rose or from her Friday bus trips to Atlantic City, she exuded the same radiant joy, and then he knew: Estelle had never played bingo or gone to Atlantic City.

She'd driven across town to Polly's house.

In the picture, one brown boy and two brown girls, smiled wide, all at the stage where their teeth were too large for their faces. Adolph focused on Estelle's smile, one she hadn't flashed for him after Gregory died in Vietnam. Two of the children—one boy and one girl—also shared their mother's and grandmother's dimples. The other girl must resemble the father, but all of them had Estelle's large, almond eyes. Both girls' hair hung long and curly like their mother's and grandmother's. The boy's hair, neatly trimmed wide curls, framed a round, dimpled face, and Adolph noticed his blue eyes that were like Greg's and his own. He'd never seen a Black person with blue eyes. The children resembled distorted brown fun house images of Estelle, Polly, Gregory, and himself. He stared at the image of Estelle before setting it back on the table.

"She looks so happy," he stammered. "She visited you," he said, thinking but not saying: *behind my back.*

"Mom didn't have the issues with Keith and me like you did," she said.

He bristled. "Don't you remember all the troubles, the riots, and the looting? The National Guard patrolling? You could have picked someone better, different."

"You mean, not Black," she said. She looked at him without flinching. "Keith and I loved each other then and now. He is an honorable man, a good husband, and a great father," she said.

"We're grandparents! Isn't that proof enough for you?"

They regarded each other in an uncomfortable silence.

"I want to tell you something," he said. He set his hands on the table, palms down, as if bracing himself.

Anticipation in her face, Polly leaned slightly closer to him. She sipped her iced tea though the straw.

Unable to find the words for everything on his mind, he blurted, "I can't remember things."

"You remember things you want to remember and forget what you want to forget. So convenient." She sounded matter of fact, but her eyes flashed anger.

The sight of her eyes—flashing just like Estelle's used to when she was angry—gave him joy. He smiled at the memory of Estelle it called up in him; a calm washed over him. He twirled his coffee cup, drank some, and then set it back on the table. He chewed the wooden stirrer and then fidgeted with the napkin strips before he methodically began ripping the strips into thinner pieces. "I'm dying," he said. "Thought you should know."

"That is what you want to tell me after thirty years of silence?"

Adolph shook his head. "That's not what I mean. I mean, I'm sick. I've been sick for a long time. I know my time's running out now, and I wanted to see you. Before it was too late. I...I'm grateful you did not hang up on me. Thank you."

Polly blinked but said nothing.

"I've got AIDS," he said, blurting it, which was the first time someone other than Doc Palmer knew his terrible, shameful secret. "I've had it for a long time, about ten years now."

Polly's head snapped up. She knocked over her iced tea.

Adolph stood, pulling away from his chair to avoid getting splattered and groaned as the pain in his foot shot up his leg. He hurriedly sat back down. She grabbed a pile of napkins from the counter to soak up the spill, and he noticed her hands trembling. She stuffed the wet napkins back into the empty iced teacup, and then tossed it and Adolph's tea-soaked tabloid into the nearby trash can.

When she sat down, he could see questions in her eyes. He held up his hands. "A long story. I've done stupid things. Stupid, stupid things." He shook his head.

Silence again. Polly leaned closer, waiting for something.

"You're the only one left," he said.

She kept her voice low, but he heard anger in her tone. "You are not alone," she said, pushing the photo toward him.

He balled his hands into fists and then flattened them again. He wanted to reiterate the reasons why he thought Keith was the wrong man, but she sat in her expensive clothes, and all his reasons evaporated. He picked up the photo, wanting to cut Estelle out of it, but that meant cutting her arms, which were wrapped around those children, who all resembled Estelle, and the boy had the ghost of Greg's blue eyes.

Polly gently lowered the photo, pulling her chair closer to him. "This is Keith Gregory Ott Henderson, Junior," she said, pointing to the boy. "Greg's a mechanical engineer known for his precision. Both Greg and Estelle Marie got mommy's smile. Stellie's a lawyer like her dad and me. And Esther Ott Henderson over here, the baby, is a dentist. They all have babies. You're a muleheaded man with great-grandchildren and a family you don't deserve, thank you very much," she said in an even voice.

He wanted to ask Polly what the children knew about him, what they'd been told, but he didn't. He wanted her to stay there in the coffee shop, sitting close to him.

"No one named Adolph?" he asked instead with a slight smile.

Polly laughed. She threw her head back and laughed so loud; it amazed him. The sounds of her laughter bounced around him, echoing Estelle's when she was happy. He considered it a gift. He waited for her to lash out at him, to accuse him of being an ass, a stubborn fool, a bigot, and to vomit all the things he'd shouted at her when he'd refused to attend her wedding, when he'd bellowed that she'd be dead to him forever. Her vitriol never came; he realized it'd be wasted on a dead man. No one would miss him much. Not Polly, her children, or her grandchildren. The weight of decades of unnecessary emptiness distressed him, knocked him off-balance more than his mismatched shoes or his injured foot.

In her mirth, Polly reached across the table, and he savored the warmth and softness of her fingers wrapped around his bony ones. He couldn't remember the last time anyone touched him, and the shock of it gave his heart a jolt. He glanced outside. The snow blanket transformed the streetscape into a Christmas card, but the reflection of him and Polly sitting side by side, mirrored on the inside window, captured his attention, and that's where he decided to look.

DAZZLE

THE BEST TIME to snatch food out of a dumpster is just after it's dropped in. It's still clean enough to eat, and the flies haven't got to it. Or rats. But that means hanging around the smelly dumpsters when the boardwalk concessions change their shifts at four o'clock or after midnight when they're all closed. Marsha Bailey, who sits on the boardwalk fence watching a couple of dumpsters, knows this. She rubs her bruised side from where her father punched her for being mouthy and waits until the concessions close, hoping her friends won't catch her grabbing burgers and fries out of the garbage in the dark.

When she's sure the last of the concessions' workers have tossed away their bags, she climbs down from the fence, winching from the ache in her side, and looks around to make sure the boardwalk is deserted before digging for the unsold fries, burgers, and chicken. Packages from EJ's Bar and Grill fill the first and second shelves of the fridge at home. No milk, no cheese, and no eggs. There's nothing. Except beer. "Bread in a bottle," her dad said when she tells him the fridge is empty. Her mother shrugs and acts helpless. Marsha thinks she's also now taking something else, but she doesn't know what it is. She just knows her mom nods out more than she does anything else, including talk to her.

"Hey, hey... Hey! Whatcha doing?" A boy's voice startles her.

Damn. She forgot about the boardwalk rides.

Mental Tommy is wearing thick workman's gloves and a blue T-shirt that says, "Do the Bump at Guy's Boardwalk Bumper Hall!" in white letters. He's holding a garbage bag and flashing a big smile.

She drops a large bag of still hot fries and looks at the motherlode longingly.

He places the garbage bag carefully inside the dumpster before removing his gloves and sliding them into his back pocket, the fingertips bent like wilted flowers.

"Whatcha think I'm doin'?" she shoots back, careful to sound mean.

"Lose something? I'm always losing something, but my mom tells me if it's lost, that's too bad." He smiles, his white teeth perfect.

"Yep. Lost something," she says.

He laughs. "Wait till I tell Guy! He has big lights. He can find it. What did you lose?"

"My ring. Yeah, I lost the ring my grandma gave me," she says, rolling her eyes right and up at the midnight sky. "She's going to kill me for losing it." She tries to look sad.

"It's fun to find lost things. My name is Tommy, Thomas Michael Hills. But it's Tommy for real," he says without taking a breath.

Everyone knows Mental Tommy. They call him the "Mayor of the Boardwalk," because he talks to everyone, and Marsha wishes he'd leave so she can grab the fries.

"I'm Tommy. What's yours?" he repeats in a singing voice.

"Dazzle," she blurts.

Dr. Hills, Tommy's father, owns the pharmacy, and Marsha's sure her parents owe Dr. Hills and a bunch of other store owners a pile of money.

He takes her hand and shakes it, shaking her whole body. "Hey, do you want to be my girlfriend? You're pretty," he says.

No one other than her grandmother has told her she's pretty before, but she has heard that she resembles her mom with her long legs, green eyes, and dark hair. She's also heard that she's got her father's height, which she believes because she's taller than her mom and nearly as tall as her dad but not as strong. She likes hearing she's pretty and weighs the angles.

"What does your girlfriend get?" she asks.

Tommy shrugs. "I never had a girlfriend before." He giggles.

"I'm hungry!" she says, looking sideways at him.

"You want some pizza?"

"I don't have money," Marsha says. She twirls her hair, glancing at her blue toenails in her platform sandals before fixing her eyes on his face.

"You can be my girlfriend, and I can get us both pizza. I got paid today! See? Guy, he's my boss. He gives me a hundred and fifty dollars every Sunday." Tommy pulls a wad of cash out of his pocket. Above the smile still plastered on his face, his blue eyes gleam under a head full of sandy hair.

He doesn't look like a retard, though Marsha knows he's older even if he doesn't act like it. His creased pants look cleaner than anything she sees her father wear, and everyone knows that Tommy works all day at the bumper car hall. She pictures melted cheese on a pizza, a milkshake, and a calzone from the same store, and she even imagines eating at a table with paper napkins and plastic forks. She allows him to grab her hand, pulling her toward the boardwalk and toward the prospects of fifty dollars' worth of fresh pizza, fixings, and whatever else Tommy's inclined to buy her with his pay.

"I'll be your girlfriend, Tommy," she says, smiling now. "Let's go get pizza!"

"*Tommy,*" a man's voice calls from the boardwalk.

"That's Guy. I'm not off yet, but I'll be finished in a few minutes," Tommy says, leading her toward the bumper car hall.

"What about the pizza?" she asks. Her stomach growls.

"We'll get pizza," Tommy says, repeating it.

She wonders if Tommy would know when he's having a bad day or if he smiles through every day, good or bad.

At the bumper car hall, Guy sits on the ground, sanding a red bumper car lying on its side.

Red chips fly like tiny gnats. Marsha sees his butt crack, plumber's ass, and his T-shirt rides high on his oversized belly. Glancing first at Tommy and then her, who're holding hands, Guy frowns, pushing his lips to one side of his face. "Where's our ice cream cones?" Guy asks.

Marsha smirks, thinks how Tommy did him a favor by forgetting the ice cream, and wonders if Fatty knows her parents.

"I forgooooooot! I'll go now," Tommy says, dropping her hand. Unable to contain his excitement, he dances from foot to foot in his cherry high top Converse. The shoestrings are a brilliant white. "This is Dazzle. She's my girlfriend. I just met her. She was digging in the dumpster for a lost ring that her grandma gave her," Tommy says. "I told her that my boss can find anything with his big lights. Can you help find Dazzle's ring?" Tommy dances his mini jig.

Guy looks at his watch. "Forget the cones. What's this ring look like?"

Marsha's stomach tenses. She thrusts her chin forward and raises her stick arms as if to block a punch but snaps her fingers instead. "I remember now. I left it home on the bathroom sink."

Guy narrows his eyes, and she can tell he doesn't believe her. "Some tat," he says, looking at her right ankle encircled by a green ivy tattoo. "Where'd you get it?"

Marsha doesn't answer. She's not eighteen, and she'd get Tony the tat artist in trouble if she tells. She shrugs. "Let's go get pizza, Tommy," she says.

Guy eyeballs her. "I asked you a question."

"Around," she says, wanting to get away from Guy.

"Why are you out so late?" he asks.

Scowling, she stares at her shoes. None of your business is what she thinks, but she says nothing. Crossing her arms, she thrusts her right hip forward.

"Dazzle what?" Guy asks, pushing the issue.

She fears he's going to ruin her chance at fresh pizza and anything else Tommy might be inclined to buy her.

"What's your last name?" Tommy repeats, moving like wooden Pinocchio.

Idiot, she thinks. "Let's go get pizza, Tommy," she says.

"Dazzle's my new girlfriend, and we're going on a date. Pizza time!" Tommy says a little too loud.

Guy mops his sweaty face with a red bandanna. Tommy dances around her, and she wishes they already had reached the pizza shop. "Too young for you, Tommy. You got to find someone older," Guy says, still eyeballing her.

"What are you staring at?" she asks, sounding tough.

"I can tell by the way you breathed in and out three quick times that your name is Elinor," Guy says. "I'm calling you Elinor, because Dazzle ain't no name for a girl who's digging in dumpsters after midnight for a lost ring. How old are you Elinor? Ten?" He is standing now, towering over Tommy and her.

Marsha's eyes widen, shocked at Guy's sheer size, and she bites the inside of her bottom lip, but she says nothing. She imagines bashing him in the face. Elinor! And she's fifteen dammit! "Do these tits look like they belong to a ten year old?" she wants to say but doesn't. She rolls her eyes instead. "Tommy, we still getting pizza or not?" she asks.

"Pizza, pizza, pizza. I love pizza," Tommy says, pulling her toward the pizza place. "You're twenty-two. She's too young. She's trouble," Guy calls after them.

Marsha twists back toward Guy, while Tommy laughs like the idiot he is. "The name's Dazzle," she yells at Guy in a clear, resounding voice.

She studies the Gemma Pizza menu, wanting all the toppings and extra cheese. She can't remember the last time she ate something fresh, hot, and not from a dumpster. "We can get a combo!"

Tommy looks puzzled. "What's a combo?" he asks, emphasizing the *bo* of the word "combo."

"Lots of stuff on it," she says.

"Even things I don't like?" he asks. "I don't like sardines," he says emphatically and scrunches his face. "Or anchovies," he spits out imaginary anchovies.

"Ew, me neither," she says, picturing gooey cheese, pepperoni, and mushrooms. "I like mushrooms."

"We match," Tommy says. "Let's get the combo."

"With extra cheese and meat sauce? Can I get something for later?" she asks. "In case I get hungry later. Like a hamburger and fries."

"You're my girlfriend so you can get whatever you want."

"Can I order?" Marsha asks, flashing a smile she hopes looks real.

Tommy shakes his head. "My job, just like my dad," he says. He leans into the table toward her. His eye are wide with expectation.

Marsha doesn't trust him to get it right, but she wants to eat and anything not from the dumpster will do. Even if he gets it wrong, it's better than what she's been eating. Tommy orders a large combo pizza and the hamburger and fries for later. The waitress asks about drinks, and she can tell that Tommy must come here often because he orders an unsweetened iced tea with lemon and nods at her. She orders a large coke. Tommy may be a retard, but he can do surprising things.

When the pizza comes, she puts her nose close to it and breaths in the smell of it. She's in love with the warmth of it, the greasy oily smell of the pepperoni, and the gooey cheese covering the meat sauce. She grabs a slice from the pan and eats it quickly. Tommy carefully cuts his slice and places it onto his plate. He sets his napkin on his lap. Marsha's napkins still sit on the table. She stuffs more pizza in her mouth, licking stray sauce off her fingers.

"Dazzle," Tommy says still smiling with those perfect teeth. "We must never, never lick our fingers at the table." He hands her a napkin, and for a minute, she forgets he's a retard and blushes. She's starving so she snatches the napkin without saying, "thank you" and grabs a third slice before Tommy reaches for a second, shutting her eyes to appreciate its fresh hotness. She spots the occupants at the two other tables, and by their uniforms, she know they also work the rides. She stares at a poster advertising Ocean Groves July 4 bicentennial celebration fireworks display with its red, white, and blue 1976 dominating it. She scoffs, knowing her parents started toasting the bicentennial year last summer.

"This is so good," she says, meaning it. She studies the song list at the tabletop jukebox. She's embarrassed to be seen with Tommy, but she's hungry. He slides coins toward her for the tabletop juke, and she selects "Shake Your Booty," instead of "Sara Smiles" because she doesn't want him knowing it's her favorite song. She's glad Cici and Jennifer, who give her rides to and from the boardwalk in exchange for beer from her parent's fridge, hang out at The Pub parking lot at the other end of the boardwalk and won't spot her eating with Tommy.

Tommy tells her repeatedly that she's pretty. He swallows before he speaks and wipes his fingers and mouth on the napkin. He reaches for her hand, asking for her telephone number and if she'd like to meet him after work again tomorrow.

She snatches her hand back but writes her number down on her napkin with a pen she borrows from the waitress. "I like being your girlfriend, Tommy. I'll come by the bumper car hall to see you," she says, unable to remember the last time she felt so full. She imagines fresh chicken tenders, burgers, and fries. And ice cream! And she doesn't have to ply him with her parent's beer.

On her way to the ladies' room, she asks the waitress if Gemma's hiring and if she can have a job. They tell her to come back tomorrow when the manager is there. When the waitress brings the burger and fries wrapped to go with the bill, Tommy pays like a real boyfriend, leaving a tip, the exact amount from a cheat sheet in his wallet. Marsha cradles the take out bag. She grabs the tip when he's not looking, slipping it into her back pocket. "Let's go get ice cream," she says.

Under a boardwalk lamp post, Tommy stops. "I waited so long to have a girlfriend, and now I have one," he says, looking overjoyed. His eyes shines like two blue marbles. He's tall. Marsha thinks if he weren't a retard, he'd have a boatload of girlfriends. The light casts a dark shadow across his face, and for a moment, he resembles an overgrown toddler: his skin smooth and his expression open. "Now I have a girlfriend," he singsongs; his perfect teeth are iridescent under the light.

She tucks the bag with the burger and fries closer to her body. She pulls him toward the ice cream store, but Tommy doesn't move. He draws her toward him with a surprising strength; bending forward, he wraps his arms around her body and kisses her, a sloppy wet kiss, on the lips. His pizza breath tongue goes in her mouth.

Repulsed and shocked by the kiss, his pizza tongue, and the hardness she feels between his legs, she pushes him away. "What are you doing?" she yells. "No!"

He blinks back tears. "When a girl says no, it's time to stop," he repeats as if remembering times tables. "Boyfriends and girlfriends kiss. I've been waiting a long time to kiss my girlfriend," he says. "I want to kiss my girlfriend. Is that okay?" Tommy sounds as if he has practiced saying this.

She wants him to think he's her boyfriend, but she doesn't want to *be* his girlfriend. "No kissing on the first date," she whispers. "You work up to a kiss," she says, keeping her voice low. "Things like that take time. I never kissed a boy before," she adds, knowing she's kissed plenty of boys, given them BJs and handies, and fucked them in her own bed after school when her parents are at EJs, which is most of the time. She gives the boys beer when they leave. "And no kissing where people can see it," she says, sure that Tommy would never be kissing her at all anyway. Imagining a hot fudge sundae with whipped cream and jimmies, she runs toward the ice cream shop, hollering "Ice cream!" with Tommy, giggling and chasing her.

In the morning, Marsha's burger and fries are missing from the fridge. She moves the beer bottles to see if the bag is shifted out of sight but finds only more beer. She finds the bag crumpled at the top of the trash can and the burger container beneath it. Except for some ketchup smears, everything is gone. Who ate it? Probably both! Bastards! She wants to kick the trash can, but she sees her father lying face down on the living room floor. His greasy hair covers his face.

Her side still hurts from the last time he punched her. She stumbles across her mother on the bathroom floor, her jeans and underwear gathered at her knees. Marsha collects empty beer bottles and debris, dumping it into the kitchen trash can atop her burger and fries bag. She straightens and cleans the apartment, one less thing to enrage them. Struggling to hoist her mother's underwear and pants up, she drags her into the hallway. In a stupor, her mother yells, "Leave me the fuck alone, bitch!" She watches her mother's eye flutter and is convinced she's been doing something else besides drinking.

An empty toilet paper roll means it's all gone. Marsha remembers Tommy's tip still in her pants pocket and considers if she should buy more toilet paper or a burger, fries, and a milkshake at Mr. Cheesy Burger. She's hungry and decides to pinch a few rolls of toilet paper from the boardwalk's public restroom and buy a burger and fries.

* * *

A month later on a Sunday in June, Marsha welcomes the air conditioning inside the Hills' home. Tommy has invited her for Sunday dinner, though everyone knows that it's lunchtime. Helping Mrs. Hills prepare dinner, Marsha marvels at two refrigerators, two freezers, two dishwashers, two sinks, and a groovy ice machine in a spacious white kitchen with bright royal blue doorknobs on the cabinets.

She examines the contents of one open fridge. Only a few beers—not from EJs—and a half-empty bottle of wine sit in the fridge, where the shelves overflow with foods she can't identify. She counts three kinds of cheeses with unfamiliar names like Asiago, Gouda, Fontina; pita, tortilla, and naan breads in plastic bags occupy one side of the middle shelf next two gallons of milk. Oranges, peaches, plums, a bag of cherries, and another bag of green seedless grapes pack the left bin. In the right bin, fresh green beans, spinach, and other vegetables burst through their brown bags. Two dozen eggs fill the door basket; packages of bacon, ham, turkey, pepperoni, and other deli counter meats cram the deli drawer.

She wonders who eats all this food. A large pitcher of iced tea and cartons of orange juice, apple juice, and cream occupy the second shelf. No colas, but on the topmost shelf, a long triangular bar of chocolate wrapped in gold foil leans on Mrs. Hills' lipstick tubes, near a box of batteries and a stack film boxes. Why do the Hills need two fridges, she wonders?

"What are you looking for, Dazzle?" Mrs. Hills asks, glancing at her. Mrs. Hills breaks the lettuce pieces up and drops them in a colander before snipping open bags of radishes and carrots for the salad she's making. She wears a strand of pearls around her neck, pressed jeans, and a sleeveless yellow, V-neck shirt. With blond hair pulled into a ponytail, she wears blush and mascara and smells like lilacs and powder. She smiles at Tommy, but it vanishes when she looks at Marsha.

"Nothing," Marsha says, shutting the fridge and planning to migrate some of the contents to her own fridge.

38

"Why don't you join Tommy and Dr. Hills in the study until everything is ready?" Mrs. Hills says. Her face is pinched.

Marsha remembers her grandmother's pinched face when her numbers didn't hit. She also remembers her grandmother's hot dogs, baked beans, meatloaf, mashed potatoes with gravy, hamburgers, rice, and baked ziti. She misses her grandmother for a lot more than what she cooked.

In the study, Tommy and his father stare at a chess board the way her father stares at the TV.

They share the same smile, the same perfect teeth.

"Checkmate!" Tommy says, snorting. Under the table, his red high tops dance.

Dr. Hills doesn't let Tommy win just because he's a retard. He shakes Tommy's hand and says, "Bravo! Well played, Tommy, my man! Persistence is the key to success."

He beams as Tommy resets the pieces. Diplomas for Tommy's whole family, including Tommy, and framed photographs cover the study's walls. In the Hills' wedding day photo, Mrs. Hills wears a poufy white gown and Dr. Hills wears a black bow tie. Tommy as a baby, as a little boy, and then as a bigger boy smiles in every photo. If you don't know he's mental, you wouldn't have guessed it from the pictures. The whole family smiles in all them as if nothing's wrong with him.

Except for the plastic EJ's clock in the kitchen, nothing hangs on the walls in her parent's apartment. A large, silver framed mirror sagged over her grandma's sofa. She remembers a picture of Grandpappy in his army uniform atop of the TV set next to one of her mother's high school graduation photos. Marsha wonders what happened to those pictures after grandma died, and she wonders what happened to the girl her mother was in her graduation picture.

Tommy and his father laugh. "Dazzle, perhaps Tommy can teach you the game?" Dr. Hills asks.

His face glowing, Tommy grabs and squeezes her hand too hard. "I can teach you, Dazzle. It's easy and fun. We can play chess when it's raining outside."

She thinks of a thousand things she'd rather do instead and pulls her hand back, wishing he was her brother instead of her fake boyfriend. He'd be a perfect older brother, and he wouldn't be wanting to kiss her. She does allow him to kiss her in the janitor's closet on the boardwalk where no one can see. Sloppy, wet kisses.

At the Hills' dining room table covered with tablecloth, Marsha pretends to be Tommy's sister, and they're all on TV. The dining room's window walls overlook the ocean, and she loves the airy feel of the house. Sunlight dances on the tall, colorful glass flower sculptures situated in front of the windows that don't face the ocean. A deck encircles the house like a bracelet. The Hills must think Tommy is an Einstein retard, because they expect him to speak to them like a normal person.

"Do you have a summer job?" Dr. Hills asks her.

She can't work without a permit and needs to be sixteen to get one. Gemma Pizza's manager refused to let her work without one, and all the other places she tried to hustle a job told her to come back next year. She shrugs and stares at the lamb chops, rice with noodles, green beans with almonds, and slices of cheese on her plate. She's never eaten lamb before.

"No one will hire me without a work permit," she says, chewing on a piece of lamb, which she decides she likes.

"What do you expect to do when you graduate?" Dr. Hills asks.

"Don't know," she says and sinks her fork into the rice with noodles. Three pairs of eyes focus on her, and she feels the heat coloring her face and neck. She can only think of getting through each day. *It's none of your fucking business!* She wants to scream, but she eats fast instead, filling her mouth with rice and bits of lamb chop. Food falls from her mouth back onto her plate.

"Sweetie, Dazzle's a guest," Mrs. Hills says, raising both her eyebrows at her husband.

"Do you have hobbies you'd rather talk about?"

Marsha swallows. She and grandma ate on TV trays and watched wrestling. "We don't talk much during dinner," she says, knowing her parents don't think about dinner. Or lunch. Or breakfast. Her fork hovers over her plate. Her cloth napkin doesn't move from its spot by the dish. She wants to eat and leave. Before her grandma died, they lived together, watching movies on Friday nights and Sunday afternoons. "On Wednesday nights, grandma and I played bingo at her church," Marsha says in a low voice, almost a whisper.

She doesn't want to tell the Hills anything more about grandma, who smelled like cinnamon, peach, clove, and orange. Who placed her lucky alligator foot, alligator tooth, and a silver dime above her bingo cards in a special order. Who polished Marsha's fingers and toe nails with fairy plum pink polish. Who took her to the ice cream shop every Friday night for a pineapple sundae for two. Who carried a rosary that smelled like roses in her pocket all the time. Who died when Marsha was twelve, forcing her to move in with her parents; her parents forget she's there. Marsha sets her fork on her plate.

"Excuse me," she says, mimicking the Hills. "I got to go." Ignoring the disappointment creeping onto Tommy's face, she leaves her plate half full, regretting the stuff she won't be able to snag from the double fridges. Outside, the heat plays bongos in her head, but she prefers it to the Hills' nosy-ass questions.

At midnight, the sky is ink, silver, and cream with a full moon shimmering in it. Filling her lungs with salty sea air, she enjoys the sounds of the waves. With her platform sandals and a brown bag in hand, she strolls along the surf with Matt, one of the boys she has fucked in her bed. His dark curly, uncombed hair flies in all directions in a wild mess, and the tattoos on his muscled arms are visible, because the shirtsleeves have been ripped off. He's twenty, younger than

41

Tommy. She admires his tats and likes his Old Spice scent mixed with weed.

They crawl under an empty lifeguard chair where Matt pulls a joint from his backpack, lights it, and takes a hit before passing it to her. She gives him her bag filled with beer and accepts the joint.

He chugs a quarter of the first bottle. "Thanks to your parents!" He belches and then hits the joint. "Why do you hang with that retard?" he asks. His voice is nasally, because he's holding in smoke.

"Something to do," she says, keeping her voice matter-of-fact.

"He tells everybody you're his girlfriend." Matt exhales and swallows another sip of beer. "And he calls you Dazzle."

She hits the joint. "Doesn't make it true," she says, remembering Tommy's stupid, sloppy kisses in the janitorial closet and wondering if Matt has spotted them eating pizza or burgers together. "No big deal. He can call me whatever he wants," she says.

"I bet he wants to fuck you," Matt says, laughing. "I bet he has a big goddamn dick."

"I wouldn't know. Never saw it," she says, telling the truth, and they both snort with laughter. "Probably wouldn't know what to do with it."

"Let's go in," Matt says, looking at the ocean. He drinks the last of the beer.

Afraid of riptides and afraid of being in the water at night, she says, "A shark'll bite your big goddamn dick." She can tell he's buzzed.

"Chicken," Matt says, removing his T-shirt. "Come on." He pulls her toward the surf.

When she steps into the cold water, she shivers. He pulls her deeper into the sea until the waves soak the hem of her mini skirt, her thighs. "I can think of better things to do," she says, trying to sound sexy although her teeth are chattering. She pulls him back to the beach, back to the guard's chair.

"I'll make you hot," Matt says, wrapping his arms around her. Leaning against the lifeguard chair's leg, she lets him kiss her. She lets him feel her tits when he pushes his hand under her bra. He unzips his fly, frees himself from his jeans, pushes her skirt up, and shoves aside her underwear. Without a rubber, his inserts his stiffening prick. Liking it, she closes her eyes and lets him.

When she opens her eyes, she sees fat Guy carrying a flashlight and walking along the surf with two toy white poodles. Sissy dogs for a big guy, she thinks. Guy spots them and frowns, watching like the pervert he is. She doesn't care. Matt's amped her up, and his dick feels good. She remembers a condom only when she feels him explode inside her. "Keep going," she says and kisses Matt. For show.

* * *

At the Fourth of July bicentennial celebration, Marsha and her friends—Cici and Jenny— occupy a bench outside The Pub, waiting for the fireworks to begin at nightfall. Marsha's parents never discover the missing beer, so she still uses it to ply favors. Slightly drunk now from the two six-packs they'd snagged from the fridge in exchange for driving Marsha to the boardwalk, Jenny lights a thin cigarette and inhales. She holds it under the bench to avoid being seen with it.

Cici eyes Marsha's white puca bead necklace, saying she's going to get one with her next allowance. Tommy gave Marsha the necklace, the matching bracelet and earrings, and the gauzy Indian cotton shirt she's wearing. She has something they don't. Cici raises her tanned arm, flicks the sheet of her sandy blond hair back, and points at Tommy coming toward them.

"There's your *boyfriend*, Dazzle," she says, laughing.

Jenny takes up the chorus. Marsha wants to deny it, but Tommy's too close now. She hates Cici and Jennifer for their 8-track players in their pretty bedrooms, for their closets full of clothes and shoes, and for their parents who feed them and give them allowances.

Tommy smiles at her and unexpectedly bends over, kissing her lips like real boyfriend.

She pushes him away. "No Tommy!" she yells, sounding harsher than she means.

"*Ew*," Cici says, laughing so hard she slides off the bench.

Jennifer makes gagging, choking sounds. "Marsha let a *retard* kiss her!"

The pupils in Tommy's eyes shrink. For the first time, his smile vanishes, but Marsha doesn't care, pushing him out of earshot. She shoots fast furious words at him. "I told you no kissing in front of people."

Confusion distorts his face. "No," he shakes his head. "I see boyfriends and girlfriends kissing and holding hands too. You're not telling the truth, Dazzle," he shouts. His feet dance a furious jig. "Hiding things is not right. Pops says hiding is lying and lying's wrong."

In one swift stroke, he yanks the necklace off her neck, sending puca beads flying in all directions. The beads tumble, hit the board walk, and slip through the slats as Tommy runs toward the bumper car hall at the other end of the boardwalk. His cherry red high tops bounce up and down like the dot on the TV sing-alongs.

Cici and Jennifer snort with laughter.

"Shit, Marsha, you let a retard kiss you for puca beads!" Jennifer says between guffaws.

"What else do you let him do?"

"Everything," Cici says.

They look at each other and laugh until they're breathless. Marsha pushes Jennifer off the bench and yanks, twists, and pulls Cici's hair. "Bitches!" she shrieks and runs away.

July flows into August, and although Marsha goes to the bumper car hall daily to see Tommy, he pretends she's invisible. He sweeps and cleans as usual. He empties the trash. He hums when he works. He flashes his radiant, perfect smile to everyone except her, and she understands that his parents and Guy have instructed him not to speak to her. She misses fresh pizza, burgers, fries, and ice cream. She misses gifts like puca beads.

She's certain that if she makes his prick stiff with a few handies, she can convince him she's his girlfriend again. She waits by the janitorial closet. Guy comes and tells her to get lost.

Hurricane Belle hits Ocean Groves in mid-August, forcing everyone into the junior high gym. Marsha looks for Tommy and his family, but they aren't in the gym. She wonders where they are since their house overlooks the beach. The wind whips, howls, and screeches around the building.

She sneaks upstairs to the first floor only to see the ferocious wind bend trees in half and soak them with horizontal sheets of rain. The storm destroys the boardwalk concessions and rides, including the bumper car hall. Boards covering the Hills' pharmacy's front windows blow off, and the store's interior is trashed. Enormous swells crash onto the beach where Cici, Jenny, and Matt ride their boogie boards, laughing like clowns. She hates them.

* * *

"Our little girl here got raped by a retard," Marsha's father says. "And now she's going to have a retard bastard."

On the sofa, her father crosses his arms in front of his dirty T-shirt. Marsha stares at the tufts of yellow sofa stuffing poking out behind him. When he uncrosses his arms, he cracks his knuckles and rubs his hands on his stained jeans. In a torn golden wingback chair rescued from a hotel discard pile, her mother nods, unable to focus on Delia or her father.

"We got ourselves a little situation," her father says, pushing back his greasy hair. "You hear me?" he asks, repeating it in a louder voice and tapping her mother's bare leg with his toe.

Eyes fluttering and with her hair haphazard and unkempt, her mother shifts in the chair. "I ain't deaf," she says.

Marsha found an old cigar box with a bent spoon, a lighter, and some other stuff in it and knows her mother's using.

"Tommy didn't rape me," Marsha says, realizing her father intends to benefit from her pregnancy. He's made it clear how much he hates doing those handyman jobs that keep the rent paid, too many of them in the aftermath of the hurricane. He has been griping about it.

"There's no way *my* daughter would fuck a retard. Who fucks a retard? Maybe another retard," he says and laughs a little, mocking her. He grabs two beers from the fridge and hands one to her mother, saying it'll make her feel better. Her mother ignores the offer, and her father sets it on the cocktail table next to the one he snagged for himself.

Marsha wishes she were in school, but pregnant girls aren't allowed. Even Tommy is going to school somewhere. Plus, he's working by stocking shelves at his dad's pharmacy. The summer paints the October sky turquoise, gold, and white, and she wishes she were a seagull soaring in the sky, flying away.

"You *let* a retard fuck you?" her father asks. His voice is laced with disbelief.

"I never fucked Tommy!" she yells.

When she told Matt she was pregnant, he asked if it was the retard's. If Tommy had fucked her, she wouldn't be pregnant now. Matt's the only boy who came inside her without a condom, so she knows he's the baby's father.

Her father settles himself back in the chair and swigs the beer. "Does the retard *think* it's his kid?"

She shook her head. She hasn't seen Tommy since July 4. "I never fucked him," she says in a flat voice.

"No proof. The retard's gonna pay," her father says, smacking the sides of one hand into the palm of the other while emphasizing each word. "We can make this work for us. He bragged all summer about you being his girlfriend. Who's going to believe otherwise?"

Marsha remembers hot pizza followed by chocolate ice cream, and she smiles.

"I ain't laughing," her father says, springing from the chair to smack her arms, her chest, and her face. "Who's going to feed you and your little bastard?"

"You don't feed me now, so why are you so burnt?" she yells.

Her father's blows rain harder, and she misses her grandmother.

"Stop it! I didn't do nothing! Even being a retard, Tommy would take care of his kid!" she yells. "He works every day and enjoys it. Not like you."

She folds her arms around her head, refusing to cry no matter how many times her father hits her arms and head.

"What the fuck, Hal? Just take her to the welfare office. She'll get a steady check, which means we do too. End of story," her mother mumbles.

Marsha imagines her parents spending all her money at EJ's on beer, chicken wings, and her mother's newfound habit. She imagines her baby being hungry all the time and blinks back tears. She decides that she'll take herself to the welfare office.

"We can get some money from Dr. Hills if his kid believes he's the daddy. And government cheese," her father says.

Her mother emits a hazy laugh.

Her father grabs the phone book from the TV table's bottom shelf and tosses it at her. "Look up the pharmacy number."

She doesn't want to call Dr. Hills, but her father shouts at her to hurry up, so she dials the number and hands it to him. "Hal Bailey here. Put Doc Hills on," he says, pacing and waiting for Dr. Hills to pick up. "Hal Bailey here. This is Marsha's father. You know her as 'Dazzle.' We have a situation here." Her father pauses. "Marsha's pregnant, and Tommy's the father. She's only fifteen, and how old is your boy again? Twenty-two?"

Her father listens and then bellows, "Who's gonna pay for a goddamn paternity test?"

"No test is going to say this is Tommy's baby," Marsha says, loud enough for Dr. Hills to hear. With his face contorted, her father pitches a half-empty beer bottle at her. She ducks, and it hits the wall, crashing onto the floor with a thud, spilling its foamy contents, and filling the room with the pungent beer odor.

Her mother barely registers anything going on, bending forward as she journeys on her trip.

Marsha runs into bathroom and splashes cold water onto her face, puffy from being pregnant. Her skin is blemished. Her bra irritates her tender nipples; her swollen tits burst the seams of her top. Her belly protrudes from her jeans and is held together by a large diaper pin. She does not have any maternity clothes.

In the living room, her father talks about her as if she weren't there. "Doc Hills says he'll pay for the test, but she ain't taking no test. The retard's going to pay, one way or another," he says. "If Mental Tommy thinks the kid is his, it don't matter now, does it?"

Her mother mumbles. "The Hills ain't going to give you a red cent."

"They should be proud that their retard made a baby." He flicks on the TV. "They can say he's a man now."

Her mother laughs. "What you got against that kid anyway?" she mumbles.

"Nothing. This here's opportunity," he says.

Marsha slams the door behind her, hitching a ride to the boardwalk where the post-hurricane reconstruction is underway. The bumper car hall pavilion is half erected. She's tried to see Tommy at the pharmacy, but he's never around when she's in the store, and she thinks his dad tells him to hide from her.

She hitches another ride to the Ocean Groves Social Services office where she waits for hours before signing papers that say she wants to be "emancipated" from her parents to qualify for her own apartment. The social worker asks her about the bruises on her arms, and she tells them the truth. She tells the social worker that she eats dumpster food, that her parents are drunk or high all the time, and that she misses her grandmother, who took care of her until she died. The social worker takes notes and then gives her vouchers for clinic appointments, for bus transportation, for emergency food purchases, and to get some maternity clothes. The social worker arranges for her to stay in a hotel as an emergency, and for the first time since her grandma died, Marsha believes everything is going to be okay.

That evening at the hotel, she daydreams about being "emancipated from her parents" as her social worker described it, decorating her new apartment, the baby's room, and shopping for items like those in the Hills' fridge. Once she's checked in, she decides to go back to her parent's apartment so that she can move her stuff into the hotel room a little at a time. She's supposed to stay at the hotel until the social worker can locate permanent housing.

After a couple of days, she goes back to the apartment where her father catches her with a laundry basket of her clothes.

"What the fuck are you doing Marsha?" he asks.

"Getting rid of these," she says. "They don't fit."

"Liar," he says. "This letter came today saying you are emancipated from us, your parents." He pauses. "You know I'm going to contest this. I'll tell them you're a little shit, and that's why you're knocked up."

"You're not getting my baby's money or the Hills' money!" she shouts.

Her father smirks. "Ain't that what you did all summer? Bamboozle that retard for money? You must have let him do something for him to think he's your boyfriend."

Marsha balls her hands into fists, jabbing her fingernails into her palms. She runs around the apartment, gathers the gauzy shirt, the puca bracelet and earrings, the stuffed animals—all the things Tommy bought her—and stuffs them into a plastic EJ's bag. She takes a bus to the boardwalk and walks to the Hills' pharmacy.

In the first aid aisle, Tommy's placing boxes of Q-tips and Band-Aids in perfect order. "I don't want to talk to you. You're not a good girlfriend, Dazzle," he says. "You don't tell the truth." He focuses on the rows of boxes. He's wearing dressy black slacks and fancy black loafers, and his feet remain still. He does not smile at her, although he does smile at the other customers.

"My name is Marsha. Not Dazzle," she says.

"You lie," Tommy says, almost a whisper. He repeats it a few times and then pauses before saying, "Marsha."

"Here are all the things you bought me," she says, thrusting the EJ's bag toward him. She remembers Cici's and Jennifer's bedrooms full of stuff. She remembers the photos of Tommy and the diplomas belonging to everyone in the Hills family hanging in their study, the food in their two fridges, and the chess games Tommy and his father plays. She wishes her grandma was still alive, but she isn't. She wants to make sure she takes care of her baby the same way her grandma took care of her and Tommy's parents take care of him.

"Yours, Marsha," Tommy says twice.

"Can we be friends?" she asks with her baby bump between them. She wants him to be her friend, a real friend, and not a fake boyfriend. "I would like it if we could be friends," she says, meaning it.

"Pops told me what your dad said on the phone."

"I told my father the truth," she says. "It's not your baby."

Tommy doesn't answer. He finishes lining boxes of Q-Tips and Band-Aids in perfect order on the shelves. Two cartons are now empty on the floor by his feet. He combines the cartons, scooping them off the floor.

"Can we be friends?" Marsha asks again. The stuffed EJ's bag dangles from her hand, feeling heavy.

For a long time, Tommy doesn't speak. He doesn't smile. He doesn't move or look at her. He stares at the Q-Tip boxes.

A minute passes, then two and three. Marsha, uncomfortable in the silence, doesn't know what else to say, although he seems to be waiting for her to say something. Silent, she stares at her feet, now barely visible beneath her baby belly.

"Apology accepted," he says. He faces her, repeats it, and flashes his famous Mayor of the Boardwalk smile. He heads toward the back of the store with a sense of purpose.

PICKING CICORIA

THE LAST PLACE Connie Sessa wanted to be was sitting in the passenger seat of her father's Dodge Dart, an old vehicle with a faded green finish, a missing muffler, and dents from his bumper car driving style. The engine coughed and sputtered before it turned over, and when it finally rumbled to life, shattering the Sunday morning silence with its roar, he shifted into gear and pulled away.

Through the window, Connie glared at her mother. Still in her nightgown, with her graying curly hair tied in a loose ponytail, her mother smiled and waved from the front window of their Little Italy row house.

"*Fai attenzione.* Pay attention," her mother had said as she handed Connie, who was thirteen years old, two large kitchen knives wrapped in butcher paper and three folded brown supermarket bags, which the girl tucked into the car's glove compartment. Cross and sleepy, Connie hadn't wanted to *fai attenzione.*

She watched a dozen gray and white pigeons strut around a pile of bread crumbs. As they pecked at the crumbs, their necks jutted in and out. She wondered if she would able to get close enough to put salt on their tails, would they be able to fly? Her father had told her that salt disables their wings. She spent countless hours as a child, with a saltshaker in hand, chasing starlings and pigeons and trying to get close enough to sprinkle salt on their tails. Seagulls competed for the crumb pile. Their huge wings swooshed away the pigeons flapping as they rose and fell away from the pile.

The sun, barely risen over the rooftops of Baltimore's soldier like homes, cast a gold sheen on the car's torn green seats. The church's bells had not yet tolled their melodic summons to the morning Mass.

Connie yawned, wondering what would actually happen next time if she refused to go foraging with her father on Sunday mornings. She much preferred sleeping for another hour or playing with her furry black cat before having to put on a lacy Sunday dresses for church, than picking *cicoria* or chicory. She had put on her worst clothes—jeans with holes in the knees, ripped tennis shoes, and an old, worn T-shirt—so to not ruin her good ones. She set her head on the window and shut her eyes.

"Ready? You no looka ready," her father, smoothing his cap, said. "Waka up."

Embarrassed and annoyed, she frowned at his black knee-high socks on his sandaled feet. She wished he would dress as if he'd been here since he was twenty, she thought. It was the '70s already. He could at least lose the black knee-highs when he wore sandals and wear regular shorts instead of those baggy things he called "halfa-pants." Her father pointed the car toward Lombard Street, away from the rising sun, and pressed his socked-and-sandaled toes on the gas.

She prayed no one would be at the Fort to notice them—especially not Tony Gardoni, who made her heart beat faster than her grandfather's sewing machine. Not her cousin Rosa or her Uncle Joe, who was her father's brother. They had the same bad taste in fashion that made them look like matching bookends. And especially not anyone from her school, the normal people who'd go to the Fort to explore its history instead of its foliage. With her whole heart, she wished she could transport herself out of the car.

Her father's rotund body barely squeezed into his plaid shorts, and a white tank undershirt revealed rolls of fat around his shoulders and back. His cap hid the ever-widening bald spot on the top of his head, and a big moustache, looking like a tarantula hanging above his lip, gave him the appearance of a pudgy bandit on vacation.

She hadn't been the only one to think so either. The salesman at a jewelry store must have fingered him for a bandit too. Why else would the man glare at them, follow them around the shop, and watch their every move when Pop had taken her and her sisters there to get a present for their mother's birthday? The man looked surprised when her father paid for a pair of diamond and pearl earrings with a wad of cash.

Although he'd been in America long before Connie was born, to her, he still looked and acted as if he was fresh from the "old country" as he called it. Some things just don't change, regardless of the geography. Just like back atop a mountainside in Sicily, the same routine dominated Sundays: pick *cicoria*, go to church, and eat dinner at noon. In Baltimore, the *cicoria* picking season started in May and ended in August. The only thing that changed every Sunday was the place.

Last Sunday, they had gone to the Green Mount Avenue cemetery, an expansive place in the middle of the city and where the most famous Baltimoreans were buried, to pick the stalks with purple-blue flowers. They had spotted heartthrob Tony, his mother, and his elderly aunt there, already bent over the stalks growing up along the graveyard's section boundaries. They had been cutting away at them like migrant workers, earning pennies per pound. Tony's aunt had twisted the skirt of her dress into a knot so that it formed a makeshift basket. Knife in hand and stooped over the plants, she cut the stalks and dumped them into her dress.

Connie's face had flushed when Tony had spotted her. She'd imagined running into Tony in a million different places but not while picking *cicoria*. She turned her face, red from embarrassment, away from him, who also looked mortified as if he wanted to shrink to the size of a gnat. She had understood perfectly. She had raised her knife a bit higher before she brought it down on a clump of *cicoria* and winked at him. She rolled her eyes toward her father.

Tony had raised his eyebrows at her in return and pointed his chin at his mother and sister. She got it: neither of them wanted to be there, and neither of them had a choice about it. He'd smiled, and her heart had thumped. She was certain that Tony, like herself, had probably visited a myriad of places where wild grasses grew on the quest for *cicoria* against his wishes.

She and her father had visited cemeteries, parks, hospitals, college campuses, elementary and high school grounds, and other places that he'd heard about through the mysterious network that also sent other foragers to the same places. Each week, they had seen the same faces at the various sites, each competing for the ever-dwindling stalks. Then her mother had heard a whisper about the Fort, supposedly filled with *cicoria* in spots that dogs couldn't easily reach—and as yet unexploited by the regular foragers.

Turning the car onto Fort Avenue, her father drove straight toward the fort. This morning, they were pioneering new territory that was safe from dog walkers and their ruinous peeing dogs. Connie could list about a hundred things she preferred to do, and at least Tony wouldn't be there. She sighed. She dreaded new territories; they always made her nervous about running into her friends and their parents doing normal things like walking around and not picking *cicoria*.

Not foraging for food.

"Maybe we finda some good stuff today," her father said.

Connie shrugged, not caring about the quality of the plants today. She clicked the button to the glove compartment to and fro and yawned.

"Stoppa dat noise!" her father snapped.

"I'm not doing this next Sunday," she said, crossing her arms.

"You donta tell me whata gonna do. I tella you, and I'ma tella you next Sunday, we picking *cicoria*."

She promised herself this day would be her last Sunday foraging for stupid greens.

Though she felt like a trespasser, the gates of Fort McHenry, like wide open arms, welcomed them. Empty and devoid of any of the other possible *cicoria* pickers, of any other people for that matter, the fort offered vast, overgrown fields below its star shaped ramparts—a *cicoria* picker's paradise.

Her father parked near the statue of Orpheus, a huge black marble sculpture near the entrance to the park that didn't even look as if it belonged there as if to call attention to his car. Why couldn't he park like a normal person? Connie thought. He thrust his socked-and-sandaled feet out the car door and rushed off to one of the areas near the harbor water as if someone else would take all the *cicoria* if he didn't arrive fast enough. In the growing sunlight, she noticed her father spot the purple-blue flowers that grow naturally like the weeds they were and resemble dandelions.

"*Andiamo*," her father beckoned. Bags and knives in hand, she followed him to the three-feet-tall stalks. "Wea lucky today. Nobody here," he grinned.

For once, Connie agreed. It was lucky that no one, especially not Tony or her schoolmates, would see them. She trailed behind her father like a duckling. Marching straight to the edges of the ramparts, he walked purposefully, placing his sandaled feet confidently on the grass. He put one foot in front of the other as if the fort belonged to him rather than the US government. "Righta here. Dese ones," he said. "Giva me de knifa."

Carefully unwrapping the knives, her father folded the butcher paper and put it in his pocket. She snapped open the brown bags, and together, she and her father chopped the hairy stalks and branched stems. A milky white sap leaked out. Working silently, they stuffed the greens into the bags, greens she knew her mother would fry with oil, garlic, and red pepper before cramming them in between two thick slices of Italian bread. Much to her chagrin, come spring, hers and her sisters' lunches always consisted of *cicoria* sandwiches that seeped oil, causing huge grease spots on their brown sandwich bags. She had longed for her classmates' lunches like peanut butter and jelly, tuna, or bologna sandwiches on white bread—not the greasy greens on football-sized rolls that prompted schoolmates to eye her lunch, asking why she ate grass. Or why she ate polka-dotted bologna when her mother packed mortadella sandwiches, which she hated.

She longed for another family, a normal family, who understood the relationship between supermarkets and food. But hunger had prompted her to eat the sandwiches daily. Though she preferred eating the *cicoria* at home, away from prying eyes of her classmates and the school where it wasn't normal to eat them.

The sappy milk from the plants itched her fingers. She and her father cut enough to fill two of the three bags before she heard a car approaching. Fearing it was Tony and his family, she looked up. The sun glinted off the roof of a park ranger's car slowly making its way toward them. With a wide-brimmed hat sitting forward on his head, the brown-uniformed park ranger slammed the door of his car and walked toward them in a wide-legged gait.

"Excuse me, sir? Sir?" The voice startled Connie into dropping the knife. She stood up. Still bent over the plants, her father ignored the voice. He continued to chop the greens as if he was alone in the world.

"Stop, sir!" the voice said. "Whatever it is you're doing, you must stop."

Her father said nothing. He chopped frantically, gathering as many of the greens as possible as if the man in the park ranger uniform, complete with a badge, a radio, and a gun belt, wasn't there. As if he wasn't speaking to him, wasn't positioning his hand uncomfortably close to his weapon.

"Dad, we gotta stop," Connie said.

"Bee qwiat," her father hissed in a low whisper.

"What are you doing here?" the park ranger bellowed.

Her father did not utter a word.

Heart racing and afraid, Connie shook. "Tell him, Pop," she said.

Silence. Instead, he chopped without looking up. He dumped them into the third bag and continued to chop as if he was in a *cicoria* picking contest. She realized he was pretending not to understand English. But he certainly can't pretend he's deaf, she thought. Afraid, she wiped the palms of her hands on her torn pants.

The ranger approached them. His shiny black shoes looked like gems in the grass. She watched the sky through them.

"What the hell are you doing here so early on a Sunday morning?" he demanded.

Her father remained mute as if she and the park ranger were figments of his imagination.

"Picking *cicoria*," she finally said. Nervous, she shuffled from foot to foot in her torn sneakers.

"Chick-*cor*-ia? What the hell's that? You can't pick whatever that is off government property without permission or a license or something," he said. "Hand me the bags. They are government property."

"You can't have the bags," Connie said. The words fell out of her mouth before she could think.

"You can't keep the bags. You'll have to stop vandalizing government property and hand them over," he repeated. "Tell that to your daddy, girl. You'll both be arrested."

The park ranger stood over her. He extended his arm, with his hand open, waiting to receive the bags. She slowly lifted the first bag off the ground to hand it off to him when her father shouted.

"Nuh! You picka you own *cicoria*. Deesa my *cicori*," her father says with an accent so thick it could have sounded Italian, waving around the knife in his hands.

"What he say?" the park ranger asked Connie, putting his hand on his weapon and backing up. "Tell him to drop that knife, missy. *Drop your knife, sir!*" he shouted.

"He said, '*Cicoria* is good to eat. You should try to eat some,'" Connie lied, stepping closer to her father. She stepped quietly but firmly on his sandaled toes with her tennis shoes. He bent over in pain but held fast to the knife.

"That may be so, but this here is government property, and your father must put down his knife. Tell him to put down his knife."

Still holding the knife, her father continued to chop the stalks, yelling that it was his *cicoria* and for the park ranger to pick his own. Connie's heart beat like a timpani drum. "Pop, *fai attenzione*! *Testa dura*, hard head!" she shouted. "Gimme it!" She pursed her lips and held out her hand for the knife.

"Sunnamabeech!" her father said, scowling. He dropped it, and she watched it hit the grass.

"Now step away from the knives!" the ranger shouted.

She pushed her father back with her body.

The ranger spoke code into his radio. Then he said, "Two subjects. Both Caucasian. One juvy female, short curly black hair, torn shoes, and jeans. One middle-aged male, fat, doesn't understand English, picking weeds..." The radio crackled.

"Mommy dips it in egg batter and puts three stalks together. She fries it with oil and garlic for lunch," Connie said. Her voice was shaky but loud. "That's what my sisters and I eat for lunch every day til the end of school. It's all we have," she said.

She was angry at her father, fighting back tears, and sounding desperate. She didn't want to be arrested for vandalizing government property. She hated her father at that moment, for his black knee-high socks and sandals and for glaring at her with that wait-til-we-get-home look.

"This here's your lunch?" the park ranger asked, sounding shocked. "You eat weeds?

You're telling the truth? You eat this stuff?" The ranger fingered the stalks in the bag. Wiping his sap-stained fingers on the sides of the bags, he spoke into the radio. "Subjects eat the weeds. Please advise."

Biting her lower lip to keep from crying, Connie dared not look at the ranger.

The voice on the other end of the radio responded in numbers. "Ten-four, Roger out," the ranger said into the radio.

"Okay, miss. You can keep the bags, but you and your Pa have to leave the fort immediately. Tell that to your Pa. That you both have to leave the fort immediately," he said. He stepped forward. His shined shoes caught a glint of the sun and the sky. He retrieved the knives from the grass and slipped them into the bag he was holding. His head under his ranger hat looked shaved and smooth.

"And don't come back here to pick weeds. I'll escort you back to the parking lot in my car," he said. He had a grim face with serious blue eyes that looked at her like he meant business. He didn't smile at them. Still holding a bag of *cicoria* in his left hand, he motioned them with his right hand toward his park ranger car. They each—first her father carrying two bags of *cicoria*, then her, and then the ranger behind her—trudged up the small embankment to the green old car. Empty-handed and face flushed, she felt naked and exposed.

Her father clutched two bags of *cicoria* to his stocky torso, looking like a fat refugee in his hideous clothes. He had an almost imperceptible smile hiding beneath his mustache as the ranger helped them into the backseat of his car. Her father beamed triumphant.

A LESSON IN COLORS IN MONEY MISSISSIPPI: PART ONE

THERE WAS A fourteen-year-old Black boy. There was a twenty-one-year-old White woman. There was a whistle. There were two White men. There was a Crow named Jim. There was a kidnapping. There was a seventy-five-pound cotton gin fan.

There was a lesson in colors, meaning that there were two White men who thought they'd teach the Black boy about a lesson in Money, Mississippi. There was a shed. There were cries in the shed over a lesson in colors, meaning the Black boy who whistles—who probably never ever kissed a girl, who called for his mama—learned a hard lesson in color. You just learned how to whistle to call your dog, Champ, but you don't want to call Champ anymore because the Crow might come instead.

There was blue. There were black and blue. There was purple mixed with red. There was a forty-five stuck inside a shiny silver pistol. There was that Crow who helped a fast, flying bullet go into a tender head. A few days later, there was the pop of the bullet exploding in the north, in Chicago where they learned that a lesson in colors in Mississippi includes topics like a beating, a lynching, a shooting, a killing, and a sinking with a seventy-five-pound cotton gin fin.

The talking White man on TV said Emmitt Till was at the bottom of the Tallahatchie River, but your Black father picked you up and held you in his arms while he yelled at the White TV man about a damned rainbow puddled around Emmitt Till, the Boy who Whistled.

There were blood red, purple, and yellow bruised arms of the fourteen-year old Black boy in the blue waters under a baking yellow sun in the azure sky in green Money, Mississippi, where horseflies with iridescent wings and the Crow named Jim buzzed like electricity. There was the pain. There was the Crow that caused the pain that leaked out of the Black boy. It made him bigger and larger than before and oozed into his Chicago mama and into your Baltimore mama, who held you so tight that you couldn't breathe. She sang "Take My Hand, Precious Lord" into your eight-year-old Black boy ears, begging for the same Lord to keep you in the palm of His. There was fear in your mama that leaked into you, who wondered what if you fell out of the giant, invisible palm of His hand or if He drops you like they dropped the whistling boy in Money, Mississippi.

There was a lesson in colors at school where Sister Ursula caught Darlene Parklee's big sister in the rear of the cloakroom, sitting on the stomach of a fourteen-year old Black boy. Her yellow hair fell over them while she tried to smear her pink lips all over his Brown ones as he yelled, "Stop it! And get off of me!"

You wanted to stay home to avoid the Crow coming to teach you about colors at your school after you learned how to whistle and after Darleen Parkless's big sister got sent home. The Chicago mama wanted everyone to learn about that lesson in colors taught by the Crow and two White men in Money, Mississippi, but just like at school, no one paid attention for long.

A LESSON IN COLORS IN ALCOLU, SOUTH CAROLINA: PART TWO

THERE WAS A ditch on the Black side of town. There was murder. There were two White girls, ages eleven and eight, searching for purple passionflowers, which they called "maypops" before they went missing overnight in Alcolu, South Carolina. There was one fourteen-year-old, ninety-pound Black boy. There was a Crow named Jim. There were horseflies following the Crow; their iridescent wings buzzed with electricity. There was an invisible line in the center of the gray railroad tracks the kept Black people on one side and White people on the other. There was an absence of red, no blood in the muddy ditch where the two missing White girls who'd been searching for purple passionflowers now lay dead with bashed in heads on the wrong side of town.

There were three White deputies, including the arresting deputy who said the fourteen-year old, ninety-pound Black boy named George Junius Stinney, Jr. confessed to killing the two White girls. There was no mention of a beating that brought the confession or the black and blue, purple and yellow, and rainbow of colors on the fourteen-year-old, ninety-pound Black boy's body that accompanied the confession.

There was Stinney's sister, Aime, who'd been playing with George at the time the two White girls searched for purple passionflowers on the Black side of town. There was cold white disbelief when little Aime said her and her brother spent the day in their father's meadow watching their brown horse. There was the White arresting deputy who collected the fourteen-year old, ninety-pound Black boy at his house to arrest him when his parents weren't home. There was little Aimee hiding in the barn when her brother was taken away without their parents being home, puzzled about a confession that couldn't be true when she knew the truth.

There were eighty-one long days when this fourteen-year old, ninety-pound Black boy sat confined in a jail fifty miles away from his family, the first time he'd been away from his mama and his daddy. There were gray walls and black bars in the jail cell that felt like forever, despite the candy bar and Bible that the arresting deputy brought him. There was a river of tears at the Stinney home and at the jail where the fourteen-year-old Black boy was given black and white striped clothes to wear. There were gold letters on that black cover and gold-edged pages on that black Bible he held with trembling hands. The thick book was almost as big as his torso; his thin short arms hugged it like a fairytale. There were no visitors allowed. No mama or daddy. No brothers or sisters. No aunties or uncles. No grandparents. No friends.

There was fear. There was terror. There was the Stinney family being run out of town, out of Alcolu, away from their farm, and away from daddy's job that fired him. There was no lawyer present when the White arresting deputy said the fourteen-year old, ninety-pound Black boy named George Stinney confessed. There was no talk of the rainbow of colors that accompanied the confession. There was no white paper with black ink signed by the fourteen-year-old, ninety-pound Black boy with blue and black, purple and yellow under his zebra striped clothes that accompanied a confession.

At the same time the fourteen-year-old, ninety-pound Black boy sat quivering in a jail cell in South Carolina while missing his mama, longing for the safety of the arms of his daddy, and clutching his black Bible with gold-edged pages, there was your big brother Clarence arrested in Baltimore for protesting police brutality when he and other Black teachers rallied in the streets to be represented on the school board. There was your Baltimore mama crying in the kitchen, wringing her hands and clutching her own green covered Bible to her heart, afraid her oldest child with his silver wire-rimmed glasses, soft voice, and head full of idealistic notions would end up dead in the Baltimore City jail, despite his hard-earned beige university sheepskin.

There was the trial for the fourteen-year-old, ninety-pound Black boy in South Carolina that lasted two and a half hours, including the minutes it took to select the all White jury, because Black people were not allowed. There was a White judge. There was a White prosecutor. There was a White defense attorney, who specialized in taxes and dreamed about political ambitions and his desire for votes. There were more than a thousand White attendees in the courtroom— potential voters—wanting revenge for two dead White girls.

There was no cross examination. There were three versions of the fourteen-year-old, ninety-pound Black Boy's confession. None on paper. There was no evidence. There was no request for evidence. There were just the White deputies and the White words falling out of their pink lips. There was no transcript.

It was for ten hours that Uncle Clarence and Baltimore's other Black teachers sat in the Baltimore jail without being charged with any crime before they were released. It took ten minutes for the all White jury to convict the fourteen-year-old, ninety-pound Black boy of killing two White girls. There was the White judge who pronounced the sentence: death by electrocution. There was no appeal. There were letters sent by citizens across South Carolina to the governor, pleading for mercy, pleading to halt the execution of the fourteen-year-old, ninety-pound boy. Letters that were ignored.

It took eighty-three days from the moment the White deputy collected the fourteen-year old, ninety-pound Black boy named George Stinney to the moment he was thrust into the arms of Ol' Sparky, the White people's name for the red electric chair with brown straps. It was June 16, 1944, at seven thirty p.m. when the five-foot-one-inch, fourteen-year old, ninety-pound Black boy, too small for the man sized chair, was forced to sit on his gold-rimmed black Bible as a booster seat, because he otherwise couldn't be secured to the chair for being too small. It made it clear that Ol' Sparky didn't want him. There was the state's too big man-sized mask that did not fit the fourteen-year-old, ninety-pound Black boy's face. There were the boy's trembling hands.

There was terror. There was fear. There was no mercy. There was the first jolt, a two thousand and four hundred electrical surge that failed to kill the fourteen-year-old, ninety-pound Black boy, but it knocked the too big mask off his face, showing his tearful eyes, filled with questions to everyone watching. His frightened child's face. His pink tongue drooping out of his red mouth. His brown lips dripping saliva.

There were two more jolts, and it took four long minutes to teach George Junius Spinney, Jr., a fourteen-year-old, ninety-pound Black boy, a lesson in colors.

There was a lesson in colors at Uncle Clarence's job where he was fired for being arrested. The White school superintendent said he would be a bad influence to his ninth grade Black students at a school where the superintendent never visited. There was Uncle Clarence's last day. The same day, the newspaper came carrying a headline about the nation's youngest murderer electrocuted in South Carolina, complete with a photo of the fourteen-year old, ninety-pound Black boy. Your mama sucked in air, squeezed your fourteen-year-old Black boy body into hers. Her sweet perfume invaded your nostrils. Her tears fell into your Black boy ears as she cried, "Please Lord. Please Lord Jesus, tell me it ain't so."

Uncle Clarence, proud of his university teaching degree that filled his head with notions of how things ought to be, punched the kitchen table with his fists. The table vibrated until your daddy held him still. There was the flap of Jim Crow's wings, nearly imperceptible but enough to hear them beating the air around.

YOU'LL DO FINE

CHARLIE ATTEMPTED TO look bored as he watched Debra tramp down the hall to their bedroom at the foot of their F-shaped apartment. He slouched deeper into his chair in front of the living room TV, gripping the remote with one hand and a can of beer in the other.

"How can you be such a snake?" she yelled from the bedroom, a habit Charlie considered rude.

He wondered if the kid living upstairs heard her rudeness, conducting mundane conversations as if she lived in a warehouse. And he didn't want to talk about it. He knew he'd fucked up. He set the remote on the chair's overstuffed armrest, grabbed his service revolver from the small lamp table beside it, fingered the barrel, opened the chamber, and dumped the bullets into his lap. He liked the sound they made—like heavy coins. Snagging the empty speed loader from the table, he set the gun, chamber still open, in between his legs and inserted six bullets into it. He wondered how long she'd jaw on tonight about the missing money.

"Charlie McAllister, I'm talking to you!" she yelled from the bedroom.

Charlie refused to engage in shouted conversations. Besides, the money wasn't missing. He knew exactly where it went. He could name each horse that failed to cross the finish line first, denying his big payout: Arcadia, Mustafa, When Lightning Strikes, Wench, Warrior, Buckshot, Ace in the Hole, and Margherita Magic. He could rattle off every football pool and fantasy football team that took his—well, Debra's money—without return, and at least—and this is where he prided himself—he didn't bet on the game day weather.

On the TV, two hands demonstrated the Veg-o-Matic vegetable slicer, and he winced watching carrots reappear as perfect orange spheres on the other side of the blade. Knowing she'd bitch at him about it, he set the sweating beer can on the table anyway, because he wanted her to shut up about the money. Maybe she'd bitch about the water ring instead. He couldn't explain how he blew through the money. It happened, slipping by in small increments. A fifty-dollar bill here, a stack, and another, up one, down two, borrowing more, and poof. It vanished.

"Did you think I'd never find out?" she asked, emerging from the hallway and using her teacher voice. She'd been crying—mascara smeared, a mask around her red eyes. It was a gross overreaction to the facts since both of them still lived. She dropped a pile of laundry onto the sofa, and he'd expected her to sit and fold it as usual. Instead, she deftly slid it into a garbage bag. Only Debra could be so neat about clothes she would be donating.

"We had this same conversation last month when the statement came. You knew I had to put the deposit down on the house contract. How could you think I wouldn't notice?" She bit her bottom lip and breathed in deeply through her nose, creating a loud sucking sound. She moved around the apartment as if she'd drunk too much caffeine. She marched in and out of every room, and Charlie wondered why the people downstairs hadn't knocked on the ceiling yet.

"Why don't you just calm down?" he asked, forgetting about the deposit. "It ain't the end of the world, you know. There are worse things. Like cancer. Getting cancer is worse, don't you think?" He dumped the bullets from the gun chamber into his lap again, just to hear the clinking sounds as they hit each other, and snapped it shut. He opened the chamber again, spun the empty cylinder a few times, and watched it whirl like a carnival wheel before loading the weapon again with the speed loader.

On the streets—especially in the red zone where he worked—a ready speed loader or two or three saved precious time and could save his life. If his partner, Jimmy, had only listened and kept a few clipped to his gun belt, he'd still be upright instead of pushing up daisies over at Holy Redeemer. He bought it on an Easter Sunday shoot-out, three years ago, that turned into an hours long siege. Why did holidays inspire the worst in people? Charlie regularly drove to the intersection where the gun battle took place, parked the cruiser, and stared at the bullet holes still etched in the red brick walls. The corner drew him as if Jimmy's ghost inhabited it.

And Debra's upset over a few bad bets? How about a little gratitude? He had made it, and Jimmy didn't. He wanted to say, "It's only money," but instead, he said, "Not the end of the world."

"It is for me. And if I got cancer, maybe that money would have saved me," she said, using her stinking teacher's voice again. "Show me what you used ten grand on, much more twenty grand. What, Charlie? What? Can you show me what you used my money for—not your money—my money from my mom's house? Do we have a nice house? Or a boat? Or something? What can you show me in this sorry apartment that's worth thirty grand?" She swept her arm around the living room, and now she didn't sound like a teacher anymore. Just a bitch.

When they'd first met, she cooed about how brave he was. She sang, "Macho, Macho Man" and danced for him in only panties and a bra before they'd have torrid sex. He smiled at the memory.

"You think this is funny? What happened to the house and children?" she asked, sniffing and blinking back tears. "This is the last straw, Charlie McAllistar. And you're a cop. Larceny after trust ring a bell?"

Charlie wanted to coax Debra's now puckered lips into her dimpled smile. "You going to make me stand in the corner and wear a dunce cap?" he asked. He drank more beer. "Okay, Teach. I'll go stand in the corner now. You can spank me," he repeated, trying for humor, but Debra frowned.

He regretted losing her money. Had he won, doubled, or tripled his bets, she'd be singing a different tune, calling him brilliant and dancing him into lusty marathon sex. She'd smile in her sunshiny way. He could survive anything to come home to that smile. During the gun battle that killed Jimmy, he'd prayed he'd live to see her smile another day. And afterward, glad he'd survived one of the fiercest shoot-outs between cops and thugs in Baltimore's history, she'd smiled, cried, and held him at Jimmy's funeral when he'd wept for his partner. He was just a rookie, a kid.

Charlie dropped the bullets from the speed loader, inserted them, dropped them out again, reinserted them, and nursed his beer.

With her eyebrows knitted, arms crossed, lips pursed, and while glaring at him, Debra stepped in front of the TV, blocking his view. "I'm talking to you. Pay attention! *Pay attention, damn it!*"

"I can hear you. I'm not deaf," he said. "Stop yelling."

"Losing that money is the last straw. We lost the contract on our dream house! I've waited for three years now for things to change, and nothing's changed except you for the worse," she said. He knew they'd become strangers with benefits. "It's over, Charlie."

"I don't believe you," he said without looking at her. He dropped the bullets into the speed loader, emptied them, and repeated the process. "It's only money. Money comes and goes. We'll get more," he said, shrugging. "I'll start moonlighting. We'll save for a down payment on another house, a better one."

"That's probably how you lost the money. Always believing it will get better miraculously. Your body comes home but barely functions. The money isn't the only thing missing," she said. "You're missing."

"I function just fine," Charlie said. He set the unloaded gun and the speed loader on the table and then crushed the empty beer can in his right hand. "See? Just fine." He held up the crushed aluminum before tossing it into the trash can. In the kitchen, he grabbed the meat mallet and pounded the kitchen counter. "You still think I'm missing?" he shouted over the pounding. He set a fresh beer can from the fridge on the counter. "What's for dinner?" he asked, examining his reflection in the glass cabinet window. "I'm hungry." Maybe he looked a little rough around the edges now, but he could still cut a sharp figure if he wanted. His hair hadn't fled, and his mustache was still thick. He patted his belly, a beer gut, he conceded.

Debra moved like a gazelle. Her frenzied activities exhausted him.

In the bathroom, he leaned against the wall to pee, but then he realized too late he'd forgotten to lift the seat. "Shit," he said, leaning over to grab some toilet paper from the wall dispenser, and that's when he saw the miniature note written in red.

His vision was slightly blurry, so he couldn't read the words but smiled. Maybe this was Debra's way of apologizing for giving him a hard time. Curious, he leaned closer, nearly falling onto the floor, and shut one eye to see it better. With his face inches away from the note, he could make it out, but it made no sense: "You'll do fine!" followed by a smile face. That Debra. What a trickster! He wiped the seat and tossed the paper into the trash can, where a blue box with white letters caught his eye. A pregnancy test.

It looked unused. Inside the box, neatnik Debra had returned everything to its original spot. Pulling the indicator stick toward him, he spied the blue plus sign.

He took the box and hurried back into the living room, where two piles of laundry occupied the sofa. When upset, she often conducted thorough cleaning expeditions, and now overstuffed garbage bags filled the sofa. He retrieved the beer from the kitchen and held up the box. "What's this?"

She shrugged. "What's it look like?"

"It says positive. That means you're knocked up. When were you going to tell me about this?" he asked, realizing he sounded as if he were mocking her about the money. He softened his tone. "I told you. I'm not ready for a kid."

She snickered as she stuffed more piles into the garbage bags. "Don't worry, Charlie. I'm taking care of it."

"Taking care of it how?" On the box, a man and woman were peering at a plus sign, looking joyful. Charlie knew they should be looking joyful too.

"I'm taking care of it." She spoke to the bag. "You can pretend we never had this conversation."

"You're not killing my kid," he said, setting the beer on the table.

"You just said you're not ready for a kid," she said. Her eyes fixed on him, looking fierce. "What I do with my body is none of your business."

"Since when? It's my kid too, and I have a say." He settled back into the chair, this time with the remote in one hand and the box in the other. "When were you going to tell me? Huh?"

"Never."

Charlie laughed. "Like you can hide a pregnancy."

"I wasn't planning to hide anything. I'm leaving."

He scoffed. "You can't leave. Pregnant wives don't leave their husbands."

Debra rolled her eyes and continued stuffing laundry into the garbage bags.

"Apology accepted," he said, popping the new can open and resettling into the TV chair. "Krug," he said, offering a toast before gulping the beer. He and Jimmy used to yell "Krug" at the shift change parties. They toasted with "Krug" only on happy occasions, and he wasn't yet sure if a baby was a happy occasion, but maybe if he toasted it with Krug, it might become one.

"Krug, Krug!" he said, lifting his can and sucking back beer in fast gulps.

"What are you talking about?" Debra asked, slipping neatly folded clothes into the garbage bags. She threw the question into the air as if Charlie was a ghost.

"That small note written in red in the bathroom. 'You'll do fine, Charlie.' And the smiley face. Apology accepted. We're calling it Jimmy if it's a boy."

She shook her head. Her black curly hair swung from its ponytail. "So, you already have a name for the kid you aren't ready to have? Oh, please," she said.

He stared at her midsection to see if she looked any different, and it shocked him that she'd gotten so skinny. Her legs—one of her most lovely attributes and still muscular—resembled thin sticks.

"You think that's an apology?" she asked without looking at him.

"Yep," he said, taking in more beer.

"Whatever makes you happy, Charlie," she said, sounding indifferent.

Relieved she didn't sound angry, he set the beer down on the table in a slightly different spot, waiting to see if she'd notice the can on the table without a coaster and the multiple wet rings. He stared at the rings, thinking they looked like the Olympics symbol. What if there was an Olympics for beer drinkers? He imagined the crowd going wild over his Olympic beer guzzling victory.

Debra traversed the F-shaped apartment as if she was training for a marathon, stuffing clothes and toiletries into bags. With a capped red Sharpie behind her ear, she looked like a construction project manager, writing notes onto the clipboard. Usually, she'd spend her evenings correcting papers and preparing for her class. She'd been teaching herself to knit, and on these nights, she would bake brownies or a batch of cookies for the kids the next day, leaving some for him. He tried to recall if she'd eaten anything that she baked but couldn't. "For Goodwill?" he asked.

She didn't respond but wrote on her clipboard instead, and he counted eight bags.

"What's for dinner?" he asked, wanting her to answer. "I said I'm hungry."

"Catch-as-catch-can," she said. "There's plenty of food in the freezer. Don't worry, Charlie. You'll do fine."

"What the fuck does that mean? I'll do fine?" Anger flashed in him.

"Must I spell it out for you?" she asked in her teacher's voice.

Before he could answer, she grabbed two bags and disappeared through the apartment door, only to return a few seconds later to grab another two. Was she supposed to be lifting heavy bags while pregnant? She returned with the large stepladder, which she leaned against the wall in the hallway.

"If you'd ask, I'd help," he said, but the door slammed on his words. Two bags left on the sofa now, and he knew he should just get up and help, but damn it, he wanted her to ask. He wanted her to need him. He wanted her to want him. Like before.

He picked up his revolver and the speed loader and practiced using it to load and unload the gun. Timing could be the difference between life and death. He'd never be caught unprepared like Jimmy, who bled to death in the middle of the Lombard and Carey intersection because the son of a bitch shooter had tried to pick off anyone who got too close.

Charlie's heart raced just thinking about it. The beer calmed him.

Panting and face flushed from running up and down three flights of stairs to and from the car, Debra let the door slam behind her. The tension seemed to have drained from her face, and he relaxed. They weren't hurting. At worst, the missing money meant a bit of a delay leaving this crappy apartment for a house.

They had a spare room, and he imagined all the work he'd do converting it into a nursery. He imagined them choosing paint colors and allowed himself to consider a son. She said nothing, acting as if he was invisible in the TV chair. Staring at the wet circles on the table, he decided to wipe them off with the hem of his undershirt. When she noticed, she rolled her eyes instead of yelling at him about being a slob the way she usually did.

He gulped more beer and resumed playing with the speed loader and the gun. He loved this gun, the same gun he'd used to finally end the standoff when Jimmy died. He'd filed the trigger mechanism down to a hair during the weeks prior to that firefight; so, instead of needing ten pounds of pressure, it'd fire at three pounds—a trick he'd read in *Soldier of Fortune* magazine.

Debra busied herself in the kitchen, banging pots and pans, and opening and shutting the freezer and oven. She emerged with a small stack of frying and cake pans, sliding them into one of the remaining garbage bags.

"You giving away our pots and pans?" he asked, raising his eyebrows.

"No," she said. "There's a few, and the microwave works just fine."

"Okay," he said, glad that the money issue flared and died faster than dice rolled. Which was so unlike her, who clung to a topic like a wolverine. "When you supposed to drop the load?" he asked, trying to sound light and funny.

She didn't smile. Instead, she looked annoyed, the humor lost on her. Angry, he flung the pregnancy test box at her, and it hit her arm before it fell with a thud. She stared at the box lying by her feet.

"You're up and down, and I never know when you'll be up or down. Sometimes, you're Happy Charlie, and sometimes you're Mean Charlie, but more often than not, you're Drunk Charlie. It comes and goes so much that I don't ever feel safe with you anymore," she said.

"Is it mine?" Charlie asked, fear prickling his skin. His muscles tensed.

Debra picked up the box and tossed it at him.

"What the hell? For real?"

She carried the ladder into the bedroom, where she stayed a long time.

He thought about their last vacation together before the shoot-out, the last time he remembered them laughing. At the Mont Sainte-Anne ski resort in Quebec, they'd rented a snowmobile, snowsuits, and helmets, accepted the French map of the route, and stopped at the stations along the way for hot chocolate. Longing for a dash of excitement and with Debra sitting behind him like a biker babe, he floored the gas pedal, imagining himself as Evel Knievel. Their scarves waved behind them before he had miscalculated a hairpin turn.

Thrown from the snowmobile, they'd crashed into each other, landing in a giant snowdrift, and the snowmobile continued riderless down the mountain. His helmet had cracked. He left Debra struggling in the snowdrift. While looking like a giant bumblebee in his black and yellow striped snowsuit, he'd chased the vehicle on the molasses-like snow path, finally running beside it and pressing the emergency stop button. It lacked a reverse gear, so he'd waited for her to come down. Face hidden by the helmet, she'd appeared around the turn like an astronaut in a blue and red snowsuit. They leaned against the snowmobile, examining the crack and trembling with joy that they'd cheated death and weren't injured. Despite snow inside their suits, they couldn't stop laughing. At the rental station, the proprietor fingered the cracked helmet, saying there'd been some snowmobile deaths due to reckless riders.

A buzzer sounded in the kitchen, summoning Debra. She brought him half a pizza on a plate.

"When's it due?" he asked, though he feared his words would start a harangue about the money again. So, he ate, shoving pizza into his mouth.

Debra shrugged and said nothing.

"Eat some," he said, trying to keep his voice even.

"No, thanks," she said, disappearing into the bathroom for what seemed like for too long. The sound of water running comforted him, though he didn't know why. She stayed there, and he finished the rest of the pizza. He wondered if he should check on her, but she liked her independence, and he knew the missing money still riled her, so why kick the shit?

With a fresh beer in hand, he channel surfed, finding another action show. The same stupid Veg-o-Matic commercial aired again, so he clicked to a different channel that had another commercial and clicked back. Grabbing his service revolver, he practiced loading and unloading the speed loader and the gun, seeing if he could complete the sequence in half the time it took the commercial to air.

Skin glowing, Debra looked refreshed when she came into the living room. She'd applied a small amount of cosmetics, lip gloss, and blush. Dark and curly, her hair hung loose, and she'd changed into a khaki miniskirt and flat sandals. She looked lovely with those dark almond eyes, and it made his heart flutter to see her. If he didn't know better, he'd think she had a date.

"Going somewhere?" he asked, sounding harsh but not meaning it.

"I told you already. I'm leaving. Don't worry, Charlie. You'll do fine. Maybe you should get a pet. A cat that you can mostly ignore."

"Ridiculous!" He sat up straight in the TV chair. His eyes were now fixed on her and not the TV. "Where're you going?"

"Sissy's. Until I can figure things out. Our lease here expires in a month. I've already told the rental office that I won't be renewing with you. You can stay here or move; it's up to you."

He opened and closed his mouth. No words came out. Then he realized she was playing him, a joke. He laughed. "You had me going there for a second. You did."

She shook her head, "Not joking, Charlie. You'll do fine."

"Pregnant wives don't leave their husbands," he said. "What do you mean until you figure things out? What's to figure out?"

Eyes wide, she stared at him for a long time. "I don't want to bring a baby here," she said, looking at the beer can, the stains on the table, and the service revolver in his lap. "A baby needs someone who can provide, not make money disappear on a whole lot of nothing. Never mind the moods. Maybe adoption," she said as she grabbed the last two bags from the sofa and set them by the door. "The freezer has plenty of stuff in it. You'll do fine."

"It's my kid too. You're not putting my kid up for adoption. You can't leave either. You just need some cooling-off time," he said.

By the door, Debra focused on him. "Oh, I've already experienced a few years of cooling-off time." The door slammed behind her.

"Wait!" he yelled at the closed door. He scrambled out of the chair to the window and threw open the sash just in time to see her walk toward her car. "Don't leave!" he shouted out the window. "Don't!"

Debra tossed the bags into her Toyota's backseat and climbed into her car overstuffed with them.

He admired her stubborn coolness. He chugged the last of his beer, refusing to believe she was gone forever. Deep in his bones, he knew she'd be back, knew there'd only be so much of her sister's family she could take.

He channel surfed mindlessly, imagining his soon-to-be-born son. He imagined playing catch with him while his mitt was too big for his little hand. He envisioned doing all the stuff with a son that his father had never done with him. Fishing. Going to baseball games or playing catch. Building model airplanes and flying kites together. Riding roller coasters. He'd done all those things with his uncle Pat and his mother while his father had warmed the same stool at Mick O'Shea's every day he could remember.

The damned Veg-o-Matic commercial popped up on every station. The blade kept slicing and dicing carrots and cucumbers. Click. Click. Click. Charlie dry fired the revolver, enjoying the sound of the clicks it made, the ease of pulling the trigger, and the hammer hitting the empty chamber. Click.

Funny that gunshots sounded more explosive on TV. In reality, they created a pop—not a boom. Like a small firecracker, it sounded innocuous, but it killed Jimmy before he could see the other side of thirty.

Why the hell did Debra get herself knocked up?

The day he died, Charlie had gotten tired of watching his partner's life slowly drain into the streets. Defying orders, he had used the cars as a cover as he went the opposite direction of the shooter to the first alley and climbed the fire escape to the roof. He had seen the shooter with his rifle barrel sticking out the second-floor window. On his belly while keeping himself low against the flat roof, he had crawled to the edge. Extending his arms in front of him with his revolver perched in both his hands, he had squeezed off a round from his newly filed firing pin, a round that had shattered the second-floor window before finding its mark: the shooter's head.

He was too late to save Jimmy. The papers and TV had heralded him as a hero sharpshooter by ending the ordeal, but the department had busted his ass for defying orders and for interrupting the negotiation that would have prompted the shooter to surrender without so much as a scratch. They banished him to permanent desk duty.

"Hell, I saved the city a boatload of money by not having to feed and shelter the cop-killing pork chop for the rest of his life," he'd told his sergeant, swallowing the bitterness that had formed in the back of his throat, two months into the desk duty. Now, he wondered if his old man, also a cop, had swallowed a hefty plate of bitter pie at Mick O'Shea's with the Jameson neat. He would wave when Charlie or his mother had walked by.

Charlie grabbed the last beer, not caring he'd drunk them all.

Click. Click. Click. Unload, load, snap, and aim. One. Two. Three. Faster.

He wanted Debra to stay. Why couldn't she understand that? He couldn't lose her too. He had to get her back, promise her the fucking moon. They'd work things out. He wanted to play catch and do things with his son that his old man had never done. He'd clean up, man up, and be ready for a kid.

Loading the weapon one last time, he snapped the chamber shut and placed it on the table before he searched for his running shoes. He saw them in the closet lined in a neat row with the rest of his shoes, but she had left the ladder standing open under the ceiling light, blocking the closet door from fully opening. Buzzed, he moved the ladder, nearly tripped, and steadied himself on it instead.

Then he saw red writing on the ceiling near the light fixture base. He read it from the third ladder step. "A hundred and thirty-seven cracks in the ceiling. I've counted them many times while waiting for you to come home from wherever you were. Perhaps I should be happy you were pissing away money and not dunking dickie, but I can't pretend it's the lesser of two evils. All of it's bad. You'll do fine, Charlie." Smile face.

At first, it riled him. These stupid notes. But then he pictured her climbing the ladder while pregnant to leave a note. He wondered how many she'd left around the joint.

He stepped into his running shoes, not bothering to tie them. He struggled to remember the directions to Sissy's house. In the living room with his pants askew, shoes untied, and a fuzzy head, he counted on his body to automatically know the way. Grabbing his trusty revolver and slipping the barrel inside his waistband, he tore out the front door. He realized he'd forgotten his car keys though, so he retreated back. Finally, ten minutes later, he found them on the key hook. Of course.

With his keys in hand, while drunk and determined, he rushed from the apartment toward Debra and his future, their future with their son. But instead he collided into the good-looking kid who lived upstairs. Maybe the kid was coming home from work, from a date, from visiting relatives, or from nowhere in particular. He was carrying an enormous cake box, running up the stairs as only a kid could. Taking them two and three at a time, he burst onto the landing outside Charlie's apartment in a midnight whirlwind.

He heard the innocuous pop at the same time the kid said, "Fuck!" and dropped the cake box. With surprise in his eyes, the kid looked at Charlie, who feared he'd shot himself and grew more alert as his training kicked in. The kid's leg buckled, and he held onto the railing to soften his fall onto the landing.

Trembling now, Charlie kneeled next to the kid, whispering "You'll do fine" like a mantra. He pulled off his shirt and ripped it into strips. He bellowed for help as the sticky wetness spread down the kid's pants and up his T-shirt, staining them red.

HIDING IN BOXES

I WIPE MY fingers—orange from Doritos—on my pants, which was already stained with snack residue. Katy rummages through the boxes in the bathroom that we don't use. She hates living out of boxes in this small apartment where we can't find things. It's obvious that everything overwhelms her.

"Tom, have you seen the iron?" she yells from the bathroom. I can hear objects shifting in boxes as she pushes them around. I consider helping her but lack the energy. Where can she iron anything in this apartment? There's nowhere to iron, even if she were to use a bath towel as an ironing pad as she sometimes did back at the house when she didn't feel like going downstairs to the laundry room, where the ironing board hung on its own wall cabinet.

Tables, counters, cabinets, and chairs lurk beneath the stuff that covers every flat surface. I know she gets anxious when she can't find things she thinks she needs but eventually forgets about them if she can't locate them right away. What does she need to iron? Her uniforms? Wash and wear. Under the pile of empty Doritos bags on the sofa, I keep a list of all the things she wants and can't find in case I come across them in the towers of our stuff that lean left and right like Dr. Seuss illustrations. Some stuff on the list is small—tweezers, photos, silver frames, and small appliances like her hair dryer and now the iron. Also on the list are her juicer, her sewing machine, and her knitting and crochet hooks and patterns, which are all still hiding in boxes.

In this too small apartment on the rougher west side of town, I catch Katy wincing in the parking lot from the window. Her hands cup and squeeze her face as if she is about to step into a precipice that drops her into the fourth ring of hell.

Katy's a nurse over at the university hospital, which is something she does to help pay bills. As a nurse anesthetist, she brings home a decent salary, better than a regular nurse. Although it pales compared to what I earned before the layoff, even with all the extra overtime she works. I miss her when she's at work, but when she's home, I miss the quiet of when she's away because she's always trying to locate things in boxes.

I'm supposed to be unpacking, arranging what we have, and getting rid of stuff. But over the past few months—well, eight to be exact—I haven't had the time to unpack, arrange, or discard anything. Time has been funky lately, speeding up or slowing down without warning that it would change its pace. I'm looking for a new job, but I often end up in a bar with my fingers wrapped around a beer when Katy thinks I'm at an interview. Dressing in work clothes for a fake interview feels odd, as if I'm watching myself perform a skit from outside my body. My work clothes—designer suits, trousers, and shirts with monogramed pockets—have grown too tight, and no one calls me for interviews.

The truth is I've stopped applying.

"Why can't we sell this?" she asks when she comes through a tunnel into the living room.

She's holding a ceramic, vintage whiskey decanter in the shape of a Revolutionary War soldier. I inherited it from my father, who kept an entire collection of such things, but the collection is now somewhere in these boxes. With its green knee-length breeches, short topcoat, painted brass buttons, and tricorn hat edged in gold, the soldier's innocent expression does not look as if he's experienced the death and destruction of war.

"It's crap. We don't need it. We won't miss it. We probably won't miss half the crap in these boxes." She palms the decanter's ceramic head.

Katy hid the decanters in the basement at the house. I'd loathe to get rid of them, one of the few reminders of my father.

Coveted like a crown jewel, a bright blue mini remote-controlled helicopter, the size and shape of a jumbo egg, nestles in the palm of her other hand, a toy. One she doesn't want me to see. It belongs to Keven, our son, who flew it around our house, delighted that the cats stalked it and leapt after it as if they were giant frogs pursuing a giant dragonfly. The day before Keven died, Scar, the oldest cat of our trio, leapt like a flying tiger and batted the thing out of the air. Keven, who was only fourteen, laughed and awed at the kitty's dare. He loved Scar more despite the crashed 'copter. The day he died, he cuddled and stroked Scar before leaving to spend the afternoon at his friend Jimmy's, where they usually played video games.

Keven and Jimmy must have spent a gazillion hours together at each other's houses. They'd known each other since first grade. Unbeknownst to us, Jimmy's father kept a loaded gun hidden, and that Saturday, the boys' curiosity unleashed a nine-millimeter copper monolithic, traveling at two thousand feet per second straight into Keven's stomach. The round perfectly demonstrated its permanent wound capacity, greater than three and a half inches in diameter. I ignored Katy's incessant cell phone calls. She knew I had to put in a few hours, the finishing touches on a few deals that would bring us a windfall. When she called the office line instead, I finally picked up. My annoyance was unchecked but unexpressed. Before I could speak, her voice crackled on the other side. She sounded breathless.

"Finally! Tom, why don't you pick up for Pete's sake? There's been an accident," she said. Her loud voice trembled as if the bottom had dropped out of it. "Keven's hurt. It's bad. I'm on my way to Shock Trauma."

She hung up, giving me no chance to ask or say anything. Shock Trauma? The next ten minutes became cataclysmic and earth-shattering. Only severe cases went to Shock Trauma. I searched for my car keys, located my wallet and my glasses, and struggled for breath from a punch to the heart. What the hell kind of accident would send my kid to Shock Trauma? I found my shoes under the desk but didn't bother putting them on. Holding them in my hand, I ran for the car. I tried calling Katy back, but now she didn't pick up. What kind of accident?

On the way to Shock Trauma, the sun bathed everything in an incandescent yellow. The sky was a watery blue, silver, and cream; it was suffocating, devoid of any birds circling in graceful arcs. The horizon was a milky white spilling toward the earth. No chicken hawks. No starlings, wrens, or pigeons. I thanked God traffic on this Saturday afternoon proved sparse, allowing me to reach the hospital in record time. My tires bounced off the curb as I shot the car into the hospital's emergency lane, parking my Mercedes haphazardly in the reserved spot for doctors and not caring so long as one of them would tell me my son was okay. I ran shoeless from the car.

Inside and unable to wait, I interrupted the clerk on the phone, shouting Keven's full name at her. She held up her pointer finger, indicating I was to wait. My eyes darted, searching for Katy. Eternity passed before she hung up the phone and turned her eyes, clinical and dispassionate, toward me. Under the florescent lights, this woman, with her garish red lipstick, teased hair, and flashing earrings, had seen all manner of emergencies without a doubt, day in and day out. My son's name just another among the latest in the parade of the traumatically injured. She would not be rushed.

"Keven Rivers," I said, spelling it and not giving her a chance to ask.

She focused on the computer screen, and two mouse clicks later, she said, "Still in surgery. Elevators behind you, second floor. The surgery waiting room is on your left off the elevator." She kept her eyes on the computer, pretending I was invisible.

"What was the accident?" I asked, hoping for some clue.

She shook her head, without looking at me, and said, "I don't have that information." Her refusal to look at me told me she did have that information.

In the surgery waiting room, Katy paced. Her face was ghostly pale, decorated by streaks of mascara. She wore her gardening clothes. The knees of her pants were stained with dirt, and she pulled at her fingers as if to remove invisible gloves. When she saw me, she rushed toward me and wept. "Shot in the stomach. A nine millimeter." The words came slowly, labored, and I could tell she held onto her professional training to refrain from sobbing.

The nine millimeter had a diameter of .355 inches, but when it struck tissue, its kinetic energy created something known as a temporary cavity, which was responsible for injuring arteries, veins, organs, and nerves not directly struck by the bullet or its fragments. The bullet did its work in Keven, who never came home. We saw him briefly, tied to machines and IVs, over the next few days. He never awoke, but each of us held his hands, which would never build another model or fly another remote-controlled 'copter. Or pet the cat. Or hug either of us.

We kissed his forehead and stroked his hair as we did when he was an infant, a toddler, and a boy. He died a few days later, the permanent damage of the nine millimeter snuffed out and erased fourteen years in a split second.

Six months later, I lost my job to the recession, and then nearly a year later, we lost the house, along with friends and family. Katy never says it, but she blames me. I was supposed to have gotten him from Jimmy's two hours before the accident happened.

A blue flash winks at me as Katy slips the 'copter into her uniform pocket. Its delicate black blades extend past the ridged welt like insect antennae. She's waving the ceramic soldier decanter by its hat, an obvious distraction.

"We're hoarders. Fucking hoarders," she says. Her tone is edged and sharp, almost shrill.

"Like on TV. We need to get rid of all of this crap."

"No, we're not. There are no dead cats and no garbage here. Just our stuff neatly packed in moving boxes," I say. We surrendered our cats to the no-kill animal shelter when we moved our stuff out of the house. I hated leaving Scar, Bella, and Spazz behind, especially knowing that Keven loved them, but we couldn't afford to keep them. Maybe they'll still be there after we get back on our feet again. "We'll need all this stuff when we move back into a house."

Our bed, an oasis in the clutter, remains the sole flat surface in the apartment not covered by stuff. Katy pitched a fevered fit about needing to sleep before work. I get it. In this oasis, the ten inches separating our bodies might as well be ten miles, ten thousand miles, or ten million miles. Neither of us finds any reason to breach the distance, although my increasing size shrinks the space between us. Also, she has been wearing gym clothes to bed as if she needs to be ready to flee in the middle of the night.

"I don't want to sell or toss a single thing," I tell her, knowing how irrational it is to want to cram a large house worth of stuff into this apartment. She would simplify to an exaggerated level, shedding everything down to the most Spartan basics.

Boxes of shoes, clothing, hangers, and bathroom products. Boxes of glasses and dinnerware. Clothing, art, furniture, chairs, mirrors, and plants. Keven's stuff. Legos, action figures, and Matchbox cars in boxes marked with his name in heavy black block letters. It appears as if we just moved in yesterday and not eight months ago. Only a small path runs like a trail from the door to the kitchen, to the bathrooms, and to both bedrooms. I cleared a space on the sofa to watch TV, despite Katy never having the time to watch it with me. She's either sleeping or working. I stopped hiding empty Doritos bags and candy wrappers, foods that have definitely upsized me in ways I don't want to think about, but I do hide beer, tossing empty bottles in the dumpster when she's at work. Beer takes the edge off, and yeah, I'm probably a little more than slightly drunk right now. Well, most of the time.

Flying things fascinated Keven, not only the mini helicopters but kites and airplanes. For his fourteenth birthday, he wanted a gas-powered, remote-controlled airplane. I got him a sweet model-sized plane—a Aeroworks Edge 540 50CC. At the time, I remember thinking it was only eight hundred dollars plus shipping. Right now, that would be a king's ransom for us, but back then, we built it together. Every Sunday afternoon, we worked on that sucker and learned how to fly the thing. That's what we were supposed to do the day after the accident, flying that damned airplane around the park. The airplane, now in pieces, is also hiding in one of these boxes.

At the house we lost, the master bedroom closet trim chronicled Keven's yearly growth with penciled lines, marking his age, the date, and the year. It sickens me to know that the new occupants have painted over those precise measurements that end exactly at five feet and a little over four inches. He would have been a tall man. I should have ripped the trim out and brought it with us. I regret leaving it behind.

A brick colonial, our house sat out on Ridge Road, back from the road and traffic. Although we weren't living large, we had granite countertops, a Sub-Zero fridge and freezer, an entertainment center in the basement, and a two-car garage. Keven went to a private school, and Katy only worked part time to keep her skills current, a decision that I at first balked at but now deeply appreciate her wisdom.

She sets a box before me. "Help me find the iron in this box," she says. Her is voice soft, encouraging, and almost a whisper. "I'll look in another box."

Her voice also sounds plaintive like a child asking for an allowance. I glance in the box full of kitchen utensils. The iron wouldn't be in there. I don't want to sort through boxes. I don't want to make decisions about putting stuff away. I want to be able to move quickly into a suitable-sized house once I find a new job. "Now is not a good time," I tell her. I shut my eyes to avoid looking at hers.

"'Now' is never a good time," she says. "Doing nothing won't fix things," she adds. "I hate this."

"I'll get to it. I promise," I tell her. My eyelids feel like weights, too heavy to open. "I'll do it later."

She pushes the box toward me and asks me to carry it into the kitchen with a voice that sounds as if she is talking to a noncompliant patient. I dislike when she uses that tone on me. She pulls a plastic grocery bag from under her arm and starts collecting the Doritos bags and the candy wrappers that cover the sofa next to me. I squeeze the list of her wanted things under my leg.

"Never mind," she says.

When she's upset, she tackles life with a frenzy. Her constant overtime is part of that frenzy, although we need what she earns.

"Did something happen at work?" I ask. "Were you fired?" My stomach curls like an octopus arm, tense with fear of her being fired. I can't imagine how she will cope without a job. She stares at me. "Nothing happened at work, just like nothing happened here. Except for your ongoing science project of becoming one with the sofa." She tucks the bag under her arm and carries the cardboard box through the tunnel to the kitchen.

I hear her say "leave" and "stay" as if she's weighing options. I follow her through the tunnel and into the kitchen, where she's sorting the kitchen utensils and loading them into the dishwasher.

"What are you doing?"

"Loading the dishwasher," she says, monotone, without looking at me. She's stacking dinner plates into the bottom basket and rummaging through other boxes labeled "kitchen." Empty boxes nestle in one another. Her hair is pulled away from her face in a curly ponytail, and she's focused on her task.

Keven had not completed his chores on that Saturday, and I refrain from asking her why she let him go to Jimmy's house without having done them in the first place. It's the one question I've been wanting to ask since the accident.

"What's leaving and staying?" I ask instead. I know she moves at a frenetic pace to avoid cracking up but watching her exhausts me.

"Bring these empty boxes downstairs to the dumpster, please," she says, pointing at them. Since Keven's death, we've been extra careful to be polite with each other as if we were strangers and not a couple with a dead son between us.

"I'll put them in storage for when we move," I tell her, failing to keep the anger out of my voice. I'm furious that she's not waiting for me to unpack them. She ignores me as I stare at her from the half-demolished tunnel. "I told you I'd get to this," I say.

"Yes. Yes, you did. You most certainly did say that," she says, keeping her face averted. "Eight months ago. Find the iron or take these boxes down to the dumpster. Make yourself useful," she says without emotion.

I'm somewhat drunk and extremely angry.

"We're not staying here that long," I explain. "This is temporary. Why do you need the iron?"

"Is that why you're not unpacking? You believe we're not staying here long?" She stops moving while her hands are filled with spatulas and serving spoons. She faces me. "Here's a newsflash for you: house or no house, I'm not moving anywhere else anytime soon."

"This place is a dump. You actually want to stay here?"

When we first married, she was ecstatic to leave our more spacious apartment after we bought the house. She was already pregnant with Keven, and he and his friends eventually crowded the basement and the yard with all kinds of activities. She loved having the boys over, serving them pizza and making cupcakes and popcorn. Our basement was three times the size of this dump of an apartment with room to spare.

"I'm not moving," she repeats. "And we don't need all this crap."

She turns away and continues unpacking the boxes, washing and organizing kitchen contents. In seconds, she assesses and discards items, tossing them with a clang into the empty boxes.

"Stop, dammit! Can't you wait 'til we get back into a bigger place?"

"We can donate what we don't need and put the rest in storage. Either way, we can't live this way anymore. Eight months is enough," she says, unpacking without stopping. She is an unstoppable force of nature, Hurricane Katy.

She begins to unpack a new box, pulling refrigerator magnets, funky things, and various colorful framed photos of Keven. Her face slackens as she stares at the photos of his baby face: of his face when his teeth were too big for his mouth, of Keven and me with the newly completed airplane, of herself and Keven sitting on a blanket at the beach, and of her sister holding Keven when he was a baby. She cleans them with a paper towel and lines them on the fridge door in the exact way they were arranged on the fridge at the old house.

"We can't afford storage fees," I say, sounding harsher than I intend.

The ceramic decanter stands guard in front of the empty boxes. His musket is perpetually pointed at his booted feet, and the whiskey it once held is long gone. "We're keeping every fucking item in this apartment until we move into a bigger house where it all fits. Do you understand me?" I shout, because she needs to understand.

"No," she says, a whisper. She shakes her head. She takes a colorful magnet frame from the fridge into her hands. Keven's face beams his smile from them. She extracts the blue 'copter from her pocket, clutching it and the photos of Keven to her heart.

I want our old life back. I want my job and our home back. I want our beautiful boy back. I want to shake some sense into her hard head too.

I lunge at her. Clumsy from my beer buzz, I glimpse the horror on her face as I plunge into the stack of empty boxes. I accidentally kick the ceramic soldier, catapulting it into the wall. My father's whiskey decanter is decapitated. Its tricorn and innocent face shatters into a million shards that drop to the floor and scatter in all directions, and it's impossible for me to put all the pieces together again.

THE ONE WHO'S LEFT

AS THE SUN rose like a giant tangerine over Southeast Baltimore, Flo Pritchard peered through her kitchen window, beyond her square patch of concrete yard and the wide alley separating East Street yards from the Fairmont Avenue ones. She glanced at the starlings and pigeons pecking away at crumbs in the middle of the concave alley. Their necks thrusted to and fro as they circled a pile of breadcrumbs that someone had tossed in a generous mood. Then Flo focused on the boy playing with his dog in the yard directly behind her. The boy tossed a Pinky into the air, and the dog leapt, with its tail wagging, and caught the rubber ball in its jaws.

She waited for the medium-sized mutt to knock him over, but the boy's spindly brown legs held fast. His two feet moved backward and forward; his body stood upright. Under his backward baseball cap, his russet-colored face laughed as the dog licked him. The joy of the boy's wide, white-toothed laugh angered her. Why should he be so deliriously happy with his dog when that same dog was the reason her cat, Juice, was missing?

"Good girl, Snickers!" The boy rubbed its sides, and the dog wagged its tail, barking a rough, high-pitched sound that was more suitable for a tiny lapdog or a fox rather than something that stood as high as the boy's thighs. The barking and the playfulness—so sneaky— exasperated Flo until she couldn't contain herself anymore. She pushed her black, cat eyeglasses, which had been slipping down her nose, back into place, threw open the window, thrust her gray head— dotted with bright-yellow curlers—through it, and yelled.

"I still haven't forgotten that your dog got my cat! I ain't seen Juice around for a month now. Right after you brought that mangy dog into the yard."

"Snickers didn't get your cat!" the boy yelled back. He laughed at her and then lobbed the ball down the narrow side yard that led to the sally port gate on Fairmont Avenue. The dog gave chase, caught it, and bounded back to the boy.

Flo sighed. "I wasn't born yesterday!" she yelled.

Ignoring her, the boy turned his back to Flo, infuriating her further.

The last time she'd eyed Juice, her thirteen-year-old orange tabby, he was sunning in her yard, sprawled longways over the wrought iron patio table. It was his usual spot. The dog was jumping like a jack-in-the-box by the fence, bellowing threats at him. Juice didn't like that dog either. He'd fluffed his fur; his tail expanded to the size of a raccoon's. He had hissed and spit at the dog before settling himself back down on the table, this time facing the alley, facing the dog. He pointed both ears—even the half-chewed one—forward, demonstrating he was on guard. Attack mode.

"Menace!" she yelled.

She could almost hear Eggy's scratchy voice behind her, telling her to leave the kid alone for Pete's sake. Flo opened her mouth to answer but then shut it again. She'd forgotten for a minute that the voice would never come; sometimes, she still expected to see him, her baby brother, standing behind her in his suspenders and red paisley bow tie. His egg-shaped bald head was a shiny version of their father's. Or she still expected to hear him. She sometimes forgot that he was gone too. He, spry for his age and nearly a whole decade younger than Flo, had been sleeping on the sofa and watching the late-night news, with Juice cuddled on the small of his back, when Flo came home from Wednesday night Bingo and found him dead.

That was a few months back—maybe six now? She couldn't remember exactly, but she did remember that he gave people the benefit of the doubt even when he ought not to, blind as he was to the snakes in the grass.

94

The riffraff changing the neighborhood brought their loud boom boxes, loud cars, loud clothes, loud dogs, clouds of intrusive spices rising up in smelly cooking aromas, and outdoor drug markets with them though. At night, the streets didn't feel safe anymore. She wouldn't be surprised if the boy across the alley, with his oversized pants, backward cap, and mean-ass dog, spent a good portion of his time courting street trouble.

"Menace!" she screamed at the boy again.

The boy shrugged.

Flo pulled her head inside and banged the window shut. "Menace," she mumbled.

She fretted over her missing cat. She poured half a cup of dry cat food into his plastic purple bowl in hope that the cat would come home, and now the bowl was nearly overflowed. With an open can of the stinkiest cat food she could find, she had walked the streets daily for two—no, three—weeks within in a six block radius, searching and calling for him. She'd never made it down to Patterson Park. The thought of walking her seventy-nine-year-old legs to and around the park and back again fatigued her just as much as the thought of clearing out Eggy's things, which still filled his closet and drawers as if he'd gone out on an errand and would return any minute.

She had only gone into his room once—to get his good suit for the undertaker. After that, she'd shut the door and never opened it again. She knew he wasn't coming back; she kept his funeral card, showing him smiling brightly from his fifty-something-year-old face the photo she provided the undertaker because in it he looked his best. With his horn-rimmed glasses below his smooth, bald dome, he looked like he was laughing as if he'd just heard a joke. His name, Frederick Pritchard, was written above in bold, black letters lined in gold ink.

And she was still mad at him. She was the older one, the one who was supposed to go first. "Lucky is the one who goes first," Eggy used to say, "because nobody will be around to take care of the one who's left." She had thought he meant, for once in her life, she'd be the lucky one, and he'd be left behind alone.

She believed he did it on purpose: flip-flopping the situation and leaving her behind. Alone. "It ain't fair, Eggy Pritchard!" she yelled at the kitchen ceiling. "You hear me?"

He wasn't coming back, but she held out hope for the cat, an animal that weighed more than twenty pounds because he never missed a meal. She hoped that the kitty would come around as he'd always done as long as she owned him. But something happened to him since he hadn't returned, and whatever happened was connected to that she-devil dog across the alleyway, the mutt that couldn't stop barking at him. Silence descended on the house like a giant cloud; the house empty of Eggy and Juice. It made her feel antsy, unable to sleep.

"Stupid, old cat," she said aloud. Her voice sounded hollow with no one else hearing it.

She missed Eggy, who began every morning with a cup of black coffee, a piece of hard bread, the morning newspaper, and a walk around the block "to get his blood moving" before he pulled out his daily list of small chores that kept the house in shape. He'd follow his list, eat lunch, and then spend the afternoons playing chess or cards with his Patterson Park cronies.

She missed Juice racing her to the kitchen every morning, meowing for his food and for fresh water in his bowl. She'd give him the water, while Eggy poured his food. She missed Juice sleeping on the upper left-hand corner of her bed at night. She missed him forming a warm feline "C" like a cap around her head. She missed him sitting on her lap when she watched the six o'clock news, purring as she stroked him behind his ears. She missed his loud meows and the tiny footprints he left in her tub, where she kept the water running at a trickle so he could drink it fresh. She missed the way Eggy used to make him jump with a stick and a string.

Eggy'd make her laugh, saying he was training the cat for a circus. He had tied a doohickey to the bouncy string attached to a stick, and Juice would jump nearly three feet, trying to grasp it. His claws on his front paws would extend like a tiny orange hand.

The day she'd found him down at the park, a tiny, orange cotton ball with a surprisingly loud meow, Eggy had thrown a fit, adamant about not keeping "a damn cat" in the house. Keeping it had been her idea, but then Eggy adopted it. The man who hated cats became so attached. He brought sardines home for Juice on Fridays.

Flo smiled at the memory. Of course softhearted Eggy would come around. Didn't he change to the graveyard shift at the factory to take care of Ma while Flo worked the morning one?

At the kitchen table with a black Magic Marker in hand, she printed letters on a brown cardboard flap she had ripped from the carton of bleach. Her hand was no longer steady, an affliction that she endured for so long now; she couldn't remember otherwise. She carefully formed each letter and held up the sign for inspection. The sign could be better, but it suited.

"Melon and Snickers are murderers. They killed Juice."

She made another sign saying the same thing and placed them in a shopping bag with dozens of similar signs. She examined the thickening shopping bag of signs, satisfied that she was accomplishing something for Juice. Outside, the dog's high-pitched bark plucked her last nerve. Melon's mother called him inside, and the backdoor slammed. Outside, the dog, panting and looking innocent as a lamb, stretched against the chain-link fence in the shade provided by fig tree branches reaching over the fence from the yard next door. A dagger of rage rose up inside her. She grabbed a couple of stale chocolates left over from the gift boxes people brought after Eggy's funeral and, from her back porch, fired one at the dog. The candy hit its haunches and fell to the pavement. The dog sniffed it, picked it up in its mouth, and gulped the candy.

Maybe Juice lay wounded somewhere, bleeding from dog bites and unable to crawl home. Her eyes watered. She flung the rest of the chocolates at the dog like stones. She looked startled at first, sniffing the chocolates, and to her horror, she ate all of them—and wagged her tail, barking merrily for more. It infuriated her, the fur-faced jaws and claws.

Flo stormed her way back into her kitchen. Stupid dog. She spied the half-dozen oranges on her counter and pitched them across the alley, aiming for the top of the dog's head. The first one fell short and rolled. The dog leaped for the second one—as it had for the ball—bit, and ate it in a single gulp. The third bounced off her head, but the dog lurched for it, snapped at it midair, and caught it; it vanished too. The mutt ran for the orange that fell short. It sniffed it, wagged its tail, swallowed it, and then barked. It happily jumped for more. She could almost hear Eggy laughing at her and saying, "Whole lot of good that's gonna do, sis."

"Damn dog!" she muttered. At her kitchen counter, she beat the cutting board with a stainless steel meat mallet, wishing she could pulverize that stupid candy-eating, orange-gulping dog. She wished Juice would come home. She wished Eggy hadn't been first.

* * *

Flo's hair was still wrapped in yellow curlers and covered by a red-and-gold kerchief. Her stockings rolled neatly at her ankles, well below the hem of her snap button, plaid housedress. Her pink mule slippers clashed with the dress's blues and purples. With her house keys bulging in her front right pocket, she carried the shopping bag of signs in her left hand and a roll of gray duct tape with a pair of scissors in her right. She gripped the bag, afraid that her trembling hands would drop it. Determined to post the signs, she held the items close to her chest, and at the first traffic sign—a no parking sign—she dug one of her cardboard signs out of the bag and taped it to the green pole. She taped another sign on the next vertical structure, a lamppost.

"You crazy?" asked a man's voice behind her. It was Pete, who stood in front of his stoop three doors north of hers. "You got any proof? Better have a boatload of proof before you go accusing a kid and a dog of murder. Far as I know, cats and dogs never liked each other anyways," Pete added. He laughed.

Flo smirked. "The boy can't control that dog," she said. "It got my cat."

"Since when do you control your cat? Everybody around here knows the big, orange tabby with the chewed-off ear belongs to you. Juice ain't a fancy house cat with a collar. He ran around all over the place, being a nuisance. You sure he's dead? Maybe somebody trapped him and turned him over to animal control. Cats got nine lives, you know. Your old friend Mary Hawkins might be keeping him in her house just to rile you," he said. He laughed again but louder, throwing back his head and opening his mouth wide enough for flies to go inside it. He repeated Mary's name on purpose, knowing the troubles she'd had with Mary and that they remain on nonspeaking terms.

Pursing her lips, Flo remembered why she never liked Pete with his fancy wire-framed glasses that made his serious-looking eyes appear enormous. His pants had crisp creases, even though his wife's been dead for an age now. His worn, frayed belt circled his scrawny waist, and the book he always carried made him look like some kind of Mr. Better-Than-You-Know-It-All-Pansy-Plumber-Man, pretending his hands weren't in other people's shit all day.

She stared at him, at his crisp creases, at the book she was sure he never read, and at his ugly, brown, rubber-soled shoes. "You sure it ain't some other orange cat you saw?" she asked.

"I saw your cat with its bit-off ear at the park a little while after Eggy died."

"It wasn't my cat. Juice stuck around the house after Eggy died."

"Maybe he went to find Eggy. Maybe he thought you'd forget to feed him, and, with Eggy gone, he went looking for a new home. Cats are smart that way. You're lucky that cat didn't go missing long before this the way you neglected it, allowing it to roam everywhere. Eggy made sure it got what it needed; he told me that himself. That dog never runs loose like your cat. The boy always keeps it on the leash, and it don't knock down trash cans like Juice did. You ain't got no proof that the kid or his dog has anything to do with your missing cat. So maybe them signs ain't such a good idea, Flo. Maybe you ought to leave well enough alone. Eggy wouldn't like it if you were about stirring up trouble now, Flo. And he ain't here to fix things no more either."

"Eggy ain't here to butt in things no more. Juice is a ratter. He's smart. Makes other cats look retarded. And he always comes home. Ever since that kid put his dog in the yard, Juice's been missing. It ain't rocket science," she said. "So, something happened to him, a set of dog teeth."

"Remember the last time you got something up your crawl? Accusing Mary Hawkins of ruining your brick wall with her dryer vent? You said it was too close to your wall—even though it was in her own yard. You insisted she was steaming your brick wall to crumble, remember that? Everybody tried to tell you bricks don't melt, but you wouldn't listen. You put up signs then too. 'Mary's Dryer Vent Cooks Walls.' Until her lawyer threatened to sue you. Eggy threatened to put you away. Don't you learn nothing? Best you keep them signs to yourself, Flo, especially with Eggy gone."

Shaking his head and with his shoes silent on the concrete like a ninja killer, Pete vanished into his house, shutting the large brown door softly behind him.

"Fool," she said to the closed door. "Pansy-assed fool."

The next vertical structure sat outside the corner store. It was a lamppost onto which she taped another sign while being surrounded by a group of boys. One read her sign out loud. "Melon and Snickers are murderers. They killed Juice." The rest laughed, taking turns reading it and emphasizing different words as if they were announcing it on the radio.

"*Melon* and Snickers are murderers. They killed Juice."

"Melon and Snickers are *murderers*. They *killed* Juice."

This stupid exercise reduced them to Silly Putty, and she wanted to smack them upside their heads with her shopping bag. Each head was covered by backward baseball caps, and the boys had gold necklaces dangling from their necks.

"Smashed Melon. Candy Juice," one boy said, snickering. "Juice *murderers*."

They all laughed. She wanted to hurl something at them, but she had nothing—no candy or oranges. But she had signs. She slipped one from her shopping bag and pummeled the closest kid with it before moving on to the next. They covered their heads with their hands and laughed harder.

"Crazy, old bat," one said.

"Jingaling, jingaling," said another, increasing their amusement and slapping each other five.

"Jingaling, jingaling!" they all shouted.

"Crackheads, you all know nothing about nothing! Probably high off your rockers," Flo yelled, frustrated that none of them considered it a serious crime: a vicious dog on the loose and a missing cat. "And you know nothing about respect. You don't even respect yourselves or you wouldn't be wearing pants that show off your drawers."

The group laughed louder at the word "drawers."

"I see your draaaaaaws,'" they mocked her.

"Ain't nothing funny about a killer dog!" she shouted before crossing the street.

A backward glance told her that one of those good-for-nothing bums was defacing her sign with a red marker. "Menace!" she hollered at the corner gang. If she'd had sons or grandsons, she'd order them to beat down those thugs. But she didn't and neither did Eggy, who at least got some respite from taking care of Ma when he joined the Navy. It surprised her when he came back to help her look after Ma, but he did without a complaint. Not one word.

Flo marched onward, clutching the bag's handles, the tape, and the scissors. She taped signs on traffic signs and streetlamps along the way. On her way home, she saw that all her signs had been ripped down. Snippets of tape were the only hint that she'd posted the truth about a killer dog loose in the neighborhood.

* * *

Eggy's and Juice's absences felt as if someone had cut off her thumbs. Or pinioned her.

She gathered her lucky trolls from the hall closet and fled the empty house for Saint Elizabeth's nightly bingo game, two blocks south. She skipped bingo on Wednesday nights now; it was bad luck since Eggy had died on a Wednesday.

At the church hall, she paid for twenty bingo cards, found her usual seat next to Mookie, and nodded to her friend, who was lining up her cards in two neat rows. Flo did the same, lining the cards in two rows. Above that, she arranged her lucky trolls in their special order. Small, tall, red hair, pink hair, and orange hair. She glanced at Mookie lining up her own lucky trinkets, which consisted of a series of pig figurines of various sizes and colors. They began with a three-inch, burgundy figurine of a sow with three piglets, followed by a pig wearing a smile and a sailor suit, followed by a series of plastic farm pigs, and ended with a glamorous Miss Piggy figure.

"Juice back yet?" Mookie asked. The words chewed along with the giant gum wad in her mouth, outlined by her garish, red lipstick.

"Dog behind me got him." She stared at her friend's red mouth, still chewing like a cow, and the sight irritated her. To hide her irritation, she buried her forehead in her left hand and rubbed her eyes. Her hands brushed against the kerchief she still wore and realized that the curlers were still in her hair. She'd forgotten to take them out.

"You pack up Eggy's things yet?" Mookie asked. "The church thrift store can sure use the donation."

Flo grunted. Why did she need to bring up Eggy? She glanced at Mookie in between number calls, watched her rub her lucky pigs, and wished her bad luck.

"It's been months now. Eggy's things ain't doing nobody no good stuffed away. Lots of people in the neighborhood can benefit, you know."

She ignored her. And as the night wore on, Mookie won more games than she lost. She won at least four times, raising her jangling-skinned arm and shouting "Bingo!" loud enough to wake the dead. Flo won nothing, not a dime. A river of bile rose in her stomach and spilled out of her mouth. "Shake 'em balls!" she screeched at the number caller. Some players laughed, but she didn't mean it in a funny way. "Shaddup!" she yelled when a woman across the room hollered "Bingo!"

"Flo, you wanna trade cards? I'll slide mine over to you if you want," Mookie said.

Flo refrained from knocking her lucky pig trinkets off the table. "Thanks, but no thanks," she said, fingering her trolls instead to keep her hands away from the line of pig figurines.

No luck came her way in any aspect of her life: bingo or otherwise. If she didn't have bad luck, she'd have no luck, she thought bitterly. At intermission, she packed up her not-so-lucky trolls, slid her twenty cards toward Mookie, and left without saying a word. At home, she lined up her unlucky trolls on the kitchen table and, with her sewing shears, cut the hair off each one. She watched the green, red, purple, yellow, and pink plastic hair wisps cover the floor like a rainbow.

* * *

The stupid dog barked all night. Every time Flo came near to dozing off, the barking started again, and she automatically reached to the top of the bed to pet Juice, the magical cat who somehow always managed to help her fall asleep. Maybe it was his purring, his body heat, his four paws touching her arms, or simply his presence, but whatever it was, she'd always fallen asleep easily when Juice stretched in his spot above her pillow. Except she'd forgotten Juice wouldn't be there, and the empty space startled her, reminding her of his absence yet again.

Eggy would've been the one to yell at the dog to shut up since his bedroom was in the back of the house.

The dog barked her head off in the backyard.

Flo padded to the back room, Eggy's bedroom, where a whiff of his cologne surprised her. She stopped in her tracks. She sat on his tan bedspread, smooth and taut across the bed. She surveyed his belongings. She saw the carefully arranged cologne bottles on his dresser. The edges of the dresser mirror were lined with snapshots: of Ma's and Da's wedding; of his First Communion; of some women she didn't know; of her younger self; of Juice; of his old pals in bowling outfits, swimming trucks, and baseball suits; of his pals from his Navy days; and the Patterson Park cronies. Another photo, slipped in the crack between the mirror and the frame, showed them at Patterson Park in the snow. She was pulling the old wooden sled they'd always used to careen down Dead Man's Hill, and red-cheeked, they both were laughing. It had to be before Da died and Ma got sick. Flo took a breath and set the picture on the bureau. A tie rack hung on the wall next to the closet; the ties were lined precisely by color from dark to light.

Outside, the dog barked and barked. She hated it more with every bark.

She opened the window. "Shaddup! Goddamn it! Shut the hell up!" she screamed as if the dog was a human who could understand her.

"Can't you get your goddamn dog to shut up in the middle of the night?" she yelled at the dark house that belonged to Melon and his mother, who probably didn't hear her anyway. Or care. The bastards were probably asleep, immune to the noise their dog was making.

Excited by Flo's screaming head hanging out the window, Snickers barked more—and louder—while jumping up and down.

"Shaddup! Shaddup! Shaddup!" she hollered, and the sound of her voice prompted the stupid dog to bark furiously.

Down in the kitchen, Flo grabbed two onions as large as Pinky balls. Outside in her yard, she hurled them at the dog with all the might she could muster; she had a vicious rage in the hope of bruising the animal into silence. "Menace!" She rued the waste of two perfectly good onions.

The dog leapt, caught both giant onions, and ate them, one gulp each. They vanished down her throat.

Flo could swear the dog laughed at her, daring her to send another edible thing. What the hell compelled her to throw food at the dog anyway? She swore and let the back door bang behind her. Maybe the boom would wake up the boy and his mother if the annoying barking hadn't. It sure did wake up everyone else. She noticed lights in all the other houses flickering on and off.

The exertion of pitching onions at the dog—even if the stupid thing ate them—fatigued her. She crawled back in bed, put the pillow over her head to drown out the sound, and fell asleep gradually. Without Juice. With the onion-eating dog barking on.

* * *

When the doorbell rang endlessly like a fire alarm the next day, Flo was napping in her TV chair. She ignored the bell, which progressed to a tapping on her front window. Between the dog barking and the doorbell ringing, she couldn't hear herself think. She heaved herself out of the chair, stepped into her pink terry cloth slippers, and dragged herself to the door.

"Go away! Get the hell away from here, whoever you are! Nobody's home!" she screamed at the door.

"Ms. Flo, open up. It's Demarco."

"I don't know no Demarcos. Get outta here!" she yelled, shuffling away from the door.

"Open up, Ms. Flo," said a woman's voice.

"It's me! Melon!" said a boy's voice.

She opened the door. A thin woman with a floozy, black skirt that was too tight, a red V-neck shirt, and red shoes stood on her stoop next to the boy. She held one of Flo's signs. The boy held a large, brown cardboard box in his hands. His smile took up all of his lower face.

"You bringing Juice's body back to me?" She stared at him, afraid to look in the box.

"Snickers didn't get your cat," the woman said. "You better stop spreading lies about my son and his dog around the neighborhood. I ain't happy with these signs you taped up all over the damn place. I spent half a day pulling them down yesterday." She shook the signs at Flo. "If I find another sign like this taped anywhere around here, I'm calling the police or whoever I got to call to get your ass locked up where it belongs. The nuthouse. Jail. I don't care where. You hear me?"

"I ain't scared of you, your threats, or your mean-ass dog," Flo said.

"I ain't asking you to be scared. I'm telling you plain and simple: another bullshit sign like this, and you're gonna wish you never met me. My son and his dog ain't had nothing to do with your missing cat. Melon has something to say. Melon...go ahead."

"I don't want to hear nothing. This boy can't control his dog, and now my cat's gone."

The woman threw one of the signs into Flo's door; it sailed like a Frisbee across the room. "I got the rest of them, proof for the police," she said. "You gonna listen to my son like it or not. Go on, Melon."

"Snickers ain't the kind of dog you think she is. She's a friendly, nice dog. She never bit nobody. But I got something for you. Please open the door, so I can set the box down." He flashed that big-toothed wide grin at her, and Flo considered how it made him look like a used car salesman.

She hesitated but opened the door anyway.

The boy pushed the box into the doorway. "Look inside, Ms. Flo."

A black and white kitten with pink lips, a pink nose, and pea green eyes peered up at her. It gave her a silent meow. She melted inside and wanted to pick it up. It was no older than eight or nine weeks, she guessed. She held it close and let it lick her face, but she wasn't going to make it so easy for the boy to give her a blood offering to make up for the probably dead Juice.

"It ain't orange like you're missing one, but it needs a home," the boy said, pushing the box toward her. "There are a bunch of kittens in one of the yards three blocks down on Fairmont in Mr. Clarence's yard, and he's rounding up the kittens. This one can use a good home," the boy said, smiling at her as if he was getting ready to snap a photo.

"Then *you* give it one," Flo said. Her voice was harsh.

"You're missing a cat. This here cat needs a home," the boy said.

The skinny woman tapped her foot.

"You think one cat can replace another?" Flo said to the boy. "You think one kid can replace another?" she asked the mother. "You think I'm simple? Get off my stoop," she said, but she didn't shut the door. She thought about it and wanted to, but she didn't. She froze.

In the moment of her hesitation, the boy shoved the box farther into her living room, and like the two cowards they were, they ran down the steps. The mother's heels click-clacked against the marble steps.

"Damn it!" she muttered aloud. She couldn't leave the box with a brand-new kitten in it unattended. Damn hussy. Damn kid.

She dragged the box to the kitchen and filled a small saucer with two handfuls of Juice's dry food. She set it in the box. She set another saucer of water there too.

Pinky in hand, the boy reappeared in his yard. He peered across the alley, into her yard, as if he was trying to see what she was doing inside her kitchen.

The kitten didn't have a loud meow like Juice. Juice, who talked to her constantly with his array of meows. Juice, who stepped in between her legs first and laid across her feet if she forgot to greet him when she came home. Juice, who had a distinctive personality that no other kitty could replicate.

She watched the boy from behind her blinds. Finally turning away, he tossed the Pinky to the dog, who leapt and caught it like a baseball player.

She took the kitten with her to Eggy's room and set it atop his neat bed. She carried two of the cardboard boxes that were missing top flaps into the room and pushed them toward the closet. She didn't pack anything into them. Instead, drawn to the window, she watched the boy and the dog like a movie. They played fetch and ran up and down the alley. The dog, on a leash, pretended to be racing. No friends joined the boy, just Melon and the murderous dog.

* * *

The next morning, when the sun beat down on the rooftops and heated the blacktop streets and concrete yards, Flo heard the boy shrieking. He screamed for his mother to come quick.

She'd already started packing Eggy's colorful ties into one of the boxes. Through his window, she saw the mother, wearing a different set of tight, floozy clothes, run in a pair of black *click-clack* heels toward her son. His smile was finally erased.

Snickers wasn't moving much. The dog gasped for breath. It had vomited all over the yard. Shit too. The boy's lower lip jutted out, and he looked ready to cry. Like a baby.

The mother ran inside, came out with a red blanket, and covered the dog. She said something to the boy and disappeared back into the house. She drove her car down the alleyway and, tiny as she was in comparison to the dog, lifted the animal like a stevedore. With the boy's help, she stuffed the dog in the back of the car. The boy climbed in the back with her, and the mother, waving a white handkerchief out the window and blowing her horn, tore down the alley like a wannabe fire truck on a call.

Later that evening, through the kitchen window, Flo spotted the mother in the yard, hosing down the concrete. She poured bleach over the areas where the dog had diarrhea and vomited. The boy, looking downcast, sat on the porch stairs. His head was in his hands. His cap was still backward, but his smile erased.

Flo stroked the kitten, which she hadn't decided to keep yet or not. She placed it back in the box it came in, and it busied itself by playing with one of Juice's stuffed mouse toys. She wondered what happened to the dog. She threw open the kitchen window, thrust her head out, and yelled to the mother. "What happened to that mean-ass dog of yours?"

The mother glared at her. "Since when are you interested in the welfare of that dog? Ain't you the one who put up them signs everywhere saying she and my son murdered your runaway cat?"

"Because he did."

"Bullshit," the mother said.

"What happened to the dog?" Flo repeated.

The mother considered. "She must have gotten into some garbage. Ate some onions. Ate some chocolates. Dogs ain't supposed to eat onions, chocolate, or garlic. Poisons them. Kills them."

Flo gasped. "She's dead?"

"You happy now? You happy now that you got your wish?" the mother asked with an edge in her voice. "You must be dancing for joy, calling my child and his dog 'murderers.' You jinxed her. You better stay away from my boy."

Trembling, Flo banged the window down. Who could have known about onions, chocolates, and dogs? At her feet, the tuxedo kitten squeaked meows and whispered gentle meows, a softie like Eggy. She lifted it up, stroked it, and named it Fred.

Outside, the mother hosed the yard, while the boy sat without moving on the porch steps like a deflated balloon. Then the mother sat on the stoop next to her son, holding him as he cried. The mother cried too.

Flo had wanted the dog gone—gone, yes but not dead. She wondered if she should give the kitten back to the boy but decided to keep it since the mother had said to stay away from him. She contemplated how unlucky she'd always been, misfortune followed her like a five o'clock shadow. She, the one who was left.

IN A STARRY SKY

POSTERS WITH LARGE, red illustrations of how various fetal organ systems function at different gestational ages brand the blue walls of the university medical center's neonatal intensive care unit—the NICU. They had closed incubators, double-glazed, and with lids and portholes; they kept the babies within them warm, protecting them from noise, drafts, infections, and excessive handling. A giant gray bunny wearing a fuchsia bonnet dances on the blue wall in the first bay and looms over Lucy, who's unable to move her lips because the tiny tube in her mouth pushes air and extra oxygen into her miniature lungs. She opens and shuts her eyes, and her startle reflex barely moves the other tubes, sensors, and monitors attached to her one-pound self. Chestnut strands of her hair border the edges of her pink and white knitted doll-sized cap, and she seems oblivious to the clinicians monitoring her vitals and noting her chart.

In the bay next to Lucy, her twin sister, Jenny, slumbers under the watchful eyes of a ceiling to floor decal of Minnie Mouse. Dressed for a party in her hot pink and white polka dot dress and matching shoes, Minnie Mouse's bow jauntily tilts on her head between her large mouse ears. Her ears were larger than Jenny, who fits in the palm of NICU nurses' gloved hands and who weighs in at a half a pound heavier than her sister Lucy. Both girls were too early to the party; the thermometer attached to the sensor on Jenny's belly rises and falls with her breaths, programmed to ring if Jenny's breathing stops.

Karen, their mother, does not notice the room's colorful walls or cheerful motif, but she does notice the antiseptic environment and the sterile gowns, shoes, and caps she must wear in the NICU. She divides her time between her daughters' incubators, peering inside them with eyes weighed down by dark circles and bags. She's blind to everything except the monitors attached to her pair of babies in their doll-sized clothes. She bounces back and forth between the closed incubators, inserting her hands through the portholes of each and stroking each child while keeping an ear on the monitors.

Jenny's monitors scream frequently, and Karen runs over to the incubator that encases her, caressing and soothing this baby with hands thrust through the portholes. Older than Lucy by a mere minute and slightly larger, Karen knows that Jenny is less strong and coos at this struggling baby, afraid of the worst.

Roadrunner dashes in from seemingly nowhere, and in the third bay, he's mid-run while keeping his eyes on a two-pound boy wearing a doll-sized purple and white knitted cap. His incubator monitor says, "Beep, beep," in longer tones than the roadrunner's, which causes nurses on duty to come running. They push Brenda, his mother, out of the way with the force of a tornado to reach the boy named Michael. He is attached to so many tubes and sensors monitoring his condition, sampling his blood, and feeding him artificially. He's scarcely visible beneath the technology. The roadrunner watches him from the wall. Brenda, who hung a medal of St. Jude, which was the patron saint of the impossible, on his incubator, mouths a prayer, begging the saint for a miracle. With tears leaking down her cheeks, she blocks the activity in the fourth bay from her sight and mind, where the Tasmanian Devil speeds in imaginary circles on the blue walls. He's only interrupted by the large window streaming sunlight into the room.

She struggles to ignore the activity in the fourth bay when she realizes what she dreads for Michael has come and swallowed the baby in number four. For new parents, Chrissy and Erik, the dappled moonlight invades the NICU's picture windows and casts aspersions on the choice of the décor element: an energetic ornery looking Tasmanian Devil decal on the wall, an element that might as well exist on another planet at a different time. They fail to notice her pretending not to see them as they fail to notice duty nurses working on her son Michael, trying to stop the incessant alarms.

Chrissy and Erik hold each other close and cradle their minuscule thirty-day old, two-and-a-half-pound baby boy between them for one last time. Leo still weighs less than a bag of flour, sugar, rice, or ice. They memorize the shape of his nose, the roundness of his ashen face, the heart-shaped of his mouth, and the familiar contours of his lips blackened by death's unwanted kiss. They cling to their dear, sweet Leo, forever stilled and as quiet as a midnight moon in a starry sky.

AFFLICTIONS

THEY LEFT. SOME of them chose to leave as volunteers, and others, drafted into the service, had no choice. They were young, just beyond adolescence when they left their families—parents, siblings, friends, and sweethearts. They left farms and tenement housing. They—those who had them—left jobs, and those who didn't left the uncertainty of unemployment. More than four million left the comfort and safety of their homes in the US to join about sixty million others just like them from a multitude of nations, and—despite differences in languages, culture and customs, and uniforms—they gathered in European trenches and battled to protect their nations or to serve their kings and emperors. They fought the war to end all wars. They wore Brodie helmets, boots, and knapsacks, and they carried gas masks, bayonets, rifles, shovels, grenades, capes, cartridge belts, eating tins, and water bottles. They carried photos and letters from home. They carried infection, trench foot, Spanish flu, typhus, and sepsis.

Homeless for weeks on end, they endured winter's cold, wind, rain, and snow and summer's heat and sun. They bore grim monotony in between the battles, longing for home, for families, for sweethearts, and for letters with news. When they battled, they destroyed the familiar, felled trees and buildings to desolate rubble. They churned up endless swatches of mud and suffered through the shock and awe of the loud blasts, thunderous explosions, and the incessant, deafening noise of artillery and machine gun fire. The sounds of grand-scale butchery.

In between battles, they lingered in the lice-filled trenches. They inhaled the indelible stench of death and rotting feet and toes. They inhaled mustard gas and died. The masked lucky ignored remnants of the dead commingled with the fullness of the living, snagging the useful items the dead left behind—their boots, their food, their weapons, their medicines, and their tools.

When ordered into battle, they climbed out of their trenches, burdened by the weight of their weapons and heavy equipment. They moved, low to the ground, over complex networks of barbed wire and through the enemy's fire field with prayers on their lips, pressed to reach the enemy's front line to overcome the defending troops sheltering in their own trenches. Despite the hype, despite the orders, and despite the hell, they knew such tactics failed, giving rise to the ever-increasing numbers of injured, wounded, and dead. The attackers suffered more than the defenders.

Some disobeyed orders to climb out of their trenches to attack, afraid of the terrifying ordeal. What was more terrifying, they wondered? The attack they were ordered to make? Or the punishments for disobeying the order? The punishments for refusing to "go over the top." By and large, most of them obeyed, but hundreds of them found death at the hands of their own armies for cowardice, for military offenses during conflict. They suffered through long bouts of boredom that were punctuated by shorter bouts of battle.

They buried their dead only after the fighting broke. Some died in battle. Others died from the flu. Others died from typhus, pneumonia, sepsis, blood poisoning, and even infections. They learned that war and sickness clung to each other like starstruck lovers. They carried their wounded and infected to field hospitals where clinicians tidied and treated the ravages of war, quarantined the sick, and revolutionized medical care, taking it as close to the front as possible.

More than two hundred and four thousand US troops, lucky they made it to the field hospitals alive, left behind limbs beyond repair. They left behind blood, stockpiled for the first time for future use, that was stored on ice. They survived battle wounds that would have killed them in the past but gained new afflictions—battle fatigue, shell shock. Soldier's heart, suicide, and homelessness. Carried home to their families, their friends, and their sweethearts. Afflictions of the terrors of wars past and present.

MIMI AND MO GO DANCING

EYES SHUT WHILE naked except for tasseled pasties taped to her nipples, a thong, a garter belt attached to white, lace-trimmed stockings, and a string of paste pearls encircling her waist, Mo Franken lap danced a dude.

It was her right now job, a lucrative right-now job. Not yet thirty, she wasn't sure what she wanted to be when she grew up, but she knew this wasn't it. The endless line of mangy dudes like the one she now lap danced for plucked her nerves, and it grew harder to hide her contempt for them. She used "Princess Milan" as her stage name at the Gentleman's Diamond Club, where she worked as an erotic dancer. The princess part allowed her a measure of callousness when necessary. She hated the job but liked the money. Hard to leave without more than a thousand bucks, give or take, for the week. Once she stepped out of the club, she didn't think of it again until she returned. She was just making money, and when she went home, she focused one hundred percent on her family—her daughter Bean and her husband. She refused to buy into the hype about changing the world. She'd swallowed enough of that for two lifetimes, and the world really didn't need any changing.

When the Liquor Board slapped a hefty fine on the club last month for serving alcohol to underage customers, Mo dismissed it. She also dismissed the five dollar per customer tax that hit all the metro strip clubs. TV news called it "the pole tax," and regulars called it the "hole tax," but the owners let regulars slide in without paying. Of course, they cooked the books, and of course, dudes kept paying for overpriced drinks and slipping fives and tens into the dancers' costume strings. Last week, an undercover vice hauled away Jewels, a skinny dancer with hip bones jutting out like bike handles. That shook Mo. But Jewels had fooled everyone. Who'd have guessed her for a fifteen-year-old runaway?

"Who do you think you are, Buster? I have a right!" A woman's voice rose above the Gold Room's sound system. The word "Buster" startled Mo. Her mother used that word, a fact Mo had forgotten, or blocked, until it drifted like an aural memory ringing a Pavlovian bell.

"Buster" threw her off her game, interfered with her rhythm. Pretending the voice didn't remind her of Mimi Franken, Mo shook memories of crowds, of holding signs, of slow-moving trains, of cops in riot gear, of soldiers in green camouflage, of her mother yelling, "Listen, Buster!" at giant black-helmeted cops, and of the sound of a man's piercing scream, a scream that still haunted her dreams and gave her night sweats.

She focused on the dude and danced. His jeans, rough against her thighs and butt, scratched her skin like sandpaper. Job drawback number one. He smelled like tuna sandwich and beer—drawback number two—and she guessed he stopped by after working at a hardware store or at a truck rental place. He raised his arms, wanting to touch her, but she pushed them down.

She appreciated the no touch rule. The slow part of "Proud Mary" reverberated, and she jiggled her butt across his lap. She wanted to entice him into paying for dance number three. At the club, dudes fought, stabbed, beat down, and shot each other over women.

The mouthy lady that sounded like her mother at the Gold Room door seemed tame. Mo offered the dude a Mona Lisa smile, pushing from her mind the image of her little brother Joey, who towered over Mimi as a teenager and was unable to break free of the "Busters." He was their mother's pack mule, carrying and packing signs, banners, flags, and bullhorns. She wondered what he'd be doing now if he were alive. If he'd be a strip club regular. Probably not. Mo raised three fingers. "Let's keep going," she said.

Despite a scraggly red beard, frayed cuffs, and threadbare jeans, the dude nodded in agreement for dance number three, and she rewarded him. Leaning closer while dangling her tits closer to his face, she performed for another two minutes and flashed him a genuine smile. Ninety bucks was ninety bucks. Quick money for six to eight minutes—on a good night, and every damned minute counted: the eighty dollar fee to dance and tips for the bartenders and DJ kept her momentum going; she thrust her tits, Goldilocks, close, shimmied her shoulders, and bounced her tits so that the tassels swayed.

"Let me in!" the woman at the door shrieked.

Something about the woman's tone leapt at her, made her uneasy. She tried to ignore it. Proud of her tight, muscular thighs, of her abs so flat no one'd ever guessed she'd been pregnant, of her athletic body, and of her exotic darkness, she twisted again, thrusting her butt toward the dude's lap. She pushed it close to his groin, knowing to push as far as possible so that he'd want to touch her. The tempo quickened, but Mo, distracted by the voice, couldn't keep up the pace with it, rubbing her butt off tempo across the dude's lap. A bulge tented the fabric of his pants. Off her game, she smiled.

A commotion rose at the entry, the woman's voice rose and fell. "What goes on in a private room?" she demanded, who was probably an irate wife or girlfriend. The end of the second tune rolled into the beginning of the third.

"Private stuff," one of the bouncers said. Everyone snickered.

"Oh baby, you're good," Mo said, wanting to focus the dude's attention away from the commotion. She kept her voice high and breathy; she moved her butt over the tent. The dude nodded.

She increased her speed and shook her ass with a nifty move she'd been practicing during isolation exercises. She longed to finish, collect the ninety dollars so that the dude wouldn't complain that the third dance had been interrupted or that he didn't get his money's worth.

"That your sweetie at the door coming to *drag* you away from me?" she asked.

The dude chuckled. "You're my sweetie, whattaya say?" He sounded hopeful.

"You know the rules. I *so* wish, but I can't," she said. Three minutes could feel like an eternity. She glanced at the entry and then spotted her mother, Mimi Franken, holding a lime green blanket and wagging her finger at the two bouncers.

"*Holy* fucking shit!" Mo said. She stopped mid-shake. Her stomach compressed into a knot. How had Mimi found her? In retrospect, she should have guessed Mimi drove the club's sudden run of legal bad luck and should have recognized her mother's activist MO, but she'd failed to connect the dots.

"No kidding!" the dude mumbled.

She caught herself standing still. "That's right. Let's keep going, babe. Princess Milan's got you," she said, moving again, counting seconds, and turning her back to the door to face the dude instead of her mother. The tune dragged, and when it finally ended, she leaned into him. "Thank you, sweetie. Pleasure's all mine," she cooed, bending Goldilocks forward and allowing her tits to dangle at a just the right distance in front of his face. "Come back soon. I'll be waiting," she breathed into his ear. He handed her a C-note and a ten. Not a bad tip. She hurried him along.

Normally, she'd persuade a receptive dude like him to go for another trio, but Mimi was heading toward her like a heat-seeking missile.

Determined to appear nonchalant, Mo sat on the lap dance couch. Plastic busts of Roman and Greek gods stared at her, and the faux marble, linoleum floor bubbled with cracks. Dusty plastic palms and ferns, the peeling mural of a fertility goddess with multiple pairs of milk spewing breasts screamed tawdry, unlike the art at the Franken home, where more than a few authentic pieces hung. Her favorite was the glittering, golden Klimt, a wedding present from her paternal grandparents to her parents. She craved a cigarette, but the club had become smoke-free a few months back, so she crossed her legs and kicked the top one nervously. Her red Lucite platform shoes reflected the room's dim light.

Mimi planted herself in front of Mo. With curly hair now streaked with gray, round wire-frame glasses, gray and pink pinstriped power suit, and no makeup, she looked aged and world-weary. She clutched a blanket to her chest. "Sooner or later, I knew I'd find you. Didn't expect it to be in this shithole," she said. "Let's leave." She spread the blanket wide, covering Mo.

"I'm working," Mo said, flicking the blanket off. It fell to the floor. "And my stage name is Princess Milan. You can call me Princess if you like."

"Give me a break," Mimi said, eyeing the fake Roman and Greek busts. "You can't possibly consider what you do in this dump important on any level."

Mo raised her eyebrows. "I come here. I do my job. I get money. It pays the bills. Sounds like a job and walks like a job, so it's a job."

She and Mimi glared at each other for a while, neither speaking.

"What are *you* doing here?" Mo asked, breaking the silence.

Mimi snatched the blanket from the floor and sat next to Mo on the lap dance couch. "I should be asking you that. This place is going down. And I haven't even started yet."

"Still kicking shit, I see," Mo said. She tried to sound nonchalant, but her stomach twisted tighter. Mimi had dragged her and Joey to a boatload of shit-kicking activities, protests, and anti-this-or-that rallies. She shuddered. "There's nothing going on here that needs your attention, Ma. No government presence and all that," she said.

"Explain Jewels. A fifteen-year-old runaway working at a strip joint, forced into prostitution by a kidnapper. The tattoo on her neck is the brand of a slave, but no doubt you failed to connect the dots."

Mo sucked in her breath. Kidnapped? Slave? That creepy guy wasn't her boyfriend? "She wasn't doing that here. Her situation has nothing to do with the club."

"Like hell. A fifteen-year-old needs a permit to work at a fast-food joint. Get real, Mo. I bet she turned over her money to that asshole." Mimi folded the green blanket.

"I'm here on my own free will," Mo said. "So are the other girls. Jewels could have escaped if she wanted. I didn't see her using any phone. Pay phone's right in the hallway outside the ladies' room."

"You don't know what her life looked like outside this joint. She's just a baby. And scared. But what's your excuse? Jimmy? You turn your money over to Jimmy? If so, maybe you're more like Jewels than you think."

Blotches of red crawled up Mo's spine and spread over her body like fingerprints left by a slap from an invisible hand. This was not the way she'd envisioned a reunion with her mother.

Her mother hated Snake, whose real name was Jimmy. She blamed him for Mo ditching college when she, sick of Mimi and her father, sick of the Must Dos, and sick of social justice protests, ditched it and her family herself.

"Leave Jimmy out of this. I like what I'm doing now, and this is what I'll keep doing 'til I decide otherwise," she said.

"You're going to need a new job soon. I'm going to shut this joint down," Mimi said.

"Who died and appointed you official social nanny?" Mo asked. Her voice tinged with anger.

"Go back to school. We'll forget this ever happened." Mimi attempted to drape the green blanket around Mo's shoulders. "Let me take you home."

"What about Snake? And Bean?" Mo pushed the blanket away. Feeling empowered in her skimpy costume, she thrust her pasties forward. "I like this dump, and we need the money." Mimi attempted again to cover Mo with the blanket. "Bean who? Daddy and I can give you money. Forget about this Bean person and Jimmy holding you back."

"Bean's our child. Jimmy's not holding me back from anything."

Mimi rubbed her temples and the sides of her eyes without removing her glasses. Mo knew she was in shock.

"Why didn't you tell me?" Her voice cracked; her eyes became wet. Mo had never heard that sound in her mother's voice or had seen her appear so undone. "I heard you had a child, but I wasn't sure."

"Look, we'll talk about this later, Ma," Mo said, softening her voice but thinking of her one thousand dollar goal. "I got to get back to work."

"Go get Bean and come home."

"I'm not leaving my husband or our home."

"You married that fool? Jesus!" Mimi set her jaw and knitted her eyebrows. Her eyes gained a steely look. Her features, which had softened at the mention of Bean, transformed into stone. She had worn that stony expression at every protest they'd attended, even on the day of the train incident, the one event Mo wanted to forget but couldn't.

"I want to meet my grandchild," Mimi said. Her voice was cold.

"Then leave this place alone."

"Impossible. A fifteen year old dancing here is illegal and immoral." Her tone sounded harsh. Just as she'd sounded on the day they'd gathered at the munitions military base in Aberdeen, an hour north of Baltimore.

Mo was fifteen then, same age as Jewels, and had held one of the signs without fully understanding it. She'd wanted to stay home to watch TV. Four people had handcuffed themselves to the chain-link fence, and a man had lain supine across the railroad tracks that lead into the base, making her stomach feel tight. She had yelled at him to get up and to move, but no one had heard her. She, still holding the sign, squeezed Joey's hand with her free one. The train moved forward, and she tried to yell again for the man on the tracks to move, but when she opened her mouth, no sound came.

Everyone else screamed, "Peace Now!" Police in black helmets and black shields arrived, and still, no one noticed the man on the tracks, heard the train whistle blowing a warning, or saw the train moving forward. Her eyes fixed to the track where the train rolled past the spot with the man lying across it. Mo dropped her sign, squeezed Joey's hand harder, and squeezed him to her. She'd found her voice, but the man had lost his legs. Both of them, the man and Mo, were screaming, and Joey was crying. She clutched Joey.

A soldier had separated her and Joey, hauling them into the base. Up on the soldier's shoulders, she had seen the man's head looking like a tiny white ball beneath the huge train. She'd lost Joey but kept the sound of the man's screams in her head, in her sleep. She trembled.

"I have a right to see my grandchild," Mimi said.

Mo sat on her trembling hands. "You've cost me two bills already."

"This job is not for you."

"Leave, or I'll call the bouncers. Or pay. Time is money."

Mimi stood. "I'm not giving you a cent unless you do what I want. I'm not supporting this," she said, gesturing around the room. "I want to see my grandchild, and I want you outta here."

Mo didn't answer. She reminded herself that she's a married woman, no longer a child, an adult, and free to do as she wishes.

"I want to meet my grandchild," Mimi repeated.

"Call off the dogs then. Leave this place alone. And go home."

Jaw set, she refused to budge. "Took a long time to find you," she said.

Mo envisioned ninety dollars and her goal evaporating. "I get it. This was never about Jewels," she said.

"I'm not leaving without you," Mimi said.

Mo rose, walked away, leaving Mimi on the couch, and entered the club's main room. She had to make some money. She signaled the DJ to start her set. Prancing onto the stage like a diva, she embraced the shiny brass pole with her right leg and extended her head backward. She danced pole ballet, took pride in her athleticism with the pole, and flirted with the dudes who threw bills onto the stage. She stepped into her dance performer zone, her Princess Milan persona, and noted the five and ten dollars collecting on the stage.

Mimi, green blanket in hand, bounded onto the stage and blocked the dudes from seeing Mo dance by using the blanket like a shield. The audience booed, yelled for her to get down, to move, and to go away.

"Why don't you just leave?" Mo said sotto voce; her lips formed a fake smile.

"I'm protecting my child from the wolves," Mimi said. "You'd do the same for your Bean."

Mo smirked. Protection? A joke. She pulled the blanket from Mimi's hands and tossed it out into the audience. "Hello, boys and girls!" she said. "Our new dancer here says you're all wolves out there tonight. So, let's all give a Big Bad Wolf Salute!" she yelled, and the dudes howled, bellowed, screamed, and whistled. "Don't be fooled. She may look official but underneath that suit is a lady wolf with some incredible moves." The dudes cheered. Mo, furious beneath her smile, sashayed off the stage, leaving Mimi alone while the dudes yelled at her to start.

* * *

On the security screens, Mo watched Mimi pacing. Mimi wrung her hands, blew her nose, and wept. She had never quit a righteous battle, persevering until she'd won, was arrested, or both. Bored as she was with her job, Mo didn't want the Diamond Club to be steamrollered.

The marquee outside blinked, a miniature red figure of a high-heeled, top-hatted woman sitting in a blue martini glass. Her neon legs moved like a pair of kitchen scissors. The marquee's blinking neon brightened and shadowed Mimi's face, highlighting the gray streaks in her hair to green, blue, and red. Mo sighed. Ignoring Mimi would make things worse.

Shivering under a bulky black sweater coat, Mo leaned against the club's brick wall, lit a cigarette, took a drag, and blew the smoke away from Mimi, whose angry eyes flashed like gunpowder.

Lips pursed, Mimi paced like a tiger in a small cage. "I don't appreciate the little stunt you pulled in there. Why are you doing this to me?"

Mo sucked on the cigarette and held it in front of her face, inhaling the smoke. She said nothing.

"Are you on drugs?" Mimi asked. She ripped the cigarette from Mo's mouth and stomped it. "And still smoking. Bloody hell."

Mo lit another and took a drag, rolling her eyes. "You're still the Drama Mamma. And I'm not doing anything to you." The questions annoyed her. "You get anybody's legs cut off lately?" There. She said it.

Mimi slapped her face, the sting tearing her eyes. "Below the belt, Mo. That man chose what happened to him. This is all Jimmy's fault. He must have brainwashed you. You couldn't call to say you have a baby? You've got to be on drugs. Your father will throw a fit."

Mo rubbed her face where her cheek stung. "You don't get it," she said.

Her father, Dino, was a moosey man, an amateur boxer with huge hands, muscled arms, and a shaved head. He had hung up on her. She'd called to tell them about Bean, and he'd answered, called her a criminal, and told her never to call back again. She inhaled the last puff and then ground the cigarette into the pavement with her Lucite platforms.

"Tell Daddy I'm no criminal," she said. Her face tingled from the slap. She imagined slapping Mimi but knew she wouldn't stop. "You haven't changed."

Mimi's face flushed red. "I'll close it down. Find regulations not being followed. The bozos who own this joint will find themselves in such a legal hurt. They'll fire you if you don't quit."

"You're free to protest whatever you want. Isn't that what makes this country great?" Mo said. "Free speech."

When the engine had rolled over the man, Mo felt as if she were floating above everyone. His screams had shaken the birds from the trees and the soldiers from the base, soldiers with radios, helicopters, and medics. Soldiers had grabbed her and Joey, carrying them inside the base.

Mimi had fought her battles to change the world but had forgotten about them. They'd stayed at the base until close to midnight when their father finally came for them. The soldiers had played games with them, given them ice cream, and brought them to the PX but couldn't erase the events that brought them into the base. When she least expected it, the smell of diesel engines, a train whistle, or the flapping birds overhead reminded her of the man beneath the train. His piercing scream lived in her head, and she often wondered if Joey had killed himself to silence the screaming he heard in his.

Newly graduated from high school, Joey had driven to a park near the base one night, and with the Baltimore skyline glowing in the distance, he took the shotgun his father had given him, wedged it against the steering wheel and windshield, and shot himself in the heart.

127

Mo had failed him, failed to protect him, but will not let Bean down in the same way.

She rubbed her face. "Do you hear them? The screams? Do you think they tormented Joey too?"

Mimi's face contorted in pain and anguish but only for a minute or so before she smoothed her features back into their righteous mask.

Mo retreated into the club. Her Lucite platforms clicked like a Geiger counter. Inside, someone had folded the green blanket and set it on a chair near her locker. She clutched the blanket in her arms, inhaling its familiar scent of both comfort and oppression. She'd bring it home for Bean. She phoned Snake to say she'd be home early.

"Whatever makes you happy, kitten," he said.

Before leaving the club, Mo checked the security cameras. Outside, Mimi, a soldier in her own war, removed a shoe, hurled it at the marquee, and cursed. The shoe hit the neon face of the top-hatted woman, bounced, and dropped, landing on its side with a dull thud. Like a small bomb.

NINE TWELVE: WE LOVE AMERICA

LIKE A GHOST in the room, the future hung between them, and the question he posed rolled around Maria's head like a handful of colorful, glass marbles dumped from a can. How could she tell him the question froze her brain? They—Maria Mannenta and Dr. Taranjeet Sodhi—sat at her dining room table. He studied a medical text, and she tapped out short descriptions of churches for a history book she'd been hired to write. Taran's white turban lay unraveled on the other side of the table, the black cap that rested beneath it—his fifty—atop the pile, and he, minus the turban with his hair still rolled in a neat bun atop his head, propped his leg across hers. He absently stroked her upper arm as if touching her would sear the medical words into his brain. He looked serious and studious in his large wire-framed glasses, glasses she'd always teased him about by saying they made him look like a bug. And she, focusing on finding the precise word, rubbed the ball of his bare foot, gently squeezing his toes as if the act would inspire words to come.

"So, *Mishri*? The verdict?" he asked. His musical accented English betrayed his Punjabi heritage. "A Thai restaurant is neutral," he added. He looked mischievous. He looked hopeful.

"Just think. Each side will have to be civil in such a public place. And we'll invite your beloved M of Cs too, for good measure."

She laughed. "First, we'd have to *tell* the M of Cs. And they may not be allowed to eat in restaurants, you know."

"We could explain that their presence is necessary to ensure peace between the two families, to quell riots between the Italians on one side and the Indians on the other," he said and laughed. "Bad press all the way around; we can tell them. Two sides with their own warriors, Mafia and Sikh." He smiled, removed his bug-eyed glasses, and set them on the text. His large root beer, brown eyes were filled with mirth. "The birth of the double-I war," he said. "It could spawn an entire Discovery Channel documentary."

Maria laughed. "Not even funny. Plus, the M of Cs won't help much after my father asks yours why he wears a rag on his head."

"I predict they will both say yes to each other all night long, because neither will understand what the other is saying," he said. "Think about it. 'Electricity' sounds a like 'I-83.' Neither of them will know what the other is talking about, and they will nod and agree with each other all night."

She stopped typing and pushed her small, rectangular glasses into her hair like a headband. "I'm not sure my family is ready for us. Timing is everything," she said.

"No time like the present," he said.

After meeting a year ago at the convent where the Missionaries of Charity, the Mother Teresa sisters, cared for dying AIDS patients, she and Taran had dated on the sly, neither having the courage to tell their families or friends about each other. Between his hospital rounds, office hours, and on-call schedules and her magazine, newspaper, and book deadlines as a freelance writer, they'd spent every free moment together and even managed to take two weekend vacations. One was to western Maryland's mountains where she'd shivered in the early morning August chill and clung to his warm, brown body under the bed blankets before daring to ride bikes up and down the hills. The other was to Ocean City, where he'd substituted a blue-printed bandana for his turban because of the sand and where he'd complained about the July sun baking his brain into a brick while they flew kites on the beach. Although they couldn't bear to be without each other during their off times, they both felt it was important to keep the existence of each other close to their hearts like precious jewels. She pictured post-announcement melodrama on both sides: her mother crossing herself a gazillion times saying, "*Puttana di miseria,*" or "Whore of misery" and his mother doing whatever Sikh mothers did under duress when sons defied expectations for suitable mates. They had a multitude of reasons such as a nine-year age difference—her being older—chief among them and her status as a divorcee, ranked high against her; she knew without him having to say it.

"Exactly right," Taran added. "Timing exactly is everything. My family is pressuring me. Already my mother and aunty have begun suggesting suitable mates. I can't hold them off much longer, especially now that they see my practice thriving."

Maria stiffened at the thought of him being arranged into marriage, but she harbored no illusions. "They are conservative, TJ. You said so yourself. They won't accept me because I'm divorced."

"We're not Hindus. Sikhs are different. Everyone is equal, and you know this already.

We're both in the same boat, *mishri*. You know this too. Your family won't be thrilled either. So, we present ourselves as a couple and let the storm rage for as long as it takes for both sides to accept the inevitable. The question becomes when and where, and my vote is for as soon as possible. Besides, I have the final say of who, and I have already decided who is you, regardless of the histrionics on either side. You just need to say who is me. That's all."

She plucked his topknot and watched the black folds fall around his face and shoulders, cascading to his waist. She loved how his hair framed his face, making his eyes look bigger under his arched eyebrows. She loved how his pupils shrunk and grew with his emotions; his eyes showed more expression than anyone she'd ever known. "Your family would never have to worry that I'd encourage you to cut your hair," she whispered, running her fingers through the shiny, black strands.

"Quite beside the point, *mishri*. Stop changing the topic. I don't care about hair since it is always under the turban except for when I am with you." He leaned forward and kissed her. "We've got to do this

131

soon, the sooner the better, because I can't hold off my family with any more flimsy excuses. Already my brother is asking if I am gay."

She laughed. "Maybe we should talk to the Sisters first," she said. "They can advise us."

Maria would never forget when she first saw Taran. She'd spotted him from one of the convent's empty hospital-like rooms she'd been asked to clean with two other Sisters. Except for Hector, who was the sickest, the residents had gone into the kitchen or the common room. She'd watched his slender, brown fingers pull the feeding tube out of Hector's black belly, and she'd watched him care for the ailing man with a rare tenderness. He'd spoken to Hector in soft, slow tones, and she remembered smiling at the cadences, his accented English sounding musical.

She'd watched him clean the tube; his nimble fingers were practiced, and his face was placid, not grimacing at the chore that she knew she'd find difficult to complete. She'd watched Hector, who probably looked older than his actual age, peer into his caretaker's face and smile appreciatively, wrapping his trembling, black, skeletal fingers around his caretaker's brown ones.

From the room where her double-gloved hands had cleaned hospital beds with bleach water, wiped down drawers and chairs, wiped the bed springs, and worked with the Sisters at the convent hospice, she'd watched him through the gap of the door left ajar. She'd watched him smile at Hector, squeeze his bony hand, joke with him, and tell him stories. His melodious voice lifted and fell as his long fingers wrung a cloth in a basin sitting on a night table. He'd gently run the cloth over Hector's thin face, across his chin, and down his wrinkled neck; he'd washed the man's hands. A Sikh with his wine-colored turban folded precisely in neat pleats, he'd wet the cloth again and washed Hector's arms and belly. When he had glanced away from Hector for just a moment, his eyes met hers, and she'd thought they looked merry. She'd known that he knew she'd been watching him. He'd smiled at her, and she lowered her eyes and looked away, focusing on the work that the Sisters had assigned her: the cleaning of the hospice rooms and the making of beds with crisp, white sheets. The Sisters—two in the room with her—had worked diligently, praying aloud and pulling her back into the task with their strong voices.

"You say the second part," one of the Sisters said after they'd completed the first half of the prayer. But the words had flown out of her head. The glance between them—her and the Sikh—had lasted only a minute, but it'd thrilled her. She felt her stomach tense and adrenaline race through her body like an electric current, and unlike the Sisters, she could only focus on the classic beauty of his face, his strong features, and his sensuous lips like David come to life.

Busy with their separate duties, Maria and the Sikh hadn't spoken to each other at all, and when she, exhausted, left the convent to walk three miles home, she thought she'd never see him again. She'd passed the boarded-up homes standing in lines like fallen soldiers; their windows looked like sightless dead slumped in a row on Monument Street in the heart of east Baltimore's worst ghetto.

She'd traveled only a mere two blocks when she heard a car horn honking furiously. With the maroon turban tight and neat around his head, the Sikh waved from a silver Toyota and flashed that brilliant smile. His eyes looked merry as if he'd just heard a good joke.

"Sister T. asked me to drive you home. She said it might be unsafe for you to walk," he'd said, still smiling. His mustache and short beard encircled his lips and white teeth like a fence protecting that smile. Instead of taking her home, he had taken her to a coffee shop, where she'd ordered a sandwich and ate ravenously. She hadn't eaten at the convent, just worked.

"I sometimes forget to eat when I'm there too," he'd said.

"I didn't forget. All their food is donated. I hold off until I get home," she said.

"Hmm," he said, smiling.

The same smile that beguiled her a year ago graced his face now, and his shiny, black eyes looked just as bemused. He took both of her hands into his. "Stop typing for one minute. I phoned Sister T. two days ago and told her everything. They know."

Maria jerked her head in surprise. "Seriously? What did Sister T. say?"

"The usual. She said she'd pray over it. She'll let us know about the restaurant. Sundays are busy days for them, especially when they visit DC."

"Was she surprised?"

"If she was, she didn't sound like it," he said.

"Such an organized man," Maria said and smiled.

"Ha! Tell that to my supervisor who's waiting for all the paperwork that still needs to be done," he said. He replaced those large-lensed, wire-rimmed glasses on his nose and pulled a paper from the back of his medical text.

"Now, voila. The Dr. Sodhi treatment plan for our future. Today is ninth of September. We invite both families to a Thai place or anyplace you want next Sunday, the sixteenth. So you can't procrastinate or hide behind deadlines. The Mannenta family—parents, siblings, and spouses—and the Sodhi family—parents, siblings, and spouses—will meet for the first time on September sixteenth, and so begins the double-I wars. They might even discover they actually like each other."

In the kitchen, Taran filled a pot with milk. He added some garam masala spice, cardamom, bay leaf, cinnamon, sugar, and water and set the pot on the burner. While moving around her kitchen, taking the bag of loose tea, spooning it into a tea egg, and dropping it into the pot before reaching into another cabinet for two mugs, he looked at home. She watched him, liking how comfortable he looked in her kitchen, how his height enabled him to reach the topmost cabinet shelves, and how he moved with self-assurance as if his being there was the most natural place for him to be. He brought two mugs of chai to the dining room table and set one before her with a napkin.

"I like your hopeful plan," she said. Her stomach tensed at the prospect of sharing Taran with her family, but it tensed more at the prospect of his family proceeding with an arranged marriage for him. To someone else, She'd seen miracles take place at the convent, miracles that had attracted both of them to volunteer with the Sisters and miracles like answered prayers and transformed lives. Their families accepting them as a couple would be nothing short of a miracle. Taran sat back in his chair and propped his leg across hers again, and she couldn't help herself. She had to touch him.

"This time next week, the proverbial muck might be flying in the double-I war, but *mishri*, at least we won't have to hide anymore. Just like a chemo treatment—it might get worse before it gets better," he said. He sipped his tea and stuffed the paper with the outline of his hopeful plan for their future in the back of his textbook.

* * *

Taran's work cell rang at four a.m. on Monday morning and shook them out of their sleep. He leaned across the bed. His loose hair cascaded around them both as he reached for the phone. Instinctively, she raised her arms around his slender body and groaned, reveling in the faint smell of the cologne still on him. He answered the phone.

"Who?" she asked as she yawns and stretches.

"Hospital," he mouthed, still leaning across her and listening.

"Uh-hm. Hm. Subdural hematoma. Fractured sternum. Broken ribs. That too? Okay, okay, okay. I'll be there." He clicked off the phone and returned it to the night table.

"*Misrhi*, I must go, but you sleep," he said, kissing the tip of her nose.

"Nope. I'll get up now, work for a few hours, and then spend the day with the M of Cs." she said. "Tea?"

He rose, slipped into a pair of socks, and stepped into his pants. "No time," he said. "Patient's prognosis is poor." When he disappeared into the bathroom to wash, Maria slipped into a T-shirt and gym shorts and ran downstairs to collect the unraveled turban and fifty from the table. In the bedroom, he finished buttoning his shirt and brushed his hair, pulling it into a neat knot atop his head. She watched him from behind and marveled how, in the mirror, their images contrasted so starkly: he, tall and brown and she, short and light olive. Her hair, honey-colored with blond highlights, looked almost golden compared to his shiny, much longer, black hair that kept with the Sikh ban on cutting it. Their eyes—both dark brown—were their only similarity. When he appeared satisfied with the way the topknot sat neatly on top of his head, she handed him his black fifty, which he placed carefully so that it covered a portion of his forehead.

"I'll help so you won't have to use the doorknob," she said.

Taran took the unraveled turban fabric and opened it, handing her the two opposite ends. The yardage—close to seven—always surprised her. "Thanks," he said. She could tell he was already thinking about the duties that faced him at the hospital. "Back up. We have to pull it—stretch it—remember?"

She nodded, backing out of the bedroom doorway and into the hallway.

He pulled the fabric and directed her to fold it in half, half again, and half again. "Stay there," he said, walking toward her and rolling the fabric around his elbow and arm the same way her father wrapped the garden hose around his when he was putting it away.

He stood close to her. His eyes shined, and he gingerly took the ends from her hands. Their fingers brushing. "Thanks for helping," he said, almost in a whisper. His arms were filled with the fabric, and he stood so close that she could feel his breath and the bottom of his short beard.

She tiptoed and hugged him. "I prefer helping you to unravel it," she said, knowing that outside his family, she was probably the only one who had ever seen him without it. Unlike Maria, who had been married before and had experienced the emotional roller coaster of the dating scene, Taran had focused solely on his education almost to the exclusion of other activities. She hadn't felt lonely so much as self-sufficient and self-contained, until he surprised her with deliveries of roses, sent her jokes through texts, and showed up with Chinese dinners when she least expected it. He had wooed her with his sensitivity and quiet intelligence. She looked into his shining eyes and ran her finger around his ear, along his chin, and to his lips.

"As do I," he said and kissed her finger first and then her.

She watched him place one end in his mouth and wrap the turban neatly and carefully until his entire head was encircled by the fabric. He pulled up a portion from behind and covered up the top of the fifty and the top of his head. He used her rattail comb to smooth the wraps in the front.

"Neat and smooth?" he asked.

She patted the wraps, smoothing them. "Give me the comb," she said and used the stem to push the remaining hair from his neck under the turban. His face, framed by the white turban and the black fifty, looked different. Of course, she preferred him without it, but perhaps that constituted a cultural bias on her part. She understood the strength of character and courage it took to set oneself visually apart from everyone else. He must have had eleven different turbans, royal blue, black, houndstooth, printed ones, and the wine-colored one, but he'd been favoring the white ones since his residency ended and he focused on building a practice. She considered the Sisters distinguishing themselves with their blue-edged sari habits and sandals just as Taran's turban distinguished him.

"Okay, Lovey. You must call the troops for Sunday. Which Thai place—Charles Street or Fells Point? I'll make the reservations later since I know you will be busy with the Sisters."

"Charles Street is bigger."

"More room for food fights?" he said, laughed, and then kissed her.

"I'm going to my parents tonight since I'm never home anymore. Later!" he shouted before shutting the door behind him.

At the dining room table, Maria fired up her laptop. She wondered how different next Monday would feel since the entire family would know that she'd committed herself to a Sikh by then. The church description she'd been working on—a contract job for a foreign publisher—the previous night popped up: Saint Therese of the Little Flower, the saint who focused on little ways to be good in this world and who developed a reputation for sending roses for granted prayers. She realized that saints and gurus did pretty much the same thing: led the faithful to the same shapeless, formless, and faceless God. She and Taran echoed each in the most important ways. So why not commit to Taran whose values weren't so different from her own?

* * *

Unable to sleep without Taran next to her, Maria awoke at dawn on Tuesday.

She missed him: missed the smell of his cologne, missed the gentle sound of his voice, missed the feel of his arms around her body, and missed the rhythmic sound of his breathing. She pulled his pillow close and hugged it, sniffing it because it carried his scent. She closed her eyes and forced herself to find sleep again, but it eluded her. She decided to start the day with a twenty-minute run before she'd clean the house, inspired by yesterday's cleaning sessions at the convent. She didn't mind the early start and enjoyed watching the sunrise over the Inner Harbor when she ran around Rash Field. The yellow sun painted the azure sky, promising a spectacular fall day.

Back at home, she switched on the stereo to listen to CDs and made herself instant oatmeal. She mapped the day out in her head: working, more working, and cleaning in between.

She cleaned her house the way she cleaned the convent the day before. But instead of praying, she sang and danced her way through the rooms, courtesy of rock and roll and techno dance music.

Later in the shower, her phone rang incessantly. At first, she ignored the rings, but when the rings failed to stop, she ran for it.

"Maria, where the hell have you been? Turn the TV on now!" her sister, Tina, shouted frantically on the other end of the phone. "Hurry up! I'll hold on."

"What's going on?"

"You'll see," Tina said. "Oh my God. Oh my God! You'll see."

"Has something happened to Mom or Dad?" Maria asked, unnerved by her sister's weepiness.

"Worse. Worse, worse," Tina repeated.

What possibly could be worse? she wondered. Still wrapped in a towel, she rushed downstairs, clicked off the loud stereo, and flicked on the TV, just in time to see an airplane fly into the World Trade Center. "Holy shit! Oh my God," she said into the phone.

"That was the second plane. A first one flew into the other tower. I've been trying to call you. Where've you been?" The cool sister, Tina, hardly ever broke down and laughed when she saw people fall in the street, not out of maliciousness but stress. She had long been tougher, whereas Maria had always cried at movies, over books, and over newspaper articles. Tina had dubbed her as "The Wuss."

Maria felt shocked into numbness. Transfixed, she watched events unfold on the TV, and news of a third plane hitting the Pentagon caused her sister to sob. "Holy shit. Holy shit," she said, shocked. "It'll be okay, Tina," she heard herself whispering monotone into the phone, not believing it. She wanted to talk to Taran, but she usually didn't call him at work.

Call waiting signals chimed in. Both her parents and her three aunts called, and she hid the disappointment that none of the callers brought his voice into her ear.

Fingering the towel, she realized she still needed to get dressed and eased her sister off the phone. She called Taran, but his cell phone took her directly to voice mail. "It's me," she said. "I guess you've heard about what's happening. Call me when you can."

Hurriedly, she pulled on jeans and a T-shirt and sprinted back into the living room to watch TV news, which now announced that another plane had crashed in rural Pennsylvania. In mute shock, she watched first tower and then the second one fall and realized she felt too scared to cry. Instead of working and calling the troops for Sunday's announcement, she couldn't tear herself away from news and even trolled for it on her laptop.

Finally, late afternoon, Taran sent a text message: "*Mishri*, too hectic to call. Tonight with parents due to today's events. Tomorrow night, dinner Mem Sahib. Urgent you are ready at six p.m. The medical center wants a group of us to go to NYC to help the injured. See you tomorrow night."

* * *

The Mem Sahib—a cozy Indian restaurant in Havre de Grace about an hour's drive northeast of Baltimore—sat in the middle of the block. Initially, they had eaten there to avoid detection, to avoid being spotted at Baltimore restaurants by their numerous family and friends, but over the year, it had evolved into their place, gaining significance with their special booth and recognition by the wait staff. Maria especially loved the restaurant's elephant décor and often stood before one of the restaurant's two wooden elephant statues. The décor hadn't impressed Taran as much as the restaurant's off the menu offering of Wazoo, a series of dishes with the main course being lamb or mutton, which was prepared almost exactly as he remembered it growing up in Kashmir. "What an unexpected surprise," he'd said when the restaurant owner had sent it out to him on their third or fourth visit to the place.

Tonight, a large sign printed in red ink greeted them. It said, "We are not Muslims. We are Sikh, and we love America."

Taran's face darkened. He glanced at the eatery's Punjabi owner and grimaced. "Let's just take our seat," he said and guided her to their booth. The owner, a heavyset man with longish hair and a face cut from shaving, came over and welcomed them. He and Taran spoke in Punjabi.

"Taran, what's going on?" Maria asked.

"Nothing. Slow since yesterday," Taran said.

The table had already been set, and a candelabra with two long, white candles aflame sat in the center.

"That candelabra doesn't look Indian," she said. "It looks Italian! And it looks familiar! My mom has one just like it!"

Taran smiled but said nothing. A waiter set a bottle of wine on the table, which Taran poured into two wineglasses.

"The usual tea replaced with wine?"

Except for special occasions, Maria hardly ever drank. While Taran had, on rare occasions, drank rum in a coke or had a whiskey on the rocks, he also tended to avoid alcohol.

"Just a small celebration that we are alive and found each other," he said. "Yesterday's events inspired me put things in a different perspective. We're not promised tomorrow, even if we take it for granted. I want to celebrate today," he said.

"You sound like you ODed on Hallmark cards," Maria said, taking a sip of the red wine.

"I started thinking about it after speaking to a colleague in the ER at Saint Vincent's, where the great surprise came from the small numbers of wounded being brought there," he said. "I ordered for us already when I made the reservation, so no menus tonight, *mishri*."

"What did you order for me?"

"The dish you've chosen to have more times than any other since we've been eating here," he said. "Ms. Eggplant. But other stuff as well. You'll see."

"I can't believe what happened yesterday," she said.

"Shocking, totally shocking," Taran said. "We were waiting to hear if some physicians were needed to get to New York to help with the wounded, but the eeriest thing happened. Only a small number of wounded showed up at ERs," he said. "So instead, a group of pathologists got on a train this morning."

"Hard to believe it happened," she said. "My sister Tina broke down and cried.

But I haven't been able to cry. I think of all those people in the buildings, the daycare center, the subways, and the planes that crashed, and I feel my brain freeze. It's like being on a roller coaster and being too afraid to scream," she said.

"People were only guilty of going to work," he said. He shook his head. "Every day, I see how delicate the line is between life and death, but yesterday just hammered it home. That's why I wanted us to be together tonight at our special place." He took her hand; the Kara on his wrist slid toward his knuckles.

When the meal began to arrive, the array and variety of foods—many she had never eaten before—surprised her. "Except for the eggplant, these aren't regular menu selections, are they?" Maria asked.

"Some are, but most aren't. They are traditional dishes from where my family comes from in Kashmir," he said. "Do you like them?"

"Very much," she said, spooning some black dal onto her rice.

"These are traditional dishes served at engagement parties," he said. He pulled a small box from the inside pocket of his jacket and placed it on the table. "*Mishri*, I wanted this night to be special. With both our families present. I was going to do it this Sunday in front of all the troops, but after yesterday, I decided not to wait and do it now with just us, the way it has been for all these months. It's just the two of us." He opened the box, pulled out a ring, and slipped it on her finger. "Say yes to a lifetime with me, *mishri*," he whispered.

She nodded. She looked at the ring on her finger and grinned. "The start of the double-I wars, I guess."

Through the rest of the dinner, Maria kept looking at the ring—a pear-shaped diamond in a platinum setting—shining on her finger. "Taran, I can't believe this."

"Yesterday, I wondered who I'd call if I were facing my last hours, and your face came to mind. I only want to be with you. Why not make it happen?"

When he asked for the check, the elderly restaurant owners refused to deliver one. Husband and wife—he, in his kitchen clothes and she, a green-and-gold sari—smiled and waved from the doorway to the kitchen. Taran left a pile of bills on the table anyway and pulled Maria out of the restaurant.

"It's done now," he said and smiled. "To the future Mrs. Singh!"

They strolled around the quaint town and headed for the waterfront. Holding hands, they sat on the gray stone bulkhead of the Susquehanna River and watched a train speed by on the bridge crossing the river and moonlight dance on the water.

* * *

In the car, before Taran slipped the key into the ignition, Maria leaned over and kissed him. "Should we announce it as soon as possible?" she asked.

"Up to you. You can do whatever you want," he said. "Because right now, nothing can make me feel unhappy, not even your dad's supposed comments about me wearing a rag on my head."

He pointed the car in the direction of I-95 South, and the both of them admired the large Victorian houses that lined some of the small town's streets. Nearly all the houses displayed American flags.

"Not even on July fourth have I seen so many flags," Maria said.

"I understand it," he said. "I was thinking about getting a small flag for the car."

"Oh, get one for mine too," she said.

Closer to the highway, he spotted a gas station and drove in. "Be right back," he said.

She watched him search his wallet for a credit card. The top of his white turban was visible in the rear car widow as he started pumping gas. She decided to get out of the car and keep him company. She kept looking at the ring on her hand. "When did you get this?" she asked.

"Yesterday. I ran over to a jeweler near the hospital. I did everything yesterday. That's why it was too hectic to call you, and I thought I would just blurt it anyway."

She laughed. "You are pretty good with secrets," she said.

"You will discover that that is a great myth," he said, "especially when it pertains to you."

"Not true, Taran," Maria said.

"Here's proof. I told my parents last night. They know now, and they're looking forward to meeting you. Like tomorrow night. For dinner." Taran smiled widely.

A gray sedan swung into the gas station. She watched two white men in baseball caps step out front, and two others remained in the vehicle. One of them pointed at Taran before they went into the store.

"Taran, I have a bad feeling. Let's get out of here," she said.

"We're at a gas station, *mishri*. In plain view."

"Please. Let's go. I have a bad feeling."

"Almost done."

The two men emerged from the store and both leaned on the sedan, staring at them and talking to the two others in the back. Finally, the larger one screamed. "Hey Arab!"

"TJ, let's leave now."

"Two dollars more to go, *mishri*."

"We don't need the two dollars that much. Let's go. Please, Taran."

"I don't want to scamper away like a coward."

The two men sauntered over to them, followed by the two others who emerged from the sedan.

"I said *Arab*," the larger one said.

Neither Taran nor Maria answered.

"If you stinking Arabs hate our country so much, why don't you just go back? Fucking Al-Qaeda," the smaller one said. The other two stood behind them. Their legs were spread apart as if they were going to spring.

"I'm not Muslim or Arab. I am Sikh," Taran said. He replaced the nozzle. "I am a Sikh from India, nowhere near the Middle East."

"You're denying it now because you don't want your ass whupped!" the bigger man shouted. "And you're going to pay for what you people did to us yesterday, you and your Al-Qaeda fuckers who hate our country but want to live here anyway."

"No!" Maria screamed. "Leave us alone."

"You're no better, fucking cunt."

"He's not Arab. He's not Al-Qaeda," she said, trying to be calm and moving closer to Taran.

"Liars!" the bigger one yelled. "Let's get 'em, boys. Show this fucking Al-Qaeda bastard what happens when he fucks with Americans."

The men—all four—sprung toward Taran, and without thinking, she placed herself in between them and Taran. She felt a blow land and another. She kicked one of the attackers but ineffectively. Someone jerked her away from Taran, and she scrambled back to him, only to be dragged away again. She elbowed the man trying to hold her down.

She saw Taran throw one punch and another. He didn't look like a fighting man. She saw him kick at one of his attackers, but the kick sliced the air. She saw him, grim-faced, fend off blows, but he was overwhelmed by the two men. He sank; his turban was crooked on his head. She dug her heel into the shin of the man holding her and ran toward where she saw Taran go down. But another man dragged her away and pinned her to the ground. She couldn't see him after that, but she heard grunts, yelps, slaps, and blows land, and she heard bones break.

"Let's show this cunt what happens to traitors," she heard one of the attackers say. She struggled to loosen herself from the grip of two pairs of hands, but they overpowered her. She raised her torso, attempting to head bang the man sitting on her. Maybe she could bite his nose, his lips, or his hands? She dug her thumb nails into the skin of the man holding her down, and she then head butted him in an effort to escape. Everything went black after that.

* * *

When Maria opened her eyes, she saw white lights, and she heard the computer beep of hospital machinery. She wondered where she was, especially when she saw Sister T.'s face. Her head was covered by the white-and-blue edge sari habit, peering down at her. Was she at the hospice? Maria wondered. She tried to move; her body ached, her muscles screamed, and she couldn't move without feeling every part of her body straining. She tried to push herself up with her legs and hands to shift herself higher in the bed, but her thighs and legs screamed with pain as did the muscles in her arms. She failed to budge. An IV was attached to one of her hands.

Where was her ring?

"Maria?"

"Where am I?"

"Don't speak. You're badly hurt," Sister T said.

Maria looked around, realizing the beeping hospital machines were not a dream. "Taran?" Her parched throat hurt when she spoke.

Sister T. did not answer. Instead, she prayed "Our Father" over Maria.

"Taran?"

Sister T. shook her head.

"You have visitors," Sister T. said and left the room. She returned with a man and woman whom Maria had never seen before. Like Taran, the man wore a turban, except his was navy blue, and he had a short beard that indented in the middle of his chin. The woman wore a white salwar kameez, and Maria wondered if she was one of the Sisters, except without the head covering. The tall woman looked familiar as if Maria had seen her before somehow and had forgotten.

She looked at them quizzically, and her head began to hurt. "My head," she said.

Her parents, both looking frail, her sister Tina, looking fatigued, and Tina's husband, followed the strange couple in with Sister M. behind them.

"You can't stay long," Sister T. told the group. "Taran's parents," she said to Maria. "They've been sitting vigil with your parents since you've been here."

"How long? Where's Taran? We're engaged now," she said with her sore throat.

Sister T. placed a pile of white fabric—bloodstained—in Maria's hands. She could still smell Taran's British Sterling cologne. She held the fabric tightly, clinging to it. She blinked her eyes in frustration. No one was telling her what she wanted to know. She smelled the fabric, the remnant of cologne mixed with the remnant of old blood. She thought about Taran. She pictured him smiling. She remembered the ring. Then she remembered his kicks slicing the air.

"Taran?" she croaked.

No one said anything. Not Sister T. Not her parents. Not Tina, whose eyes blinked. Not her husband, whose pursed lips looked as if they were locked shut. Not Taran's parents, who looked like tall statues. No one uttered a syllable. She looked at their faces, one by one, and then fingered the bloodstained white turban, unraveled in her hands.

SAVED

LOTTIE SWISHED HER hips first right and then left, controlling her belly muscles to shake in time with the strains of bouzouki music coming out of her stereo. Clicking tiny thumb cymbals in each hand rhythmically to the beat of the hollow drums, she danced around the living room, practicing the steps—sway left, then right, then isolate the ab muscles and the neck, head in the opposite direction—and humming the familiar melody. Her hair, jet-black and curly, cascaded around her shoulders in unruly corkscrews—her best asset, she thought.

If she tried hard enough, she could almost hear her teacher's husky-voiced directions. "Zat's right. Move hips left and right. Swish, swish. Move ze belly, not ze body. Move ze belly, not ze body. Two, three, four." It was ingrained in her psyche after almost four years of lessons. "You dance iz good. A natural wit'a passion," her teacher had said, elongating the first syllable of the word.

Lottie worked to keep her ab muscles flat, although she noticed that, despite the exercise, she was developing a slight pot anyway. "Love belly," Sammy, her boyfriend, had teased her, pulling up her shirt, pinching her belly into a roll, and kissing her belly button. "More to love!" he'd laughed. They'd been lying across the carpet in the living room after an impromptu picnic, in the days before Aunt Dorothy moved in with them. Impromptu picnics. One of the many sacrifices they'd made to accommodate the old woman's presence, the woman who refused to accept Sam.

Although he shrugged it off, asking, "How's 'The Saint' today?" and laughing before racing out the door for work every day, it bothered Lottie.

The drum on the stereo boomed. Aunt Dorothy whined, "Evil walks in this house." She was sitting in a hospital bed in Lottie's dining room.

She hated when her aunt threw a tantrum, so she squeezed her eyes shut and bit the inside of her mouth to avoid snapping at the old lady. She envisioned herself smacking her into silence. The thought frightened her. She had no penchant for violence and found herself wishing the Lord would call Dorothy home. She knew moving in with her probably hadn't been number one on Dorothy's dance card either.

Lottie stopped dancing. The music played over her aunt's complaints about evil and Satan. The old lady rocked on the hospital bed, begging for mercy and covered her ears, which were already covered by the cream-colored linen scarf tied in a knot at the back of her head.

"Was just exercising," Lottie said.

"You are not walking the Lord's path," the old lady said. Her thin lips formed a straight line. Her face was filled with bitterness. "That dance is obscene. A sex dance."

Lottie sighed. "We've been through this already. Keeps my belly strong and flat. Well, flatter," she said, patting her belly and frowning. At dance class, aspiring belly dancers dressed the part with coin belts that jangled, flowing, sheer harem pants with slits at the side seams, beaded or coin halter bras, veils, anklets, jingly bracelets, and earrings. She loved the clink and jingle of the coin belts and jewelry, the shimmering cacophony on the beat when everyone performed the same movement. And shopping for costumes. Pre-Dorothy.

"I can tell you *like* the sex dance. For someone so smart, you know nothing. You can run up and down the stairs or around the block. Or you can get one of those machines and run on it.

That's what a God-fearing woman would do," Aunt Dorothy said.

"This is way more fun," Lottie said.

"The same dance the harlot Salome did before she asked for the baptist's head on a platter."

Lottie laughed. "You're so dramatic."

"Obviously, a certain someone who shall remain nameless didn't teach her child anything important," Aunt Dorothy said, almost spitting. "If I were your mother…you wouldn't have grown up to be a childless spinster living a heathen life."

Lottie shook her head. "No wonder you and Mom didn't get along."

The old woman scoffed.

Resigned, Lottie flicked off the belly dancing music and switched the stereo to a rock and roll station. Aunt Dorothy pushed herself toward the bed's edge and searched around for her stainless-steel cane, which helped her lean onto her stainless steel walker. With the walker, she navigated the first floor of Lottie's house. She looked like she intended to hobble over to the stereo to switch to the preachy religious station she listed to all the time.

"Those preachers don't like anyone who thinks for themselves. Con men hiding behind the skirts of the church," Lottie said.

"You sound just like Tina. Your Uncle Clem and I tried to save Tina and you. We couldn't save Tina, but I can still save you. That's why God put me here. Thank you, Jesus! You can do it now, Lottie. You can accept Jesus as your personal Savior. Let me save you. I can die in peace if I know you're saved for all eternity."

"It'd be a heck of a lot more peaceful around here if you'd stop harassing Sammy and accept him as my boyfriend," Lottie shot back.

Aunt Dorothy said nothing. She banged her cane on the floor, leaned on it with her right hand, and raised her left arm to the ceiling. She intoned, "Demon of Fornication. Demon of Rebellion. Demon of Ignorance. I bind you in Jesus' name. I command you to leave my niece, Carlotta Penn, free of your plagues and to depart from this house in

Jesus' name, the name of the Son of God who lived and died for our sins. Oh, Jesus, I ask that you come and sanctify this abode. I pray for the banishment of Satan's lapdog from this home."

Still leaning on her cane, she pulled a small bottle of holy water out of her pocket and splashed it in every direction but mostly toward Lottie, who felt the wet and cool water drops her sweaty arms, neck, and face.

"I thought Evangelicals didn't use holy water," Lottie said. "Aren't you the one who said my mom and me were Papists?"

"I blessed it myself. I don't need any magical man leader to connect me to the Lord.

Weak as it is, I like using it for protection."

"And I hope you're not referring to Sammy as 'Satan's lapdog' or as one of those demon names you just mentioned. Any other man would have demanded you to be gone and wouldn't have put up with those relentless insults in his own house," Lottie said, arching her eyebrow.

Aunt Dorothy smiled wide. "By the grace of God, you will be saved. The Lord can move mountains."

* * *

Upstairs in her attic studio, under a skylight with sun streaming into the room, Lottie worked. She drew fish—all kinds of whimsical fish. She drew some fat fish, some with glasses, some with moustaches, and some with hats. All were surrounded by squiggly circles, a design to be used in a print ad for the local aquarium.

Downstairs Jennie, the day nurse, looked after Aunt Dorothy. Her aunt disliked Jennie and raised a daily commotion. Lottie could hear it three floors up and tried to ignore it. She drew a fish that resembled Dorothy and added a tall, bouffant hairstyle to disguise the fact the scowling face was based on her aunt. Sometimes she smiled when she saw her mother's face echoed in her aunt's, the way her left eyebrow raised itself when she felt skeptical. Her mother had laughed more and worried less than Dorothy did.

Jennie, a heavyset Black woman with short, dreadlock hair and black horn-rim glasses in front of her large, almond-shaped eyes, used her no-nonsense nurse voice on Aunt Dorothy. Her Jamaican accent overpowered the old lady's cranky whine. Lottie smiled and sketched a fish that looked like Jennie into the fish mix. And another that looked like her mother as she best remembered her face: joyful. And another that looked like Sammy.

Since Aunt Dorothy's arrival, Lottie ate lunch with her instead of at her light table or with friends at restaurants. With the living room, the dining room, and the kitchen linked together like a train car on the first floor of Lottie's town house, the space proved to be enough room for her eighty-year-old aunt but only with a portable commode tucked discreetly behind the hospital bed. Lottie had handrails and a metal chair added to the first-floor bathroom so her aunt could sit and shower, although she still required assistance with the task.

At lunchtime, the three of them—Dorothy in her hospital bed, with the food tray in front of her, while Lottie and Jennie sat in folding chairs with TV trays before them—sat in the dining turned hospital room. A preacher intoned a sermon on the stereo speaker, set on low. Jennie had given Aunt Dorothy tomato soup, a scrambled egg, and cherry Jell-O.

"Are you having a good day today, Aunt Dorothy?" she asked. She bit into her grilled cheese sandwich and stabbed a black olive in her salad.

"Compared to what?" the old lady snapped. Her wrinkled fingers played with the soup spoon. "No, I'm not, since you asked. I prefer you to spend time with me during the day. Not a nurse with ties to voodoo. I'm not sick," she said.

"Keepin' you company is all," Jennie said. "You want Lottie to lose her job, nah? We can sit outside on the bench with the neighbors if you like. And who said anything about voodoo, nah?"

"I'm not decrepit either," Dorothy said. "I'm not sitting on a bench where all the old men sit."

"What do you have against old men?" Lottie asked. "I don't blame you for not wanting to sit with old men. It's a lot more fun to sit on a bench with young men. Like Sam."

They all laughed.

"First, I'd save them, and then I'd invite the best one home to meet my niece," Dorothy said.

"After you save them, none of them would want to meet me anymore, because I'd still be...a heathen!" Lottie laughed.

"Until they see your Salome dance," said Aunt Dorothy. "Then I'd have to get them all to repent and be saved again."

"How many times can somebody be saved?" Jennie asked.

"As many times as it takes," Aunt Dorothy said with conviction. "The spirit is willing, but the flesh is weak."

"Maybe those old guys outside on the bench are waiting for you to save them," Lottie said. "Even Jesus ate with tax collectors, prostitutes, and lepers. And here you are, eating with me, who is also unsaved."

Dorothy snorted. "Not for long."

"I can take Dorothy outside today. Warm spring day. Looks like it would be a big job, Dorothy, because every day about seven of them men sit outside on the bench, feeding the pigeons. Same pigeons. Same men," Jennie said. "Maybe the Lord is waitin' for you to start working."

"I don't want to go outside without Lottie." Drops of tomato soup dribbled down her chin. Jennie held a napkin toward her, who ignored the offer and pretended Jennie's hand was invisible.

"Get some fresh air," Lottie said. "Anyone who feeds the pigeons can't be all bad. God made pigeons too. Give them a chance. Maybe you can make some new friends, and maybe you'll find one or two of them already saved, a partner in the saving business or something."

Lottie took her plate with her unfinished sandwich and her salad upstairs. Back in the studio—her haven—she listened to the radio and glued the fish characters she'd illustrated onto a poster. She wondered if an assisted-living home somewhere in Baltimore could accommodate her aunt. She picked up the phone, dialed Sammy's work number, and listened to the first ring but hung up before he could answer or before the voice mail clicked on. She's already lost time on this project and procrastinating on the phone with Sammy wouldn't make up for it.

She forced herself to focus, although, honestly, all the changes to her house and the inconveniences of having an elderly relative live-in had disturbed her rhythm, disrupted her discipline, and cost her time.

* * *

Later, the phone rang, startling Lottie out of a deep concentration. She answered without looking away from the light table. "Carlotta Penn."

"Lottie!" Sam's voice sounded enthusiastic in her ear. "Hottie Lottie! Hottie Lottie with my fabulous totties! How's the fish poster going? And how are things with 'The Saint'?" he asked.

"Marching along," she said. "Fish poster is nearly done. If I work straight through until you get home, I'll make the deadline. And Dorothy expelled the demons again today. She also doused me and the house with holy water."

Sam chuckled. "I didn't know our house was possessed. Maybe that explains the creaking and moans it makes at night, just demons getting comfortable. Any luck finding suitable places that will take her?"

"I know. I made a few calls but not many, and so far, there are no openings. Plus, when there is an opening, they'll want to interview her."

"Oh, great!" Sammy said. "That'll go over like a lead balloon. She'll hate every place and won't hesitate to say it. Then we're stuck 'til she kicks. That can take forever."

Lottie said nothing. She hated the trouble, but right now, her aunt was her last connection to her mother, her only living relative. The thought of just dumping her at any old place left her feeling unsettled.

"Thanks for being patient. I appreciate it. Maybe her attitude toward you will improve once she gets to know you better..." Lottie knew how feeble she sounded. "Satan's lapdog" wasn't exactly a term of endearment.

* * *

When Sammy came home, Lottie was sitting with her aunt. Dorothy was eating mashed potatoes, creamed corn, a chicken fillet cut into pieces, and spinach thanks to Jennie, who had prepared and served her dinner, which was her last task of the day.

He came in through the front door, carrying a huge bouquet of flowers—pink, white, and red camellias, purple hyacinths, and spider flowers. The bouquet nearly obscured his face: his father's Chinese nose and his Swedish mother's deep dimples. His long, black hair was tied in a neat, black braid. He had said his hair harkened back to his father's heritage, because ancient Chinese scholars had always worn long braids.

"For 'The Saint,'" he said, smiling at Lottie and showing his deep dimples but extending his hand to the old woman.

"Not for me?"

"You get something else better later," he said. "These are for you, Aunt Dorothy."

Ignoring his hand with the bouquet thrust almost in her face, Aunt Dorothy looked him up and down, stared at the slashes in the knees of his jeans, pursed her lips at his green T-shirt, which featured an alien face—black with white eyes—and frowned.

"I expelled the demons of fornication, ignorance, and rebellion this morning," she said. "I see I should have included the demon of sloth too."

He laughed. "Dorothy the demon slayer. Lottie told me. Maybe the house will stop creaking at night. How was your day?" he asked in a loud voice.

"I'm not deaf," she snapped. "And I'm not blind either."

"Well, can you see the flowers then?" he asked.

"I can," she answered tersely. "That don't mean I have to accept them. If I could walk faster, I'd drop them in the trash can."

"Thank you for the lovely flowers, Sam. You're welcome, Aunt Dorothy," he said, giving the bouquet to Lottie, who carried them into the kitchen and hunted for a vase. She returned with the bouquet and put it on one of the tables near the hospital bed.

"Lottie doesn't need a boyfriend living here. Her jezebel days are over, especially now that she's practically saved. You can go back to your own home."

"This is my home, Dorothy. If you want, I can show you my driver's license with this address listed on it. In case you need further proof."

"Did you say practically saved? That means you accepted Sammy as my personal boyfriend?" Lottie asked.

Aunt Dorothy's steely eyes regarded him. "Why don't you want a man who wears a respectable suit and who knows the Lord?"

"This is a respectable suit!" he said. "I don't want to wear fancy clothes to the lab.

They'll just get ruined. And who says I don't know the Lord? Maybe I just call him by a different name."

"Highly doubtful," she said.

He shook his head. "Let's go out to dinner, Lottie," he said.

Lottie nodded at her aunt. "No sitter. It's like having a kid but with bigger diapers," she said in a low voice so that only Sam could hear her.

"Pizza in?"

"Staying away from it," she said. "Had to cut down on my workout time. Aunt Dorothy here doesn't appreciate belly dancing, and it's been hard to get to class or to the gym.

My belly is getting bigger, and I'm hating it."

"*Love* belly," he said. "We can work on that tonight if you want. Salsa in and out," he said, dancing around the room with an invisible partner. He laughed, and she smiled.

"I can cook us something light. Fish? Veggies? Pasta? A salad? That work for you?" Lottie asked.

He nodded. "Any more beer in the fridge?" he asked.

"No, but there's some wine in there from the other night," she said.

"No alcohol in the house!" Aunt Dorothy yelled from her hospital bed. "How many times do I have to tell you, Lottie? No alcohol in the house." She looked as if she was about to cry.

"This isn't a church or some kind of dry religious compound, Dorothy," he said. "It's our home, so you need to get used to it and our heathen ways if you plan to stay here."

She slipped the bottle of holy water out of her pocket and doused him with a spray of it. "In Jesus' name, demon of self-indulgence, demon of pride, and demon of sloth, be gone."

He laughed, but he sat with the old woman while Lottie prepared dinner. Aunt Dorothy glared at him and the wineglass he held. "Unforgivable," she said in a hoarse whisper. "Unwise man."

"Correct me if I'm wrong, but didn't Jesus turn water into wine?" Sam asked.

"The wisdom of the Bible tells us to stay away from a strong drink. Proverbs 23:31 says, 'Look not thou upon the wine when it is red, when it giveth his colour in the cup, when it moveth itself aright.' And Proverbs 20:1 says, 'Wine is a mocker, strong drink is raging: and whoever is deceived thereby is not wise.' Jesus only did that to please his mother. And you are leading my niece straight down the road to hell with all your Satan-loving activities. Like living under this roof like husband and wife without being married."

Sam took another sip.

"The Bible is filled with things we now consider wrong. Slavery. Multiple wives. Concubines. Murder. Adultery. Betrayal. And stories about how the Lord vanquished those things. It hurts me to see Lottie flying down the wrong path toward eternal damnation with you."

"There are many paths to God. And many definitions of a strong drink. What about coffee drinkers? Caffeine is strong a drink, and the Catholics use wine at every Mass, so alcohol can't be that bad. What's that saying? 'Everything in moderation.'"

She snorted. "Papists. They also worship Mary like a god. They aren't true Christians. Clem taught me that ages ago when he saved me, and I converted. We tried so hard to save Tina, but she refused, calling Clem vile names. And now, Lottie, poor child, remains in the dark. I pray every day for her to come into the light."

"Maybe she's already in the light, and you're just blind."

"Not with you around, tempting her off a righteous path, living in sin, drinking beer and wine, and everything else like living together without the benefits of marriage. And she's doing that Salome dance to exercise of all things. Lord have mercy!"

"Dinner's ready!" Lottie called from the kitchen.

Sam served the steamed white fish, asparagus, and pasta with butter onto paper plates and carried them into the former dining room. They ate off TV trays. Aunt Dorothy accepted some fish. Afterward, he cleaned the kitchen, while Lottie set up the Monopoly board. The three of them played, each wanting to win. Dorothy got angry, yelling "Snap!" when she landed in jail.

"Snap?" he asked. "What's that? Oh *snap*! Bull*snap*! *Snap* a brick!"

Lottie giggled, and Dorothy cracked a smile.

When Lottie saw the old lady fading, they finished the game. She helped her aunt prepare for bed, while he put away the game and grabbed some CDs before they tiptoed upstairs to their bedroom.

When they reached the middle of the stairwell, Dorothy hissed from the hospital bed. "Is he sleeping here again tonight?"

"He sleeps here every night," Lottie called down the stairs. "For the hundredth time, he lives here."

"Where's he sleeping?"

"With me. Not that it's your business, Aunt Dorothy."

"He won't marry you if you sleep with him," she called as if Sam wasn't there.

"I can *hear* you," he said.

"Maybe I don't want to marry him," Lottie said. "Maybe I don't want to marry anyone, but it's my choice."

"Tina indoctrinated your evil!" the old woman yelled. "But you can commit to the Lord. Come, Lottie. You can do it now. Come to Jesus. Come let me save you tonight!" she shouted.

Lottie snickered.

"Good night, Dorothy," he said. In the bedroom, he plopped on the bed. "Man. She drains the life out of anything around her."

Lottie laid across the bed on her stomach. "Honestly, I'm not sure how long I can do this." She sighed. "No wonder my mother butted heads with her."

"Chinese honor the elders, even difficult ones, and respect their wisdom, so don't worry about me in all this. This is between you and your aunt," he said. He slipped a CD into the stereo. "That said, I hate the dining room looking like a nursing home with an Asian influence."

"I think Uncle Clem left her destitute."

"That sounds a bit odd to me. Doesn't it sound odd to you? What do poor old people who have no one do? They end up somewhere."

"I had this naive idea that I could bond with her and get to know my mom better through her. She looks like a version of my mom."

"The evil twin version?"

She laughed.

"She only wants to save *you*. As far as she's concerned, I can rot in hell. Dorothy's heaven is a selective one." He leaned in to kiss her. She turned her face so his lips landed on her cheek.

"Well, Hottie Lottie. What's that? No kisses?"

"From Satan's lapdog?"

"She said that?" His dimples formed deep parentheses around his lips. "Come sit on my lap's dog," he said, grinning.

She kissed him and pulled him into her. She loved the contours of his body—compact and hard-muscled—next to hers. She undid his braid. He slid his fingers up her blouse, running them along her belly and toward her breasts. She sighed at the touch. Piece by piece, their clothing sailed across the room, and she welcomed him.

* * *

On Saturdays, Jennie didn't come, and not having a nurse present ate into Lottie's leisure time. Before Aunt Dorothy moved in, she had worked a few hours on Saturday mornings before she ran errands, had a manicure or a pedicure, and maybe got a facial. Or she and Sam would go to festivals, craft and art shows. Something. Today, she promised herself that she'd make the effort to get Aunt Dorothy and herself outside with a small shopping excursion to the mall, a test-run trip before taking her to places with porta-potties. Sam offered to come along. Dorothy appeared excited by the prospect of going outdoors too but not by the prospect of Sam's company.

"You need to accept Sam, Aunt Dorothy."

"I'd rather be alone with you," she said.

"We're a package deal. Since you've been here, you've done nothing but upset him in his own home. He's a good man. He's *my* man, and you better start respecting him."

"He's going to be gone from here anyway, so there's no point," Dorothy said. "God moves mountains. You'll see. Paul was Saul before he was Paul."

Lottie rolled her eyes. While Sam showered, she gave Aunt Dorothy a sponge bath. She helped the old woman dress in a pair of blue polyester pants with a matching blue-striped shirt. She offered to wrap her aunt's thin, gray hair in heated curlers, but the old lady insisted on keeping her head covered instead. She hoped to persuade her to put on a bit of lipstick, but Dorothy refused, saying it was immodest.

When Sam came downstairs, he wore tight black jeans and a muscle shirt.

"Maybe you should go home and change like a big boy," Aunt Dorothy said. "Put some decent clothes on."

"Aunt Dorothy must have eaten chicken's ass for breakfast. That's why she's so shitty first thing in the morning," Sam said, smiling. His dimples were polka dots on his cheeks. "We're taking you to the mall. When was the last time you went to a mall? What a thrill, don't you think?"

Aunt Dorothy's eyes widened, and Lottie thought she could see an imperceptible smile play across her aunt's face.

"I'll go get the car ready," he said. He winked at the old woman.

Lottie helped her aunt to the front door. Dorothy's feet were encased in new double-knotted running shoes instead of the terry cloth slippers she'd arrived with, and they moved forward, step by slow step. Impatience bit into Lottie's heels; her feet were used to a faster pace.

"What happened between you and Mother?" Lottie asked.

Dorothy stiffened. "I prefer not to talk about it."

"Why didn't you come to her funeral?"

"She did me wrong," Aunt Dorothy said. She inched another step forward. "I'd hate to see you turn into a fast number like your mother, but that's what's happening. Good thing God sent me here to save you."

Lottie bugged out her eyes.

"Lucifer was God's most beautiful angel. The devil still always comes dressed like a gentleman. Except Sam, who doesn't bother with suits or with being a gentleman."

"Don't talk about Sam that way. I'm not having it."

"You don't know anything about your mother. She lived a whole life before you were born, so how could you know anything about her? She didn't tell you anything important either."

"We had no secrets between us," Lottie said.

Aunt Dorothy humphed. "That's what you think. Doesn't matter. She's dead and so is everybody else."

"It matters to me. What happened between you two?"

"Nothing you need to know about."

"What kept you away from her funeral?"

"There's no point in talking ill about the dead," Dorothy said. She pursed her lips and then stepped forward. She breathed out loudly. With her white-knuckles on her walker, she banged it on the floor.

"Must have been something. Just thinking about it makes you angry. You look like you can beat something up."

The old woman stood still for a minute. She pursed her lips, and she stood as straight as she could. She said nothing. Instead, she banged the walker down as hard as her nonexistent muscles would allow again and took the next step toward the door. "What kind of sister is she when I can't trust her alone with my husband?"

"That doesn't sound like Mom," Lottie said.

Dorothy snorted. "You don't know anything about your mother. She always had wild hair, and you seemed to have inherited it."

Lottie guided her out the door, slowly down each of the three steps, to the pavement.

Dorothy's large, white old lady purse dangled from Lottie's shoulder as she helped the old woman. Sam had unlocked the doors of his blue Taurus and helped her ease the old woman into the seat and buckle the seatbelt.

"Except for those coal-black eyes, you look just like her. A spitting image," Aunt Dorothy said when she was finally situated in the backseat. "You got your daddy's eyes, for sure."

"Nope. You're mistaken," Lottie said. "Don't you remember? Daddy's eyes were pea soup green."

Aunt Dorothy looked at her quizzically, and then she looked angry. "You don't know anything," she said, folding her hands on her lap just as Lottie shut the door.

"Ready?" Sam asked, while Lottie climbed into the front seat.

Aunt Dorothy grimaced as he pointed the car forward. "The question on my mind is when are you going to make Lottie here an honest woman and marry her? That's the question if you ask me. Are *you* ready?"

A tension settled in the car. "Go with the flow. Bend with the breeze. You'd be a lot happier, Dorothy," he said.

Now she laughed. "So the breeze can blow you all over hill and gone? Lottie, there's still time for you to embrace the Lord. And then maybe you can save this alcoholic man from bending so far with the breeze that he bends himself parallel to the ground."

He flicked on the radio, and heavy metal guitar licks filled the air. Aunt Dorothy yelled a prayer of lament, asking for God to have pity on her during the torture. She began to sing the hymn "A Mighty Fortress Is Our God" loud enough to drown out the radio. He turned up the volume and so did Dorothy.

Lottie sighed. The ride to the mall promised to be torturous for all of them.

* * *

Lottie obtained a courtesy wheelchair for her aunt, who sat lopsided in it, clutching her white purse on her knees, gazing around with a dumbfounded expression, and gaping at the storefronts, the decorations, the parade of people, and the gangs of teenagers. Sam pushed the wheelchair toward one of the major department stores, and they browsed at items sold at the kiosks and carts situated in the center of the walkway.

"You have brought me straight to Gomorrah," Aunt Dorothy said, gaping at a group of young girls with their exposed bellies sporting navel rings while arm in arm with boys wearing oversize pants and backward caps. She scowled at shoppers with tattoos and jewelry piercings on their faces, at teenage couples holding hands, and at the window ads with women in thong underwear. "I want to leave," she whined.

"We just got here," Lottie said. "You want anything in particular?" she asked Sam.

"Just along for the roller coaster," he said. He rolled his eyes downward to the top of Aunt Dorothy's head. "And it's a level one for impossible." He hummed the opening melody of *The Twilight Zone* over her whine to leave.

Aunt Dorothy turned her neck to glare at him. "I can hear you. I want to leave. I want to go home. Right now." She began to sing another hymn.

"Sing louder, Dorothy. This way people will think you're senile or crazy. I mean, here we are in the middle of the mall, and you're in a wheelchair, singing as if you were in some church choir. Then we can commit you to the loony bin instead of a nursing home," he said.

"Smarty-pants," she said. "I won't be the one turned into a pillar of salt."

He hummed *The Twilight Zone* tune again. "Nobody will, Dorothy. No matter what. When I was a kid, my father used to say that wise men create their own heavens in this world and the next, and foolish men create their own hells in the same way. So, Dorothy, can you say you have had more pleasure or pain in your life? Has your life been more heavenly or more hellish?"

"Blasphemy," she said. Her eyes widened, and her fingers grew rigid around her white purse. She pursed her lips in frustration.

He continued to push her chair. "Absolutely not."

They meandered to the department store and stopped at one of the perfume counters. Lottie picked up a tester bottle. "Smell this!" she said and sprayed it into the air. She sprayed her aunt before the old woman could object. She noticed the old woman stiffen at first and then sink into the fragrance. "I love this smell," she said. "I have a bottle at home already."

Dorothy smiled but said nothing. Her blue eyes were teary and wistful.

"Look! Here's the lotion," Lottie said and dropped a small dabble into her aunt's hands. She massaged the lotion into her aunt's wrinkled fingers. She worked it into her palms and the tops of her hands. She rubbed a bit more onto her aunt's forearms and up to her elbows. She felt her aunt lean into her touch. "Your skin feels so soft now! Doesn't it feel good? With a little bit of perfume?" She rubbed her aunt's paper-thin arms. "Relax, Aunt Dorothy. God can't possibly mind a bit of a fragrant massage with lotion to soften your skin." She massaged Dorothy's shoulders through the blue polyester shirt. The perfume's sweetness rose like a cloud enveloping them.

The old lady whispered, "I loved Tina. I hated her too. She was so fearless. So alive and so pretty, while I was so plain. I couldn't forgive her for fooling around with my Clem and then denying it, acting all innocent even after you came with those coal-black eyes like his. His eyes. Her hair. His expressions. Her smile. His kindness. Her passion. That is why I must save you, a child born of sin and betrayal."

Lottie stared at her aunt in disbelief. She and Sam exchanged glances, and then she squatted to be eye level with her aunt. "What are you saying, Aunt Dorothy?"

"You heard me," the old lady said. Her head hung low; her thin, gray hair exposed her scalp. Her paper-thin skin smelled like the perfumed lotion, and the old lady reached for Lottie's hands and clutched them tightly as if she never wanted to let them go.

SISTER RAFAELE HEALS THE SICK

SISTER RAFAELE WAS to be unceremoniously ousted from Josephine's tiny row house in Baltimore's Little Italy. Later, she was also to be welcomed into and kicked out of three other houses in the same neighborhood, mostly because their owners had come to believe her to be mad and hateful instead of holy and loving. She, who had once been known simply as Mrs. Caterina Della Vecchio and the former wife of a renowned mobster, had been occupying one of the neighborhood benches, telling anyone who asked that she was awaiting guidance and direction from her boss. She pointed to the sky.

Wearing a navy-blue skirt hemmed at her knees, a loose white blouse, no stockings, thick brown sandals, and a huge wooden cross on a rawhide strip around her neck, she looked like one of the nuns from a Catholic grade school. Except, surrounded by large brown supermarket bags filled with her belongings, she also looked homeless. Stained, broken teeth marred what could have been a beatific smile, a smile she flashed when she explained to those who asked that her mission was to be assigned to a household that needed her and that God would, as He would invariably do, guide her to the next assignment.

"I'm being called to this neighborhood," she'd explained on the early spring day when she showed up on the bench.

Waiting for her "instruction," Sister Rafaele had occupied various neighborhood benches over the spring months, and the neighbors could never discern if she was mentally ill or holy— at times, she seemed to be one and then the other. They remained content to figure it out from the sidelines; no one came forth to offer her a place in their homes. Until Josephine.

In all those stories about saints that Josephine had read over the years, none of them did normal, everyday things that regular people did. St. Francis of Assisi's own father, embarrassed by his own son, considered him a nutcase. St. Lucy plucked out her eyes to avoid marrying a monied, older, non-Christian man, embracing a lifetime of blindness. Joan of Arc, burned at the stake, was considered crazy for putting on armor and riding into battle.

In Sister Rafaele's case, God had spoken, and Josephine, an unlikely candidate, heard.

At thirty-tree, Josephine—also called Jody—smoked cigarettes and pot on the sly. She cursed; the words slid out of her mouth as easily as breaths. She loved all kinds of men freely, saying she was advancing world peace one man at a time. With a head of black curly hair, doe brown eyes, and olive skin, she loved her twins—two eight-year-old boys, who were products of her individual world peace campaign. She single-handedly raised them with the dedication of a Madonna.

Jody, who hadn't considered either holiness or insanity, merely decided it would be a win-win situation if she provided Sister Rafaele with a home and meals for a few months in return for babysitting the twins after school and doing some light housekeeping. On the face of it, when Jody had first thought of the plan, it did sound foolproof. Having a helper like Sister Rafaele around the house could be a boon. Except, she hadn't considered all the changes Sister Rafaele would bring about.

Immediately after the freelance nun moved in, she discouraged Jody from listening to CDs and to rock music on the radio. Instead, they listened to the Christian radio and endless sermons. When she noticed the navy blue tapestry with a gold sun and moon border hanging in the second-floor hallway, she encouraged Josephine to remove it, saying the sun and moon designs were evil and frightened her so much that she couldn't go upstairs to bathe as long as it hung on the wall. She also fined Jody a quarter every time she said the word "shit" and a dollar for every other profanity. And soon, Jody smoked only on the front stoop and not in the house since the smell of smoke sickened the nun.

"*Wach*. I can't breathe," Sister Rafaele had gasped after Jody lit up as usual. "Help. It smells so bad. My lungs can't tolerate the pollution." The nun hung her head out the front door, gasping and sucking in fresh air.

Behind the nun's back, Jody rolled her eyes but willingly overlooked the increasing number of small inconveniences in exchange for a cleaned and reordered basement and kitchen.

While she said she didn't mind the hymns in the evening, Sister Rafaele's increasing restrictions frustrated her over the next three months. By the fourth, she sat in her friend's living room at least one night a week, repeating the word "fuck" and listening to rock and roll cranked up.

"Nothing comes for free," she told her neighbors. "I don't mind some of the things, like the cuss cup, because it sets good examples for the boys. I do miss listening to my music though. She cleaned the basement and mopped the floor. She took a big load off my mind when she caught the laundry up," she said. "She picks the boys up from school, brings them home, and gives them a snack. They seem to like her so much."

Sister Rafaele had insisted on prayers before meals. Once the boys had been put to bed, she and Jody would sit in the living room and sing hymns. Jody didn't mind. Having someone to talk to filled an emptiness in the house. Though smoking outside, paying the cuss cup, and listening to boring sermons felt like a nuisance, she'd liked the changes she saw in the boys, who started beginning most of their sentences with "Sister Rafaele says."

Jody started rushing home from work to see the changes Sister Rafaele had made. Sister Rafaele had busied herself by cleaning the house. She organized the insurmountable stacks of papers scattered on the dining room table into piles, so all Jody had to do was sort, discard, or file them. Though the nun didn't cook, she kept the house meticulous, so that coming home to a clean kitchen to prepare dinners felt like a dream. By the time Jody had returned from work, Sister Rafaele had already overseen the boys' homework assignments, and she just had to review them and praise the boys' work.

"I don't know what I'd do without Sister Rafaele," she said, while smoking, to her neighbors shortly after the freelance nun had moved in. This was before Sister Rafaele, a woman unattached to any specific community of religious women, established all the house rules, which included no fornication in the house, the one rule that set Jody's teeth on edge.

"You going out tonight? Let me use your apartment. I need to see Mr. Kung Fu and fuck his brains out," she said to a coworker. "Sister Rafaele is crimping my love life," she added.

"You need to divorce Sister Rafaele," her coworker said.

* * *

The July heat beat down the streets, cooking the blacktop even though, close to five p.m., the sun slowly made its way toward the western horizon. Jody walked the half block from the bus stop toward her house, gazing at the line of people and not knowing why it had formed. Yawning, she continued toward her house, thinking that perhaps one of the twenty-two neighborhood restaurants was giving away free food to attract such a mangy crowd, until she saw Sister Rafaele praying and touching people. She approached the line.

"They've been waiting in the long line for what seems like hours. She's telling them that they're now healed and can go with God," one of her neighbors said. She noticed that many of her neighbors had come to watch the spectacle.

Astonished, Jody gasped. "Holy shit!"

"That'll be a quarter," one of them said with a laugh.

She only scowled.

"I wonder where they all came from. Looks like every homeless person in the city found your place," another neighbor said. "It's a wonder that nobody got robbed yet with all these strangers hanging out here for her."

"They ain't staying in front of my house. Sister Rafaele is gonna have to move these fuckers someplace else," she said. Her lips formed a straight line across the bottom of her face.

"Looks like they're people coming to be healed. An encounter with soap and water would have one powerful healing effect on them," the same neighbor said.

Jody didn't laugh.

The people—unshaven men in raggedy clothes and busted shoes, skinny women with unkempt hair, and children with dirty knees and cheap plastic shoes—quietly waited in a line that stretched across the street to the next block. Some of them held prayer beads. Some of them carried plastic bags that appeared to contain all their worldly possessions. They smelled rank too like old body odor and dirty hair. It smelled so rank that the stench of the unwashed assaulted Jody's nose from where she stood about six feet from her stoop.

"Pew! The great unwashed," she said, "congregating in front of my house. That fucking nasty smell is going to invade my space."

Hair peeking out from her homemade white linen veil, Sister Rafaele, head bent in prayer, touched them all. She laid her hands on their heads and prayed in Jesus' name for them to be healed from demons and diseases, from addictions and disasters, and from anything that might be plaguing their spirit with her eyes shut.

"They can get healed someplace else," Jody said through clenched teeth.

"Hard making this crowd move," her neighbor said.

"That's Sister Rafaele's job," she said. "She attracted the horde here; she can get rid of them."

* * *

Now the long line of believers, desperate for Sister Rafaele's healing touch, stretched for a block and a half. Embarrassed by the sight, shocked by the diversity of the people in line, and confronted by the strangeness of it all, Jody searched for a cigarette, muttering, "Fucking a."

Another neighbor's face, an old man named Mario, scrunched into an expression that suggested extreme constipation. He flashed her angry looks and raised his cane at her. "What da hella is dis?" he asked. "Where dese bums come from? I can't get into my house."

She shrugged.

"Disa no right. We noncha wanna dese people here," another older neighbor said.

She waved to Sister Rafaele who stood on the top step of the stoop to her house.

Sister Rafaele waved back and continued with her healing work. This time, she put her hands on the dirty gray head belonging to a disheveled man.

"Uh, Sister Rafaele. Can I have a word with you?" Jody asked. She stood on the top step of her neighbor's stoop and climbed to the top of her own.

"Not now, dear. Can't you see I'm a little busy?"

"Now, Sister Rafaele," Jody said through clenched teeth.

"I'm doing the Lord's work. The Lord's work doesn't wait," Sister Rafaele said as if she were talking to a child. She smiled with her broken and stained teeth that were in need of dire treatment themselves and turned away from Jody, dismissing her like an errant child.

"You're going to have to do the Lord's work elsewhere. This crowd is disrupting the neighborhood," Jody said. Her face flushed. She searched her purse for a cigarette and lit one.

"It's a wonder ol' Mario over there hasn't yet called the cops."

Without even looking at her, Sister Rafaele said, "Impossible. The Lord has directed me to heal His flock right here."

Jody spotted the twins. Their dark heads bobbed and weaved on either side of the line, passing out cups of water. "You have three minutes to move these fucking people someplace else, other than outside of my house!" she shouted.

Sister Rafaele ignored her. Head bowed, she laid her hands on the next seeker of her healing, who was an obese woman in red polyester shorts and a black striped shirt. "Demon of gluttony, leave this woman...in Jesus' name," she intoned. She prayed over the woman, whose eyes fluttered in the back of her head.

Jody disappeared into her house; the door slammed behind her. A few minutes later, she emerged from the basement doorway that fronted the house, hauling a long green hose.

"Time to be baptized!" Jody yelled and pointed the nozzle at Sister Rafaele. A blast of water streamed from the hose and drenched the freelance nun, who stared in stunned silence. She then pointed the nozzle at the long line of disciples and soaked them, walking up and down the long line and wetting them all as they dispersed, unhealed.

MOTHERS BECOMING

DORI WATCHED HER mother count pills from numerous vials situated in an old shoe box. Her bony fingers trembled as she placed each of the tablets in her wrinkled palm and then gingerly dropped them into one of the pill holder's five slots.

"These two are for my heart. So is this one. It's a baby aspirin. I have to take one every day after breakfast. This little blue one is for my diabetes. I have to take one after each meal. It's either these or the needle, and I'm not up for that. These yellow ones here are for my high blood pressure, and these two red ones are for my high cholesterol," her mother said.

Fumbling with the plastic pill holder, she nearly pushed it off the table in an effort to reach for another medicine vial. "This one is for pain. You know, the pain in my hip. I always forget them, though I don't know why since the hip pain should remind me, but it doesn't." Her mother sighed. "I'll tell you something, Dori, getting old isn't for the faint of heart."

Dori looked away, lowered her eyes, and noticed the grayness of her mother's once white kitchen floor tile. Fatigued from the cross-country, red-eye flight from Las Vegas to Baltimore, she sat with Betts, her mother, in the cramped kitchen, shaking off the irritability from the trip. "Nobody wants to get old, Mother," she finally said.

She hated aging and hated turning sixty. She hated looking in the mirror and wondering who stared back at her when she did. She hated the wrinkles and the laugh lines now lining her forehead and her eyes. She hated wishing she had the courage to undergo surgery to erase them. She hated dreaming about the failure of Ponce de Leon to find that damn fountain. She kept her hair dyed black to hide the gray and rode her stationary bike to keep the pounds off—albeit unsuccessfully. She didn't want to look like an old lady, act like one, or smell like one either.

When she was drinking, she hadn't cared much for how she looked. Win and Lindsey had suffered as children, and Dori spent a sober decade making up for the lost years—too late. Win had already paid the price for her drunkenness; he was killed during a stupid bungie jumping accident at the age of twenty-one. Had he been trying to get her attention? Trying to break through her drunken haze? When she became sober, she'd vowed to earn Lindsey's forgiveness, and she'd pardon her mother for abandoning her with the rest of her family in Nevada. Her mother, who had become an old lady and whose bare feet now barely touched the floor, dangled them childlike under the kitchen table.

Crumbs lay scattered on the sticky kitchen table and on the floor. Mail, papers, old bills— some stained with round tea mug imprints— current bills, letters from friends, greeting cards, and magazines covered every flat surface in the condo. They leaned in piles on the kitchen counters. On the dining room table. On the desk. She was a hoarder. Her mother owned a cat and transformed into a hoarder old woman, the kind often written about in the offbeat news sections of big dailies. A stack of newspapers climbed halfway up the wall in the corner opposite of the refrigerator, and another pile of magazines and mail-order catalogs butted into the newspapers. Two small ceramic bowls, one half full of dry cat food and one half full of water, sat near the magazine pile for Blue, her mother's black cat.

The teakettle shrieked, and her mother looked anxiously toward the stove.

"I'll get it, Mother. What kind of tea do you want?" Dori lowered the heat under the kettle; its whistle irritated her. She needed some sleep, if only for a few hours, especially now with every little thing annoying her. Uncomfortable with flying, she'd kept her trips to

Baltimore to a minimum, and now she wondered if she should have come more often, perhaps on a train.

Maybe she would've seen the gradual downward spiral and could have slowed its progress. Though as she looked around the condo, slowing down her mother's penchant for keeping things might have been a little like slowing down a runaway train.

"Green with just a little sweetener. Not sugar. That other stuff," Betts said, pushing papers and clutter to one side of the kitchen table. Two wrinkled white papers fluttered to the floor. "Don't make it too strong, or I won't be able to sleep."

"It's still morning," Dori said with a yawn. "Though sleep sounds good to me right now."

She picked up the papers from the floor and flicked them into the overflowing trash. Betts had never been the most organized person, but she usually kept things clean, if not tidy. At least it had appeared that way during the short visits Dori had made over the years. Betts had long demonstrated a method to her madness, but this mess offered no method.

She searched the kitchen cabinets for mugs or cups and found none. All of the glasses, a pile of dirty dishes, flatware, dirty pots and pans, and the caked remains of onion and carrot peelings filled the sink. "Mother, why don't you use the dishwasher?"

Her mother looked at her blankly.

"Why do you let these dishes pile up like this? You live alone, Mother. It's ridiculous."

She chafed. Her mother knew she was coming. Why hadn't she cleaned up just a little? Betts had never been the Susie Homemaker type; she was the woman who left her family to pursue college and beyond in an era when most women focused on landing the perfect husband or perfecting the juiciest pot roast. But Dori didn't expect this level of mess, not even from her mother-the-artist, an artist who thrived in chaos.

177

"Don't you ever clean up anymore? Not even the minimum?"

Betts shrugged and pursed her lips.

Reciting the serenity prayer to herself and allowing frustration to wash over her and float away, Dori opened the dishwasher and gasped. Neatly folded sweaters and sweatpants filled the machine. The overflow spilled out when she opened the door. She counted to ten. In the old days, she'd reach for a drink, but a childhood trick she'd learned from her grandmother coupled with the serenity prayer and other tricks she gleaned from Janine, her AA mentor, helped her cope. She wished she had stayed home.

"We're supposed to have a nice visit, and you're already badgering me. You haven't been here for half a day even. Don't be a bad daughter," Betts said.

She didn't respond. She chewed her lips instead. She unloaded the clothes from the dishwasher and loaded the dirty dishes into it, leaving out two mugs to hand wash. She filled the door cavity with the last of the dishwashing detergent and switched on the machine before searching the cabinets for green tea. She found jewelry, old coins, tidbits of faded paper notes, empty medicine vials, paint tubes, stained paint brushes, a booklet on how to crochet, and Velcro hair curlers cramped into the cabinet spaces in between spices, packages of soup, boxes of instant soup, gelatin, and a stack of tea boxes.

With tea bags seeping in their mugs, she emptied the sink of the vegetable peelings, and she wiped down the kitchen counters and the portion of the table minus the papers. She also wiped down the refrigerator and sprinkled powdered cleanser into the sink, scrubbing it until the brown rust stains and water marks disappeared from the porcelain.

"Agnes helps me every day," Betts said. "I don't know how things pile up so fast because she washes the dishes every day. I don't know what I'd do without her."

Dori hunted for a box of garbage bags.

* * *

A huge self-portrait in oils of Betts, at age eighteen, graced the wall over the faux fireplace in the living room, almost mocking the real white-haired Betts sitting in the chair beneath it. Dori looked at her mother and saw the ghost of herself reflected in her features. She decided to make a salon appointment for Betts during this visit, an idea that seemed especially appealing since her mother appeared neglected whereas Agnes, on her daily visit, looked like a fashion plate with her chunky gold earrings, eye makeup, bright red lipstick, and crisp white slacks. She was a woman who obviously understood the value of keeping up with appearances.

Dori sat on her hands to hide her own neglected fingernails.

"Your mom has told me all about you," Agnes said, flashing a white denture smile. Her voice sounded husky, damaged by cigarettes.

"All good stuff, I hope," she said.

"Funny how you both ended up being teachers," Agnes said. "That's an amazing—uh—I can't remember the word... Oh darn! It's on the tip of my tongue," Agnes said. She pinched her face in concentration.

"Feat?" Dori suggested.

"No. Oh Betts, what's the word for something that happens—like when two women show up in the same dress, and they don't know each other?"

Betts hesitated. "I don't remember either." Blue, her mother's old black cat, jumped on her lap and circled before curling up in a ball. She stroked the cat.

Still fatigued, Dori rubbed her eyes. She'd never been a teacher. Her mother knew she'd worked as an accountant—the antithesis to Betts' life as an artist—and had managed to keep her job only by a miracle. She had managed to show up for work hungover and keep columns balanced and numbers straight. Numbers were easy compared to achieving the impossible top-of-the-line art maven of her mother's dream. She hadn't wanted to achieve immortality as Betts had. "Coincidence?" she asked.

"That's it!" Agnes said. "A coincidence… What was I saying now? Oh yeah. It's a coincidence that you both became teachers."

"Dori taught math," Betts added. "She taught elementary school, and I taught college. My mother was a teacher too. The women in our family represent a long line of teachers."

Dori didn't know how to respond. Should she contradict her mother? Announce that she'd never stepped foot in any classroom, not even for Lindsey or Win, which was something that shamed her to this day? She gazed around the room, wondering if she ought to correct her mother but then decided that Agnes didn't really need to hear the truth.

Dust-covered whimsical pottery sculptures of clowns with brown patched hats and red conical ones, with black and white cats, with Little Boy Blue with a trumpet, with a little girl asleep in a flower bed, and with Dori herself as a child adorned the condo's end tables and bookshelves. All of which were objects her mother had made. She picked up the one of herself as a child and marveled at the accuracy, wondering if Betts had used a picture of her or if she had simply remembered what she'd looked like. Had these sculptures always been visible? Why did she notice them now with the apartment in such disarray?

"Even my grandmother was a teacher, but in those days, she had to quit when she got married," Betts added. "She taught in a one-room schoolhouse out west."

"How fabulous is that? A long line of teachers…" Agnes said. "It's fabulous. Simply fabulous." She smiled vacantly.

Her mother, beaming with pride, laughed, and for a moment, Dori saw her as she had looked as a younger woman. With golden hair cut as a thick bob, wire-framed glasses, large dimples forming parentheses around her heart-shaped lips, and washed-out sky blue eyes on an oval face, she'd have been considered a classic beauty. Dori recalled the endless stream of men accompanying Betts on her Vegas visits and decided her mother knew how to use her looks to manipulate men without putting much stock in the traditional trajectory of relationships: marriage, house, and kids. She had refused to remarry after divorcing Dori's father and described numerous subsequent boyfriends as "friends with benefits," a progressive idea for a woman now pushing eighty.

She had applauded Dori's own divorce, saying she didn't need a man to make her whole and dismissing the fact that the divorce had been an unwanted, painful thing, because John no longer loved her *that* way. He'd loved a man instead. She had never once asked how Dori felt about it or even why it happened. She assumed it was the best thing in the world and had pronounced "good riddance."

Dori could still feel the sting. She had expected to grow old with John, and despite such a mundane expectation of growing old with one's husband compared to Betts' revolving door of boyfriends, she and Betts—and Agnes even—had found themselves in the same place. They were alone after all. They had all just arrived by different routes.

"Do you have any children?" she asked Agnes.

"A son. He visits every day. He's fabulous," Agnes said. Her white dentures were slightly askew. She wondered if Agnes had forgotten other adjectives.

* * *

Dori noticed dust balls clinging off the corners of the curtains, covering every available flat surface not already taken up by catalogs. Stacks of clothing occupied the sofa, and edges of papers stuck out from under the cushions. Small paper cups filled with colorful tablets and capsules sat forgotten on the dining room table, under the lamps, and on the end tables. Only a small passage from the kitchen to the bathroom and to the bedroom existed. How on earth did her mother live like this?

"Mother, why don't you hire a cleaning lady once a week?"

"Why waste money on a cleaning lady when I can spend it on other things?"

"Like what?"

"Art supplies."

She shook her head and broke four eggs into a bowl. Adding milk, salt, and pepper, she whisked it with a fork and then searched for a clean frying pan. The once lush indoor jungle, evidence of her mother's knack with green things, had been reduced simply to dead plants. Their withered and brown leaves littered the floor by their pots; dried branches touched the floor and reached out like tired hands. Her mother used to be able to make anything grow. Now orange and grapefruit seeds were carelessly tossed onto soil. The ruin depressed her.

"You were always a spendthrift. Some things don't change," Betts said.

"Okay, Mother," Dori mumbled. How would her mother ever know that? She poured the egg concoction into the pan with some butter and scrambled it with a spatula. Omelets for a late lunch.

"Why aren't you having any tea?" Betts asked. They had retreated into the kitchen after Agnes left.

"I drank mine already. Don't you remember?"

"Stop teasing me, Dori. It's not nice."

"I finished my tea. You watched me put the mug in the sink." She held up the mug in the kitchen sink for her mother to see.

Betts looked confused, but the sound of the toaster popping distracted her. Dori wiped the table clean of the sticky crumbs and set two plates with omelets on them down. She buttered the bread and set two slices on each plate. Rummaging around in the flatware drawer, she found two forks and washed them before setting them on the table next to two small glasses of orange juice. "Let's eat," she said.

"Tell me about Win. What's new with him?" her mother asked.

Dori flinched. "Win's dead. Don't you remember, Mother?" Setting her fork down on the table, she clenched her hands into fists. Her fingernails dug into her palms, a far more acceptable pain than the loss of her only son. "But Lindsey's fine. You should see little Myles. He's a lot like you," she said.

"Dead?" Betts looked horrified. "My God. When?" She started to cry. "I wondered why you came all this way, and it's to tell me Winston's dead." Huge tears streamed down her mother's wrinkled cheeks.

"Mother, don't you remember coming to Vegas for the funeral?"

In a rare fit of maternal care, Betts had flown to Nevada for the funeral, had orchestrated the service, and had taken care of every minute detail, leaving Dori and Lindsey free to grieve. The wound of Win's death had barely scarred over and probably never would. Dori understood that she indirectly had been responsible for it by her drunkenness. She, like Betts, had abandoned her children even if she hadn't left them anywhere else.

She reminded her mother of the by then openly gay John showing up with his new friend, Andrew, of Win's friends who wept all over themselves, of the oak casket Betts chose herself that carried the remains of Dori's son to the graveyard, and of the achingly beautiful spring day they laid him to rest. Her mother had no recollection. None.

"This is too much for me. Poor Win," Betts said. She had eaten only one bite of the omelet.

"Here's a picture of Myles, Lindsey's child," Dori said, fishing one out of her wallet and wanting to change the subject to distract Betts. "Look. He's five now."

Her mother held the picture. Her trembling hand pulled it closer to her eyes. "He looks familiar," Betts said wistfully.

"That's Lindsey's little boy, your great grandchild, Mother," Dori raised her voice, almost as if shouting would help her mother understand better. She caught herself, lowering it to a normal range. Speaking loudly wouldn't induce her mother to remember. "He looks like you, don't you think? Same blue eyes. Same nose."

Setting Myles' picture on the table, Betts said nothing about the little boy. Slowly, she rose from the table, picked her way through the small pathway around the clutter to the large, brown recliner chair, sank into it, and rubbed her forehead. Could all those medicines have disoriented her? Dori made a mental note to bring them all to a nearby pharmacist to find out. She scraped Betts' uneaten omelet into the trash and put the dishes in the sink before gathering the stack of clothing from the kitchen chair and picking her way through the clutter toward the bedroom.

The bedroom contained its own version of a mini storage flea market. Old wooden chairs and small four-drawer bureaus surrounded the bed, covered with bags of fabrics, bags of draperies that needed dry cleaning, stacks of sheets and blankets, piles of clothes, and piles of shoes. No wonder her mother slept in the recliner chair. Covered with junk, the bed offered no place to sleep.

She examined the contents of a bag, fingering dry-rotted skeins of yarn—mustard, gray, pink, and black. She recognized the colors immediately. It was yarn left over from the animal hand puppets Betts had sent her for her tenth birthday: a lion with a golden mane, an elephant with a pink tongue, and a pink and black cow. She had first pinned the animals to the walls of her room, wishing instead that she had a mother who was around to sing "Happy Birthday" and cut the cake at a party with a piñata. Grandmother Winslow had done all that for her. Betts had sent the animal puppets but forgot to phone. Angry at Betts for not calling on her birthday, she had unpinned the puppets and threw them into the trash, kicking over the can after Grandmother Winslow had dug them out again.

"Dorothy Ann. Your mother made these puppets for your birthday," she'd said.

She pushed the dry-rotted yarn bag back into the junk pile on the bed where she spotted a large black lacquered box with cloisonné floral inlay. The unlocked box contained every letter she'd ever written to her mother and every drawing she'd ever made and sent. It had photos of Dori at every age and at every special occasion, including her wedding and even baby pictures of Win and Lindsey. She found receipts for payments to Grandmother Winslow to support her: the private school tuitions, piano lessons, roller skates, swimming lessons, prom dresses, and shoes. It had the cost of her life chronicled by money orders and canceled checks—regular as morning—and letters from Grandmother Winslow about her advances, scrapes, successes, and failures. Grandmother Winslow had never mentioned her mother's financial support.

She lost herself by skimming through the letters, letters between a mother and a daughter in which Betts called Grandmother Winslow, "Mommy," and letters from herself to Betts, including the period when she had been so angry at Betts. All the salutations had said, "To Mrs. Betts Stapler." She smiled, having forgotten her childish rage; warm memories of Grandmother Winslow and a younger Betts rushed to her. True, Betts had left her in Nevada, but she obviously had not forgotten her. She, in a drunken stupor, had remained in the same house with her own children, absent in another way and wrecked her own kind of carnage.

"Dori?" her mother called. "Dori, where are you?"

In the living room, Betts appeared troubled. Her lips formed a line across the bottom of her face, and behind her large owl-like spectacles, her steely washed-out blue eyes avoided Dori.

"The bed is covered with junk," Dori said, trying to sound neutral. "It's hard to move around in there."

"All because of that stupid flood," she said. Her face flushed red. "The pipes in the basement broke and ruined everything. I had to take everything out of the basement."

"It's okay, Mother. You just have a little too much stuff," Dori said, touching her mother's papery thin arm. Her mother's condo was on the first floor. There was no basement. She cleared the remainder of the sofa clutter and piled it onto the bed but kept the lacquered box out of the pile. At least she could sleep on the sofa now. "Maybe you need to be someplace where you're not alone. Why don't you move back to Vegas? Or consider assisted living here?" The words slipped out before she could stop them.

"I'm not alone. I have Blue," her mother said. She looked past Dori's shoulder. "I'm in my own home."

"You know what I mean. Someplace where people can help you bathe and keep your clothes and living room organized."

"Dori, don't. Don't. Don't start on that. Stop badgering me. I am perfectly capable of taking care of myself, and if I need some help, I have wonderful neighbors who help me in a pinch. Agnes looks in on me every day. I like my apartment and my friends." Betts blinked, focusing on the dark TV screen.

"What happens if Agnes can't drop in on you anymore?" she asked.

Betts sighed deeply. "I'm not moving anywhere."

"You might not have a choice."

"Says who?" Blue jumped onto Betts' lap. "Blue likes to watch TV," her mother said. "I got him a special video from one of my catalogs. It's a tape of birds flying to a window. Do you want to watch it with us?"

"No thanks, Mother. And changing the subject doesn't change the situation," she said.

Using the remote, Betts clicked on the TV, which all the stations featured snow. She finally found the VCR button and started the tape consisting of birds flying toward a window filmed from inside the window. Blue's ears pointed forward; he hissed at the TV.

"Kitty TV," her mother said. "I have to take care of Blue, you know. He's old. Nobody'll take an old cat. Old cat. Old people. Doesn't matter," she muttered. "Nobody wants 'em around anymore. I don't want to put him down out of convenience."

"Don't you get tired of Kitty TV?" Dori asked.

"Don't get any other stations," her mother said. "Cable stopped working."

"I'd better get the sofa vacuumed since it's my bed for the night," she said.

"I'd help, but my hip hurts," Betts said before nodding off in the chair. Her wrinkled hand rested on Blue's torso, stopped mid-stroke.

* * *

While Betts slept, Dori worked. She collected newspapers, magazines, and catalogs from the kitchen, and using a hand-pulled shopping cart stored in the living room closet, she hauled them to the condo's recycling bins. She filled three large garbage bags with the boxes of stale food from the cabinets and molded food from the refrigerator. Interspersed between the papers, she found legal papers, condo notices for late fees, months-old cable bill, and small plastic containers of forgotten pills, medicine not taken. Then fatigue slayed her. She covered the newly cleared sofa cushions with a clean sheet, slipped off her running shoes, and slept. Her eyes were closed for the first time since she had left Vegas.

"I'd like to take a bath now," Betts said, seemingly just as she had closed her eyes.

"Okay, Mother," she said half asleep.

"I'd like a bath now,"

"In a minute; I'm so tired, Mother. Just let me nap for about twenty more minutes."

Eyes closed, she could feel her staring—no, *glaring*—at her. "What's the matter?" she asked with her eyes still closed.

"I'd like to take a bath now."

"Wait twenty minutes, please," Dori said.

"I'd like a bath now." Betts said.

Helping Betts out of the chair, she noticed that a towel on the chair's seat reeked of urine. So did her mother's already dirty housedress. The accident disgusted her. She realized that the urine smell in the apartment had nothing to do with cat piss.

"Mother, you peed in the chair." She felt stupid announcing the obvious.

"Okay," her mother said, looking surprised, embarrassed, and almost childlike in her acceptance of Dori's announcement.

Leading Betts to the bathroom, Dori instructed her to undress and to throw all her clothes on the floor while she searched for clean clothes in the flea market of her mother's bedroom.

She stuffed the soiled clothes in an old plastic grocery bag with the intention of trashing it all.

Her mother's sagging nakedness, the atrophy of unexercised muscles, the thinness of her body, and the purple bruise on her mother's hip caught her off guard. She fumbled with the clothing and the plastic bag. Her mother blushed.

"We both have the same things," she said, trying to sound nonchalant. "Except I have more fat, the thing no one else wants more of."

"I don't know how things got out of hand," Betts apologized. "I sometimes don't feel the need to go until it's too late." She cried.

188

Dori had never seen her hard-edged mother cry, not even when Grandmother Winslow or Win died. "Shit happens," she said, scrubbing the filthy tub.

Worried that Betts would slip in a shower with no shower mat, she ran a warm bath and helped her step into the tub. She gave her mother soap and a clean face cloth. "I can wash your hair when you are done washing yourself."

"Okay," her mother agreed plaintively.

She saw that Betts needed help washing herself. "How about you soak for a while and relax?"

She poured ancient-looking bubble bath into the tub and turned the faucet on to churn some bubbles. While her mother soaked, she cleaned the soiled chair, tossed the urine-soaked towel into a trash bag, and sprayed disinfectant on the cushion. In the bathroom, she scrubbed her mother's head, building tall mounds of hair and soap into odd shapes and showing them to Betts in a hand mirror.

"Tokyo after Godzilla smashed it," Betts said about one of the soap mounds, and Dori, appreciating the humor, laughed out loud. Betts grinned.

* * *

Freshly bathed with her hair still wet, wearing clean clothes, and watching Kitty TV with Blue on the sofa, Betts talked about the basement flood again: how the broken basement pipes had ruined all her artwork, how she had to move her clothing, how she couldn't stop the flow of the water, and how the plumber had joked about needing a rowboat in the basement when he'd finally showed up. Too late to save Betts' things. She talked about the event as if it happened yesterday and flicked the remote control to other snowy stations before flicking it back to Blue's Kitty TV.

"Aren't you bored with that video?" Dori asked.

189

"Blue likes it. It's one of his only joys now."

She gave her mother some dinner—canned baked beans, which was the only thing left in the cabinets that wasn't spoiled. And while Betts ate, she attacked the clutter on the bed, throwing everything into the trash: the ancient bag of yarn; the dry-rotted thirty-year-old dresses, blouses, skirts, slacks, and fabrics with golf ball-sized moth holes; a glue gun; and small vials of paints. She kept the crochet blankets, the crochet, the knitting needles, and the buttons but tossed reams of water-damaged construction paper and leftover materials from art projects long gone.

Betts hobbled into the bedroom, hovering over Dori. She went through all the trash bags, retrieving items. "Not this. I want to keep this and this and this. This too," she said, snatching objects out of the trash bag. "These are still good," she said, clutching them to her chest. "There are still art projects waiting for these materials."

"We can get new stuff from the craft store. I found bugs in this stuff," Dori lied. She removed the retrieved trash from Betts' hands and returned them to the trash bags. "I'm sure you'll want some new materials for your art projects too," she continued.

"Oh yes. I'd love to go to a craft store. I'd love to go to the supermarket even. I haven't been able to get out or to drive the car since I hurt my hip," Betts said, and new worries sprang up in Dori's head: the car. Goodness. Her mother probably still had the old gray Impala parked in the lot outside.

* * *

Betts grew more confused as the sun set and then transformed into a raving lunatic after dark. She accused Dori of being a bad daughter, of wanting to lock her in a nursing home, and of being a saleswoman. She ordered her to leave since she didn't want any stinking saleswoman or her wares in her house. "Get out! Get out!" she yelled.

Trembling, Dori felt lost, angry, and sad. Resentfulness and fatigue rose up like bile, but she beat it down.

"I'm calling nine one one," her mother threatened. "I'm telling them that a strange saleswoman is robbing me in my home!" she yelled. "Taking all my stuff away in black garbage bags!"

Later, finally subdued, Betts slept on the sofa. With the bed still covered in clutter and no other place to lie down, Dori arranged blankets and a pillow in the tub. Uncomfortable but exhausted, she slept.

* * *

"Why are you sleeping in the tub?" Betts asked, looking innocent of the upheaval she'd created the previous night. Dori looked at her mother peering down at her. "If that's not the darnedest thing I ever saw."

"You can go back in your bed tonight," Dori said.

"I'm not stupid, you know. Why didn't you wake me and ask me to move?"

The question seemed sincere enough. She wondered if her mother had recalled anything from the previous night. Or realized there was no place else to move. She stepped out of the tub with her joints aching. Her body punished her every move for foisting such an unsuitable sleeping place on it.

The desire to escape enveloped her. She could book herself on a red-eye flight back to Vegas, pick up her bag, scoot out the door, step into a cab, and escape a problem that wasn't hers. Except by default, it was. With Win gone and Lindsey occupied by her own family and job—rightly so—she and her mother had no one else but each other. They were two women bound by blood, by old scars and fresh wounds, by funerals and births, and by mutual love for the now late Grandmother Winslow who once said, "Your mother's my baby too,

191

and don't you ever forget it," when Dori, as a teenager, had raged against Betts after one of her in and out again visits. "She is what she is. That's what love really is, you know, accepting people for who they are and for who they aren't."

After breakfast—tea and crackers—she bathed Betts again and helped her into a fresh dress. She moved six giant garbage bags out of the apartment and into the trash bin. She called the doctors named on the medicine vials and apprised them of the situation. "Sundowners," one said. "Dementia that unfolds only at night. It'll get worse over time until she has more moments of dementia and less of lucidity. She shouldn't be living on her own."

She didn't need doctors to tell her that.

"Let's go!" Betts said brightly. They took Betts' car, which was still working because Agnes' son had regularly started it over the past few months and ran the engine when he visited Agnes.

At the supermarket, Dori's body still ached from sleeping in the tub, and Betts, eyes bright, laughed gaily and chatted about how great it was to be out and about again. Dori wondered how long it had been since her mother had gone outside. Betts talked about making a cherry pie and listed the ingredients she'd need. As a child, Dori dreamed of such mother-daughter moments, the ones that most people took for granted—simple things like grocery shopping or running errands together. Together, they filled the shopping cart.

"We have to hurry home," Betts said, dropping a can of pineapples into the cart. "There's a leak in one of the basement pipes. Water will ruin everything if we don't get home in time."

Knowing there was no basement, no broken pipes, no flooding water, no number of things to be ruined, and no reason to hurry home, Dori pushed the cart. "We're nearly finished," she assured her mother. "We'll be home before the water ruins everything. Let's talk about that famous cherry pie."

She led Betts slowly down the supermarket aisle, an aisle that looked remarkably like any aisle anywhere: in Vegas or in Cincinnati or in Los Angeles or in Baltimore. It was an aisle so similar to the ones where she lived, where Lindsey and her family lived, where Grandmother Winslow and Win were buried, where her family can visit, and where Betts wouldn't be able to distinguish between the two.

UNCHARTED STEPS

T-BONE BECAME CERTAIN he'd made a mistake by bringing Juice and pussyboy Lewis to his Aunt Clara's place as soon as he—using Ma's keys—opened the door and saw his eleven-year-old cousin looking startled and scared in his Catholic school navy-blue uniform pants and blue polo shirt. He knew they should bounce, should find another place to chill with their hostage, pussyboy Lewis, but Juice pushed his way past him, looked around, and deemed the place perfect. He and Juice had planned to hang there with pussyboy Lewis for a few hours, unseen and unnoticed, and leave before the family returned— no one the wiser. Except now Onion, whose real name, Patrick Fisher, was spelled out in blue block letters on his plastic school name pin, beamed at him.

"Guy! Aunt Jilly told you I got out early?" Onion asked.

T-Bone had nodded vaguely. "Came to keep you company for a few hours," he lied. Ma didn't know his whereabouts or that he was with Juice, who she'd disliked and said looked creepy. Nor did she know that he'd brought Juice to his aunt's apartment. The four boys crowded the small, shabby living room. Pussyboy Lewis sat on the threadbare, gold wall-to-wall carpeting because T-Bone occupied most of the sofa, and Juice was in the one chair. Gold dime store drapes with thin threads and loose seams drooped from bent curtain rods that covered two dirty, undersized, painted-shut windows. They allowed neither air nor light into the second-floor apartment. A hole in the dining room ceiling gaped like a toothless yawn over a dining room table cluttered with unopened mail, magazines, and papers.

T-Bone inhaled stale air. His breathing labored like any fat boy's. Eying the others and uneasy at finding Onion home, he channel surfed, ignoring the television's kaleidoscope images, and watched Juice instead. Onion fidgeted on the sofa's overstuffed armrest; his army-green eyes fixed on him.

"Daddy got me Dance Dance Revolution for my birthday, Guy. It's fun. Wanna play?" He bounced off the sofa onto the balls of his feet.

"Not now," T-Bone said with a wince. Juice didn't know his real name was "Guy," a much worse name than "Lewis," and he didn't want Juice knowing his suck ass, uncool real name. Juice had told him that the only person to call him Rodger was his probation officer; he rose higher in T-Bone estimation for having a P.O. T-Bone didn't know anyone else with a P.O.

Pussyboy Lewis sat cross-legged on the floor next to a pot of plastic ivy near the TV, just in front of the cherry wood shelves Uncle Bill had built in the niche there. The football player took care not to lean against the shelves and grimaced when his sleeve brushed against the dusty plastic plant. He gawked at his aunt's place as if he'd been transported to Mars.

"What are you looking at?" T-Bone demanded.

"Nothing much," Lewis said.

T-Bone ignored the slight and checked his watch. Every minute he spent with Lewis felt like an hour, and so far, twenty minutes felt like forever.

Juice, with his fluffy, curly shock of red hair and cornflower blue eyes, slouched in Aunt Clara's brown chair, watching pussyboy Lewis with catlike alertness that made T-Bone feel invisible. He enjoyed being around Juice, being part of his posse, being around all the girls who wanted Juice to be their main man, and being the one they'd called when Juice was dissing them, but he didn't like feeling invisible, not in his own aunt's apartment. After this whole kidnapping business ended, T-Bone and Juice would never see Lewis again anyway.

Although they hadn't yet decided what to do with the money pussyboy Lewis' parents would pay to get him back, T-Bone imagined a fifty-fifty equal split. He imagined him and Ma—and even Aunt Clara, Uncle Bill, and Onion—sitting on a fancy beach, maybe down by the ocean. He imagined Ma relaxing. He pictured her happy, surprised face when he'd hand her a wad of vacation money. She always talked about how different things would have been for them had Guy Sr. not run off with that whore of a bimbo when he was a baby. They wouldn't have to be robbing Peter to pay Paul.

Onion bounced from the floor to the sofa and back to the floor.

"Settle down," T-Bone said. "You're a fucking live wire."

Juice laid the gun he'd hidden in his waistband on the rickety coffee table.

At the site of the gun, Onion squirmed more. T-Bone could tell the boy itched to touch it. Onion adjusted his thick, wire-framed glasses, which had slid down his nose, and gaped at it. His eyes the size of tangerines. He pointed to the weapon. "Where'd you get it? Can I hold it?"

"It ain't real," T-Bone lied to his cousin again but looked directly into pussyboy Lewis' eyes. "And no, you can't hold it, so don't ask no more."

"Guy, where'd it come from?" he repeated.

T-Bone didn't know. Juice always packed some heat, and he wished Onion would stop using his real name, the same one his bastard runaway father went by. He preferred his new nickname Juice had laid on him a few months back when they first met at the Square. "T-Bone" sounded cooler, a welcoming change too since the skateboarders there had always laughed at him, singing, "Fat Guy in a little T-shirt." They called him "Tiny," snickering at him because of his size. They called him "Pizza Guy" because of his acne. Little punks.

"Where'd it come from?" Onion persisted. "Did you buy it? How much did it cost?"

"Mind your business, Onion," T-Bone said, looking first at Juice and then at Onion.

"You don't need to get all bent."

Lewis eyed the gun too and then eyed Juice, but he didn't say anything.

"Hey, let's do DDR now," Onion said. No one responded. "Ma said it's good exercise," he added. "It's fun." Every now and again, he glanced down at the gun and then at T-Bone with questions in his eyes, questions T-Bone plain ignored. He wished Onion was still at school, out of the way.

Twenty minutes ago, corralling Lewis into Juice's vintage Mustang was easier after Juice had flashed the heat—a pearly gripped revolver—and stuck the barrel into the football player's side. He'd stopped struggling immediately. T-Bone marveled at how light reflected off the revolver's steel parts, making it look like a shiny jewel on the coffee table.

Onion bounded around the apartment like a caged monkey, stealing glances at the shiny wonder. "Is it loaded?" he finally asked.

"No," T-Boned lied again. He also wanted to touch it too, wanted to shoot it. He chewed on the inside of his mouth. "Don't be stupid," he added. Juice shot him an appraising glance, and he felt good about it, though he wished they could leave the apartment and go elsewhere. The plan—Juice's Plan really—didn't factor Onion being home; Aunt Clara's place was supposed to be empty. The hideout was T-Bone's own suggestion.

The plan had formed when they were smoking weed at the Square. He and Juice jokingly hatched half a dozen fast money schemes—snatching a rich kid was one of them. He never thought any of them could become real, not caring either. He just liked Juice, who treated him with respect, who had his back, and who did things like build his yellow Mustang from an old junker. The skateboarders stopped messing with him once he began hanging out with Juice. He had acted nonchalant the day Juice had outlined the plan and asked him to think of some down low place until they could conduct the switch: the snatched kid for the booty.

"Best neither of us know all the details," Juice had said, dismissing his questions.

Not wanting to disappoint, he could only think of his Aunt Clara's place. He hadn't considered Onion being home.

"How about some snacks?" he asked Onion. "Got anything good here?"

"Chips and dip," Onion said, disappearing into the kitchen.

"What about some drinks?" he called after his cousin. "Go help him with the drinks," he ordered Lewis. Lewis followed Onion into the kitchen, and they emerged carrying bags of chips, tubs of dip, and two liters of cola.

Juice snickered. "Where's your cell, pussyboy?"

"Don't have one," the football player said. He sat again, shifting his legs so they looked like Vs, hiding the outline of a cell in his sweatpants pocket if he had one.

"Everybody has a cell," Juice said, sounding matter-of-fact.

Lewis shrugged. The football player's easy confidence annoyed T-Bone, mostly because it reminded him of his father's two new sons with similar pussy names. The runts were ten and eight. Who the fuck names a kid Guy, Xavier, or Isidore? "Zave" and Iz played football and soccer at Blakefield High's sports fields. When they get to high school, they'd be just like Lewis, driving their own cars and navigating around as if they owned the world. T-Bone quit school, hung out with Juice, and earned his own coin signaling when competition or cops came. He worked his way into Juice's crew. He'd be finishing up his senior year if he'd stayed and wasn't failing. Ma didn't know yet. He'd been snagging school letters from the mail.

He tore open a bag of chips and stuffed a handful into his mouth. No one else ate any, including Juice, who never turned down food and often saved it for his brother Jimmy.

If he had gone to Blakefield High instead of to Highland Public, maybe those Blakefield kids wouldn't harass him about his size or his pimples, and he would've gotten better grades. He'd be graduating in a few weeks. He'd asked Ma about it when she was ranting about Zave and Iz, but she'd dismissed the idea, saying she wasn't about to ask his father for a shittin' thing. Instead, she worked endless odd jobs for little pay, singing at night in a Podunk rock and roll band she felt certain would hit the big time. He finished the chips and rubbed his greasy fingers on his pants.

"You're both fucking nuts, man. This is so fucking stupid," Lewis said. "Man, I thought my buddies put you two jokers up to pranking me. An end of year joke or something. Talk about a fucking bad call." He rubbed his forehead and eyes.

"It sucks to be you," Juice said.

"Guy, what are y'all talking about?" Onion asked.

"Nothing. Nothing at all," T-Bone said. "Lewis here is referring to a misunderstanding between him and some of his Blakefield buddies."

Blakefield High sat at the top of a grassy hill near his father's house. He knew his way around the neighborhood better than Juice from the few times his asshole father had invited him there for weekend visits. The other Guy Cantor had ferried Zave and Iz and a car full of sports equipment to and from soccer and lacrosse practice held on Blakefield High fields. His father called T-Bone, the extra wheel, "Sport" the whole time as in "Hey, Sport! We gotta run some errands." He had waited, but his father never asked if he wanted to play soccer or lacrosse. Not that he would've said yes, but the offer would've meant something. His father also never asked about his mother as if he had been inexplicably dropped into their laps by accident like a turd dropped haphazardly by a giant pterodactyl.

Earlier that day, when they had driven the Mustang past his father's house on their way up the hill toward the high school, T-Bone peered out the window to see if anyone were home, to catch a glimpse of his father, his brothers, or his stepmother, but there was nothing. He pictured their big, sunny yellow kitchen with the white-tiled table where they ate like a TV family. He remembered the basketball hoop in the backyard and the giant, rectangular trampoline. The garage was filled with equipment and bikes. In Zave's room, Spider-Man ruled the curtains, the bedspread, the rug, and trash can. Superman lived in Iz's room.

He didn't point his father's house out to Juice, who probably wouldn't believe him anyway. Juice and his little bro Jimmy didn't have any father they could talk about, and T-Bone didn't want brag about having an asshole one.

"What's wrong? You got quiet all of a sudden. You gonna chicken out on me or something?" Juice had asked, facing him and leaning onto the steering wheel.

"Nah, I'm in," he had assured him, not believing they'd succeed, but he allowed himself to imagine Ma resting on a powdery white beach, being happy and not complaining about stuff they needed and couldn't buy for once. He and Juice were about to hit a giant payday thanks to Lewis.

"This is such bullshit," Lewis said. Moving toward the door, he pulled a cell phone from his sweatpants pocket.

"Thought you didn't have a cell," Juice said, spitting a curse word, which prompted Onion to giggle. With his face tense and red enough to match his hair, he rose to his feet and faced the football player, who ignored him. "Where the fuck you think you're going?" he demanded. His wiry arms were held slightly apart from his body; his feet were spread wide as if he were ready to spring.

"Away from here and you two clowns," Lewis said.

He nodded at the gun. "It'll end bad," he added.

"Yeah, right," Lewis said without stopping. He punched his phone's buttons, saying, "Shit" into the mouthpiece, which caused Onion to dissolve into uproarious laughter.

"They're saying bad words," he said in between guffaws.

When Lewis grabbed the doorknob, Juice sprang, tackling the football player, who hit the floor sideways with Juice on top of him. They wrestled. Lewis gained the advantage, trying to put Juice into a half nelson. T-Bone heaved himself off the sofa. Onion swallowed his laughter and trembled. The two struggled. The cell phone was opened on the floor nearby, and Juice lunging for it.

"Stop! Stop!" Onion shouted. "T-Bone, make them stop. We'll get into big trouble if they mess up the place. Make them stop!" He shuffled from foot to foot.

"Yo!" T-Bone bellowed.

Juice and Lewis' faces were flushed. Lewis' jaw was clenched. His hand pulled a fistful of red curls; Juice's nails dug into his wrist before he elbowed the footballer in the ribs. They thrashed, knocking over a table. The lamp on it crashed down; its lightbulb shattered. T-Bone hesitated and thought about tossing water at them as if they were dogs, but he didn't want to soak Juice, risk his anger, or make a mess. Or leave telltale stains on his aunt's floor.

"T-Bone, make them stop!" Onion shouted, frantic.

Unsure of how, T-Bone moved slowly toward the fight. He picked up the pearl handled gun, aimed, and shot Uncle Bill's built-in wood shelves. Onion jumped at the sound of the blast. The sound, not as loud as on TV but louder than T-Bone thought, stopped the fight. The others looking stunned, staring at him holding the gun. He trained it on Lewis.

"This ain't a game; we ain't playing," he said. "Get back over there by the plant."

Juice nodded slightly with an imperceptible smile on his face, an appraising glance. He reached for pussyboy Lewis' phone, pocketed it, and motioned for T-Bone to hand him the weapon. He slid it into his waistband as Lewis took his place on the floor next to the plant. Thrilled he'd made the right call and that he got to handle Juice's heat, T-Bone resettled himself on the sofa.

Onion ran toward the shelf like an old lady. "Guy! You shot Daddy's homemade shelf! You said that gun wasn't real. You and your friends ruined Daddy's shelf and broke the lamp. You gotta leave. Or just your friends got to go, but all of yous can't stay here. What am I going to tell Ma about the shelf? You know it's going to be the first thing she notices!"

"I'll pay to get it fixed," T-Bone said, thinking about the ransom coming to them. He thrusted his chest, basking in the powerful feeling that came from shooting the gun.

"Where you gonna get the money? You don't have a job!" Onion's voice cracked.

"Dig the bullet out," Juice said.

T-Bone heaved himself off the sofa and examined the hole. The bullet bored deep inside the wood; the impact buckled the joint. "Man, must be solid wood. It ain't coming out in this lifetime," T-Bone said. "Maybe your Daddy won't notice right away, and it'll be fixed in no time."

"Anybody can see it's ruined! You just got me in trouble." Shaky with his green eyes big as apples, Onion lifted the overturned lamp and examined the dented table before returning them to their original places. Pieces of the shattered lightbulb lay almost embedded in the carpet.

"Did you say you got DDR? Turn it on," Juice said.

"You got to go," Onion said, returning from the kitchen with a broom and shovel. "You can come back when Ma is here."

Juice rubbed the top of his forehead where Lewis had pulled his hair. "We got to make a phone call first though," he said, pulling Lewis' cell from his pocket. "Give me the digits," he said to Lewis.

"I prefer not to," Lewis said, deciding to Bartleby him.

Juice laughed incredulously. As he scrolled through Lewis' phone's directory, he listed all the things he'd preferred not to do. He'd preferred not going to jail for a burglary because it was a necessary job. He and Jimmy needed to eat when their mother was cracked up, drunk, or busy with one of her johns. He'd preferred not to be locked outside day and night, summer or winter, with Jimmy when their mother was working. He'd preferred not to hear her stories about spitting a john's jism out the side of her mouth in a way to conceal what she'd done and charging extra for swallowing it. Mostly, he'd preferred not to have gas and phone bills in his name that he couldn't pay, thanks to his mother who hadn't paid them either. "I could continue, but there's nothing nobody can do about it," he said. His incredulous smile made his face look like a mask.

He pointed his thumb backward at Lewis. "What a laugh riot!" he said. "What the fuck makes you think you got a choice here? It is what it is, so spill the numbers to talk to your daddio—or whoever controls the purse strings at your house."

Lewis remained silent. Neither spoke. Onion fidgeted. T-Bone watched, astonished at Lewis' refusal to cooperate. He was either brave or stupid; T-Bone couldn't figure out which. Maybe neither. Maybe the football star was just stubborn or proud.

"So let's see if the parents who gave you that pussy name will hand over some dough to get you back," Juice said, breaking the silence

"They aren't home," Lewis said. "They're at work."

"How much you think, T? What do you consider substantial?" Juice asked T-Bone, who straightened his posture, pushed hair away from his face, lifted his shoulders, and raised his head.

Shooting the shelf had been an excellent idea. Juice now respected him more, asking for his opinion. He shrugged, careful to sound nonchalant. "What do they do?" he asked Lewis.

"Mom's a nurse. I don't know what my dad does. Some kind of analyst. Works in an office," Lewis said.

"Maybe twenty to thirty thou? Thirty-five sound good?" T-Bone, careful not to show too much interest, asked Juice. He calculated a cool seventeen thousand dollars coming his way.

"You asking or telling?" Juice said, squinting his steely blue eyes.

"My parents don't have that kind of money," Lewis said. He wiped both of his palms on his sweatpants.

"T-Bone, you got to go," Onion said in a fast, bright monotone.

"Relax, Onion," T-Bone said. "I got you. I got you covered."

Onion ran his forefinger over the bullet hole, rubbing the buckled joint as if massaging a broken elbow. He looked worried about the injury to the wood. "I thought we were buds," he said in a stage whisper.

T-Bone looked away, lowering his eyes and focusing on his wide knees. Lewis grunted, rolling his eyes. T-Bone regretted dragging Juice and Lewis to his aunt's place. Onion acted like such a baby.

Lewis pointed to Juice with his chin. "That's his bud," he said. "Nobody else."

"We'll bounce soon," Juice said. "So, T, thirty-five Gs. Sounds right to me."

"My parents are broke," he said. "You got the wrong guy."

"I bet pussyboy Lewis here ain't never went to bed without eating the whole day or never slept on a mattress with no sheets. Them shoes alone probably cost a few Benjamins. That school ain't for poor boys."

"Whatever you say, man," Lewis said. "But I'm telling you, my parents don't have that kind of money. I have to play sports to get into a good college. Otherwise, I can't go. Ditto for my sister. She plays lacrosse in the hope of a scholarship because they can't afford college for us."

"An even thirty-five thousand dollars," T-Bone said, thinking of seventeen thousand five hundred dollars with his name on it.

Ma had never mentioned the word "college" to him. Or "good college." She had said, "job," as in "get your lazy ass a job."

Juice raised the gun. "Spill the digits," he said.

"T-Bone! Whattaya all doing? What's he doing?" Onion shouted.

"Shut up," Juice snapped.

Onion contracted, pulling himself away from his spot near the table and lamp. T-Bone ordered him to go sit in his parents' bedroom for a few minutes, but the kid stayed rooted to the same spot, and T-Bone wanted to smack him.

Even with the gun pointed at him, Lewis refused to tell the digits, remaining immobile on the floor by the planter. He smirked. "So after you shoot me, how're you going to explain that a stranger was shot dead in your aunt's apartment? And how do you think your aunt's going to explain that to the cops? She sounds like the kind of person who'll go straight to the cops. And how do you expect to collect ransom on a dead person?" he laughed, a snarky sound, as if he anticipated that the events these clowns had initiated would end badly for them and never for him.

T-Bone considered pussyboy Lewis' points valid, but Juice held the gun steady, and Onion whimpered.

"Nobody's home. It's pointless," Lewis said. "Mom gets home seven-thirtyish, and Dad gets home after midnight."

"We have time to kill then," Juice said. "Turn on DDR, Onion."

Onion looked at T-Bone. His eyes pleaded.

"We got less than an hour," T-Bone said. The lie slipped out of his mouth easily, though he'd never lied to Juice before.

"We'll bounce on time," Juice said. "We'll even take you with us, Onion."

"I can't leave without permission," Onion said.

Juice snickered. "Baby Onion. You two years old? Your Mama knowing where you are every minute? Ha. We got ourselves a pair here, Baby Onion and pussyboy Lewis."

"I'm not a baby," Onion said, crossing his arms.

"Leave the kid alone," T-Bone said, hoping his voice sounded important.

Onion laid the soft plastic dance pad on the floor. Its neon-blue arrows pointed north, south, east, and west. He attached the wires from the pad into the game console. A green screen flashed on the TV screen, and words in red block letters said, "Hottest Party Mix," "Ready," and "Here We Go." "Who's first?" he asked. "It's set for three songs for one game."

"You," Juice said. "Then Lewis here." Lewis glared at Juice.

Wearing just socks, Onion positioned his feet on the pad, using the control stick to set the level to standard before hitting play. The dance gauge representing the player's life bar appeared, and the music began. It was a techno rock version of "Everybody Dance Now." He missed a few steps, and the word "Miss" appeared in red on the TV screen, but his score quickly rose. Red numbers sped upward like those on a gas station tank. His feet moved fast, always returning to the center. A computerized male voice said, "Keep on going!" and "Well done!" which made T-Bone laugh. He finished three songs with a healthy dance gauge.

"Just try it, Guy. You might like it. It's fun," he said, breathless, handing T-Bone the controls.

"Lewis's up," T-Bone said.

"Come on, T," Juice said. "It's just a game. You're good at videos."

"This is going to be rich," Lewis mumbled.

T-Bone had heard the derision, that same tone toward his size, hundreds if not thousands of times before. "It's Lewis's turn," he said.

"Pass," Lewis said, holding both hands up. His palms faced toward Juice and T-Bone.

"You don't get to pass," T-Bone said. "Your turn."

"Ready" and "Here We Go" appeared on the screen in red. A techno tune began, the dance gauge at the top of the screen flashed green, and Lewis moved his feet. At first, a wooden Pinocchio with the red "Miss" popped up at each missed step. As the game continued, he began to follow the patterns better, and soon the computerized voice called mechanical encouragements. The score scrolled up faster as the music sped up, and he scored a string of blinking orange, happy-looking words. "Perfect!"

To T-Bone, they looked more like angry scars. Of course, Lewis would be good at it. Of course. He played football and got all the girls. Of course, he'd be good at any fucking thing he tried. "Change the level," he said.

Lean and muscular, slim-wasted like a movie star, and graceful as a ballerina, Lewis danced nonstop with a strange joy, and for a second, T-Bone wished he could be as free as Lewis, as Zave and Iz, and not nameless "Sport."

He had asked his mother why his father didn't see him more and didn't treat him like the others. "He's an asshole, Guy. We don't need him. We don't want anything from him neither, so forget him. I'm all we need," she'd said, flashing a fierce look as if him wanting to be with his father who had betrayed her. He had never considered that she'd betrayed him instead, punishing the man who'd fucked her and her son over at the same time. He had always wanted them both like Onion and Lewis, who both accrued points so easily because of feeling confident. A hole inside him widened.

Lewis' turn ended again, but T-Bone told Onion to set it at the highest level. He wanted to see perfect Lewis trip, maybe for the first time in his life. Lewis danced "Perfect!" combos again with few missed steps, calm as a clam. He clenched his jaws, seeing his cousin obviously taken with the flawless Lewis.

Refusing to be bested, T-Bone removed his shoes and positioned his feet on the dance pad. Onion reset the game to the easy phase, forgetting to turn off the nonstop mode before hitting play. T-Bone danced, and the word "Miss" popped up on the screen like a hoard of red ants. His belly jiggled, and his face reddened. His dance gauge bar fell to nonexistent. A tiny sliver of green kept his character barely alive; it rose slowly and steadily on the second song though. He willed himself to move faster and began scoring some of the orange letter "Perfect!" combos like Lewis, prompting the mechanical encouragements despite his low score. But he stumbled, fell, and rolled like a barrel off the pad. His dance gauge bar reduced to nothing—zero life left in the bar. He barely missed the rickety TV stand but crashed into the cocktail table. Flimsy or not, the table's edge hurt his side and back. All of them laughed. Juice, Onion, and pussyboy Lewis. Humiliated, his face flushed, and he blinked back moisture forming in his eyes.

"Not bad for a first timer," Onion said, glancing at the console's digital clock.

Red faced and dripping sweat, T-Bone sat on the sofa, struggling against his belly to retie his sneakers. He was careful not to show that his sides and back hurt. He decided to play it with Onion again later.

He watched Juice's skinny legs flying. The red "Perfect Combos!" words were constant on the screen; the score was rising. He saw in Juice's eyes that winning meant everything.

When Lewis cracked the front door open, the door whined. Seeing his potential thirty-five thousand about to vanish, Juice leapt off the dance pad toward the door like a gazelle. Lewis dashed out, went down the steps, and jumped over the front stoop. His practiced football feet carried him away.

T-Bone lumbered out the door, impossibly slow compared to the others. Onion locked the door behind him. Juice tossed the Mustang's keys at him before disappearing outside.

Astonished that Juice trusted him with his car, T-Bone pressed the gas pedal, wondering how they were going to force Lewis back inside. He caught up with Juice and slowed the car so he could hop in on the passenger side. "You seen where he went?" he asked.

Juice sucked in his breath. "Turn right at the next light. He won't expect us to come from that side."

T-Bone followed directions, and they saw Lewis running toward them. Juice pounded the dashboard. "Let me out," he said, bailing before T-Bone came to a full stop.

Spotting the neon yellow car, Lewis turned, retracing his steps. T-Bone couldn't believe it. Incensed, he sped up and banked into the alleyway just before Lewis reached it. He scrambled out just as Lewis ran around the back of the vehicle.

"Damn," T-Bone said. He lunged for the footballer and missed the boy, but Juice sprinted from behind, wrapped his arms around the athlete, and shoved him into the car through the passenger side door. T-Bone shut it once Juice and Lewis were both in the backseat. Juice punched Lewis. The footballer used wrestling moves against him, but Juice fought dirty, thumping the footballer in a fury with balled fists.

"Fucking try that again, and you're history," Juice said, out of breath.

T-Bone hadn't seen this side of Juice. Lewis writhed in the backseat. Juice slid behind the wheel, beckoned T-Bone into the passenger seat, and pointed the car toward Aunt Clara's. He double parked in front of the apartment's entrance and hit the flashers.

"*No!*" T-Bone yelled. "You said nobody gets hurt. That was the plan."

"He knows too much," Juice said, stone-faced.

"He doesn't know nothing. All he knows is that I brought two jerky friends there."

"It's a problem we deal with now or later," he said. He disappeared into the building and returned with a whimpering Onion. T-Bone's heart pounded, but Juice smiled a fake smile.

He pushed Onion into the backseat and retrieved Lewis's cell from his pocket. "The number," he said.

Lewis grunted. T-Bone trembled, feeling sick when the red-haired boy put the car in gear and drove away from Aunt Clara's apartment.

"Come on, Lewis. Tell him," T-Bone whispered, afraid for the first time since the plan was set in motion.

"ICE," Lewis said. His voice was hoarse.

Sitting next to Lewis, Onion whimpered. He stared at Lewis' bruised, puffy face and reached for his hand.

Juice found ICE and hit the button.

A man answered. "Lewis? Where the heck are you?"

"This ain't Lewis, but we got Lewis," Juice said into the phone with a tone that T-Bone hadn't heard before. "If you want to see Lewis alive again, we need thirty-five thousand dollars in a brown bag taped underneath the first bleacher row closest to the parking lot at Blakefield. Got it? This ain't a game. Call the cops, and Lewis here bites it." He listened and then handed the phone to T-Bone. "He wants to talk to pussyboy there."

T-Bone twisted his oversize body and held the phone to the footballer's ear. "Dad," Lewis said. His tone was calm, but his voice was hoarse. "Dad, I love you. Tell Mom I love her. Ellie too. Take care of Spazz and Mr. Boots for me, okay?"

When T-Bone removed the cell from Lewis' ear, he heard the man's voice crack. "Lewis, did they hurt you? Lewis, I love you too. Hang in there, son. Oh, Jesus Christ. We'll do what we have to. Don't worry. We'll do what we have to get you out of there."

Juice demanded the ransom by eight p.m. He sounded practiced as if he'd said those words a hundred times before and drove in a direction that T-Bone didn't know.

He couldn't remember ever saying, "I love you" to his mother or to his asshole father. Worse, he couldn't remember either of them saying it to him. He wanted to hear his father say, "I love you" with a cracked voice and not just "Sport" as if he'd forgotten they'd shared a name.

Juice pulled into a gas station. "You're on watch," he said, sliding out of the car.

"You going to let that dickhead treat you like a flunky?" Lewis asked. His voice was strained. "He didn't even ask if you agreed with his idea of taping the money to the bleacher. He didn't tell you what he's up to. I bet he's calling his real partner, and it ain't you. He's going to do us all and keep the cash to himself," he said. He pointed at Onion, who was still whimpering. "That what you want?"

T-Bone's heart beat faster. Sweat dotted his forehead. "Shut up. Shut up! Juice ain't like that!"

"Thirty Gs changes people. Let us go, and I'll tell the cops you helped us. You know they'll be cops. There are always cops."

"Shut up. Just shut up," he said. Something inside T-Bone felt unhinged.

Juice climbed back into the Mustang. "They can ID us," Juice said, locking eyes with T-Bone. "You hear?"

"I won't rat you out," Lewis said.

Onion sniffed. "Guy?" he said in a plaintive voice.

"We never talked about hurting nobody," T-Bone said.

"It was part of the plan you didn't need to know about 'til it became necessary. Now you know," Juice said matter-of-factly.

"I ain't doing that," T-Bone said. He felt his heart pound.

"It's them or us," Juice said. "Don't get much clearer than that."

T-Bone shook his head no.

No one talked. They killed time, circling the Baltimore beltway for hours. They stopped at a drive-through for burgers and fries that only Juice ate. Two hours after the appointed time, Juice pulled into the Blakefield High neighborhood, driving through the campus toward the wooded area behind the sports fields.

T-Bone's heart banged like a kettledrum in his oversized chest. He felt the seat's plastic upholstery underneath him. It stuck to his pants.

Juice pointed the shiny gun at him. For the first time, he realized how lucky he'd been before meeting Juice, how lucky he'd been as a fat boy with acne on his face, and how lucky he'd been with his Ma, his asshole dad, and two new brothers. He wished he'd never offered his aunt's place, that Onion had a full school day, and was at home playing DDR. He watched himself push open the car door and hold the front seat back so Lewis and Onion could climb out of the car. He watched the three of them huddled under the moonlight. T-Bone held Onion's trembling hand, and Lewis shielded the boy's smaller body with his own. He saw the full moon shining its dim dappled light on the treetops beyond the sports fields, and Juice, with the gun behind them, pointed it at their backs, marching them toward the fields.

MOTHER'S DRESSER

IN THE EVENING, after dinner, the grownups drink espresso laced with Sambuca or anisette. The aromas of licorice, of anise, and of coffee rose up like extended fingers and mingled with whiffs of garlic, tomato, and basil, remnants of the now finished dinner. The guest declines the espresso and instead wants the Sambuca as a shot "with the fly." Three coffee beans anchored at the bottom of the glass—the Holy Trinity of health, happiness, and prosperity. "Chin-chin," they say, toasting with demitasse cups and shot glasses. They lift them high above the table, giddy with relief that among them is a newly minted citizen of their new country. "Chin-chin," they toast the guest, a lawyer who helped them file the correct papers.

They stuff cannoli with sweetened ricotta cheese dotted with chocolate chips, and their rough, calloused hands pass them around on pure white, fine china with gold rims and hand-painted peonies. The women cut wide circles in the centers of cakes; one is a giant rum cake, shiny with thin, sugary icing, so that the slices, layered with vanilla and chocolate cream and flavored with real dark rum, will be even. The men cut and light cigars. Spoons and forks clink against the delicate, hand-painted peonies as they reprise the journey to the exalted summit of citizenship. Their words bounce back and forth between their old and new tongues. Words reverberate through the home like racing soap bubbles.

None of them—the extended family and the one honored guest—notice the two tiny girls, in their special, matching dresses and shiny, black, patent-leather shoes over lacy, white ankle socks, slip out of the kitchen. They run to the bedroom, where the mother's dresser sits against the wall between two lace window curtains.

The almost twins, in polka dots, bows, lace, and ribbons, hold hands as they gaze at two statues atop the dresser. The statue of the lady in a blue gown with extended arms beckons the girls with her serene smile. Under the blue gown, the lady's bare foot treads on a brown snake as she balances on a blue and brown half circle. Next to her, an even more intriguing boy with golden hair stands by himself. His child's head is topped with a large, golden crown. He wears an astonishing silk, white cape with a fur border. Longing to touch them, the awestruck girls stare at the lady and the boy, unaware that their own small faces and polka-dotted dresses reflect in the dresser's polished sheen.

In the kitchen, the grownups' laughter sounds far away and does not disturb the silence of the bedroom. Together, four small hands pull open the dresser's bottom drawer. Four small patent-leather shoes climb onto the open drawer's ridge, where they stand close enough to extend their short arms. They stretch their fingers toward the statues, trying to touch the beautiful lady and the crowned boy. They fail.

Each clutching the dresser's top edge to grip with one hand, they reach with the other for the lady and the boy. With their combined weight, both statues slide slowly and then quickly toward them. The dresser pitches forward, toppling over and hitting the floor with an explosion. Its drawers escape in all directions; silk, lace, pressed linen, and cotton fling wide. With a bang that rivals thunder, the dresser delivers the lady and the boy to the girls.

The lady flies into the arms of one girl, but she's too heavy. The girl watches the lady roll sideways over her patent leather shoes, surviving the fall with a chipped nose and scratched gown. The boy with the shiny crown rushes past the other girl, soaring like Icarus for a half a second before he plummets. He smashed into pieces on the hardwood floor. Only his silk and fur cape are still intact.

All the adults—the extended family members and the one guest— burst into the bedroom, talking at once with old and new world words. They survey the damage, snatch both girls, who are now crying from the wreckage, and thank God in two languages for a tragedy averted. It is a minor miracle that the fallen dresser did not crush the girls under its solid wooden weight. The grandmother sweeps the pieces of the shattered statue of the boy into a dustpan; the pieces clink as they tumble into the trash can. The girls know that after the guest leaves, they're in trouble, but they do not understand that they're the real jewels.

LAZARUS DIED TWICE

BEFORE, I DIDN'T think about things. I didn't gaze at the sky, wondering where exactly Elohim lived beyond the ceiling of the stars. I didn't study the earth beneath my feet to explore what lay below. I didn't consider the ants, the worms, the beetles, or the swarms beneath the limbs of trees—the bees, the wasps, and the flies—and the hordes of winged insects. I didn't consider the network of roots beneath the trees or what allowed the olive and palm trees, wheat and beans, fruit and vegetables, and figs and dates to spring up from the earth.

Now, of course, I've seen that Elohim's breath created all, down to the smallest rock and stone. I've seen how easy it was to notice every grain of sand at every beach in the world. And yes, I saw the entire world from far above, unimaginable distances even from the moon. I can talk about what happened now, but for a long time, I told no one about what happened to me in the four days before Yeshua called me back. Ironically, no one asked me what it felt like to be dead. They all wanted to know what it felt like to be resurrected, and I always told everyone that it felt like waking up from a deep sleep. In reality, it felt horrible as if my essence had been shrunken and forced back into this body that meant nothing to me the moment I left it. I looked down and, shocked at how ugly that body looked, almost failed to recognize myself.

Before falling ill, I supported my two sisters, Mary and Martha. I danced and drank wine with my friends. I gave my heart to loves, aching and longing for the men who dared to love me back in secret, lest we come to bad ends. I'd always kept that part of me hidden from everyone, including Martha and Mary, because I wanted to avoid being stoned to death or murdered in some bloody way. If only we had known then that the ends would have been pleasant.

Despite the desires of my heart considered sinful, I kept holy the Sabbath, recited the Shabbos prayers, and loved Elohim. I lived an acceptable, mundane life, although I admit I could have worked harder to find suitable matches for Mary and Martha. Separating them would have been difficult since they acted as if they were joined at the hip since our parents died. I prayed to Elohim, whispered the Kaddish—"*Hineni, hineni*"—and recited the Passover passages. After Yeshua called me back, every night and every day was different from the rest; everything changed. I wept more in this dusty world than I did in all the years before I died.

"Lazarus, would it crack your face to smile for once?" Martha said soon after my return, kissing my cheeks, squeezing my hands, and then squeezing me in a hug so fierce that I felt my eyes would pop out of my head.

"We are so happy you're breathing. And alive!" Mary said at that time, bringing me a plate of figs and dates. She worked hard at keeping an endless succession of foods for me to eat, saying, "We're so happy you're back." She touched my arms, hands, and face in utter disbelief that my chest continued to rise and fall with each breath. She affectionately pulled my hair and pinched my nose and my cheeks as if I was a child instead of a grown man.

Before I died, Mary and Martha treated me like a king. They showed no concern that no one would hire me after my return. After Yeshua called me back, potential employers acted too frightened to hire me, and my sisters treated me like a demigod, permitting me to do nothing helpful or useful. They accepted the endless supply of foods and gifts that people brought to pay homage to Yeshua's miracle that defined me. I wept uncontrollably, oppressed by the happiness radiating from their faces. With my face buried into my arms, I longed with my whole being to return to Elohim.

When I closed my eyes and imagined that perfect place beyond the stars, beyond the sun, beyond the moon, beyond the dark tunnel filled with warmth and love, and beyond the beautiful, bright Light of Love who welcomed me home, I felt Elohim's unconditional love wash over me again. In that other ethereal place, I learned what it seemed I had already known and somehow forgotten: that every grain of sand glowed with life, that every rock and stone vibrated with life, and that this dusty blue Earth quivered and trembled with Elohim's breath. In that perfect place, our parents and their parents welcomed me with love and joy that no words could describe. It seemed I only had just arrived before Elohim told me—with words that came into my being—that I had to return to Earth. I fought. I begged Elohim not to send me back. I refused. I argued that I'd only just arrived and didn't want to return. I couldn't bear being away from Elohim's presence and the deep, unconditional love that enveloped me while there.

"Lazarus, you still have work to do," Elohim said.

"No. I won't go back. You can't show me this, let me feel this love, and then try to send me back."

Elohim's sternness washed over me. "Only I can give this to you. You must go back." His thoughts rushed into my mind. He wasn't angry. He seemed amused, stating facts as a parent would do with a child running too close to the rim of a well.

I then found myself traveling down a tunnel; demons on the periphery tried to capture my soul. Aware of their torment and that they'd never know that they'd never capture any souls, I felt compassion for them. Back in my body, I awoke, confused, in the sepulcher and still wrapped in burial shrouds. My body felt too heavy and too constricting like sandals that were too tight.

Yeshua's bellowing voice called out to me. "Lazarus, come out."

Yeshua's voice sounded like rolling thunder. I obeyed. Still wrapped in burial strips and barefooted, I moved myself off the cold, stone slab, leaned against it to steady my wobbly legs and feet, and slowly ambled toward the front of the tomb, where someone had already removed the boulder that sealed it. I was stuck in this constricting, heavy body, this overweight lump of flesh and bone, and this heavy clay pot on unsteady legs. While holding onto the stone ledges around me, I emerged from that tomb, fell into Yeshua's warm arms, and wept. In despair.

"What work must I yet do?" I asked, whispering to Yeshua.

"You've just completed it, Lazarus," he whispered back.

"Send me back then," I implored. "I didn't want to return."

"I know," he said with tears in his eyes.

He held me in silence. Like Elohim, his thoughts came into my mind as I heard him thanking Abba and Ema for sending me back. It never occurred to me to refer to Elohim as Abba and Ema, but after being with that bright Light of Love, it made perfect sense. I glanced up at Yeshua and saw, in his eyes, Elohim's bright light peering back at me and unconditional love filling me as if I were an empty jar. It filled me to the point of tears. The shock of it astonished and comforted me, and from that point forward, I knew something about Yeshua that I couldn't articulate.

He laughed. "Welcome back, Lazarus, my dear friend," he said in a loud voice.

In a quieter voice, he said, "Abba and Ema will always be within you. Look within to find the light you seek."

The sickness that killed me remained a mystery. After Yeshua brought me back, it was cured. Every ailment in this heavy, constricting body was cured, and I felt as fresh as a young bull. The sickness that killed me began with stomach pains, loose bowels, and vomiting. Mary and Martha cared for me and embraced the impossible task of keeping me clean as my body expelled all its fluids from both ends. The stench disturbed even me, and I felt ashamed and humiliated that my sisters were forced to care for me so intimately, like a small baby. In desperation, they had called for healers, only to be vilified by neighbors accusing them of using magicians and witchcraft. But the healers' teas, oils, plant concoctions, and poultices failed me, and my sisters' desperation infected me too. Fearing a bad end, I so desperately wanted to recover. At that time, I wanted to live. When Mary and Martha finally sent for Yeshua, he couldn't come right away, and neither could any other rabbis.

Mary had battered me with questions I couldn't answer. "What did you eat? Where did you eat?"

"Maybe you drank dirty water?" Martha offered. "Maybe dropsy, but your belly isn't swollen. A reverse dropsy maybe? Why did God send this sickness?" she wailed, wringing her hands. "What will become of us?"

They both said, "*Mi Shebeirach*" for healing. Though instead of feeling stronger, I'd grown weaker and eventually allowed myself to slowly succumb to the deep sleep calling me. Once I succumbed to the sleep, a unique thing started happening. I popped out of my body and began floating in a white space, feeling light as a feather and free. I felt better and unafraid. Dying felt incredibly pleasant. The brightest thing one can imagine in the world would be a dark hole compared to the light and love I saw. The beautiful bright light and love astonished me. In this white space, where I possessed no real form despite still feeling my arms and legs, the burdens of everyday life fell away, and I understood that Elohim consisted of love. I felt connected to Martha and Mary but also to our parents in that other realm. In an instant, I became conscious of those around me—their feelings, their emotions— as I expanded far into the reality that overflowed the world we know into a different realm.

It was a beautiful reality with simplicity and joyfulness to it, knowing that we are all One. I was remembering what I had forgotten. I could see every molecule of existence. Elohim surrounded me, making His thoughts known to me without a voice. My essence felt huge, powerful, amazing, and available to me, an expanded knowing of all the universal information. It was connected to all existence and time.

"Expand out into the cosmos and know all things," Elohim said in my head.

I grew cocky and said, "I'm a god!"

Amused, Elohim showed me a vision of myself as a tiny baby, proud of me like a parent. His thoughts pushed me out into creation to be everywhere at once. As I experienced all these things, love—a pure love so strong—proved to be the only constant, and it overwhelmed me with happiness. Just as suddenly as I had expanded, visions of every detail of my life bombarded me, free of Elohim's judgement, and was presented simply as a fact. It was also shown to me how my every action afflicted everyone else around me. I judged myself for all the times I behaved in unloving and hurtful ways to other living beings. Yet Elohim let me know that as powerful and large as I had become, my small baby being could not begin to fathom His greatness, and it immediately humbled me. I never wanted to leave His presence in a perpetual unfolding of now.

Before I died, I worked as a carpenter in Bethany. That's how I first met Yeshua, a beautiful young man who was learning the trade from his father. A head for math, that one. He had no errors in any of his measurements, obviously gifted, but unlike the other apprentices, he dedicated himself to the Mishnah without caring about the earnings that such a talented carpenter would bring. Clearly an exceptional Mishnah student too, we all knew Yeshua wouldn't work as a carpenter.

When Yeshua and his father, Yusef, visited our home, Martha and Mary prepared us elaborate dinners. One of them could make a suitable wife for Yeshua, and I wondered about raising the issue with his father at some point, but neither Yeshua nor Yusef ever deviated from the topic of the scriptures. We understood then that Yeshua's Mishnah path would take him to Galilee to become a rabbi. We watched him grow into an exceptional rabbi, unconcerned about the coins that would fall into his coffers from any number of sources. He busied himself teaching and treating everyone with kindness, including the healers—considered magicians—and tax collectors—considered cheats—prostitutes, and others usually avoided by decent folks. Anyone who heard him teach followed him, yet he still found time for us, just like the old days, and shared a meal as our humble brother. Mary, Martha, and I offered him succor, an oasis of rest and relaxation from the maddening crowds he loved so dearly but which allowed him little respite.

After my resurrection, I was stuck in this hefty body, this constricting clay vessel, and plagued by sadness. I longed to return to the other side. I longed for Elohim, the unconditional love so freely given, and the different expanded reality, but I couldn't disappoint Yeshua or insult him by dispatching myself there on my own. Besides, Elohim had already warned me that what I experienced wasn't mine to take, only His to give. I felt stuck and angry. I hung around the house, doing nothing, saying nothing, and trying not to disappoint my sisters with my unhappiness and sorrow. It hurt to smile and show joy. The neighbors called me "Lazarus of the Four Days," as if "of the Four Days" were part of my name instead of the amount of time I spent with Elohim—which, truth be told, felt more like four seconds than four days. While there, I learned time doesn't exist the way we know it. Eternity doesn't feel like eternity. The other secret I held—although both Yeshua and the healer my sisters had called knew—was that I returned with special gifts.

I could hear other people's thoughts, the good and the ugly. I could hear plants and animals speak. When I slept, without working hard at it, I could escape this restrictive clay vessel and roam the earth, adventures that I recalled as vivid dreams. I forgave everyone and anyone for the largest and the least transgressions. My new persona frightened my sisters. Like Yeshua, I loved everyone, making no distinction between the tax collectors or the prostitutes or between the poor and the wealthy. The healer worked hard collecting leaves and flowers, drying them, sorting them, preparing them, and storing them to treat others. I sometimes helped her to feel useful. She'd used these leaves and poultices on Yeshua's swollen, cracked, and dry feet from all the traveling he did and used them to help me feel less sorrowful.

Months later, Yeshua rode into Jerusalem on a donkey. Everyone waved their palms, greeting him with "Hosannas" falling off their lips. The crowd and his followers said he rode into the city like a king, and I scoffed while hearing this. No king would ride a donkey. They'd be atop great horses like the Romans or camels like the desert tribes, not the lowly donkey. Knowing Yeshua, his feet pained him no doubt, and the donkey allowed him to advance at a better pace. Neighbors told me he went straight to the temple. Enraged by the money changers cheating the pilgrims who were buying animals for the Passover sacrifice, he threw everyone out of the shul, especially those selling special temple coins. He drove out both the merchants and their animals with whips made from some cords. It must have been quite a sight! After that, he preached there daily, angering the high chiefs and elders who challenged his teachings and failed each time. They grew jealous of the rising numbers of followers hanging on Yeshua's every word.

I visited him in Jerusalem on Passover in that upstairs room where he urged me to gather my things, leave my sisters, and flee Judea because our enemies were plotting to kill us. They wanted to kill him for upsetting the status quo and me because I was the living, breathing evidence of his works. He knew that because of the knowing that came back with me, I already knew about this terrible, murderous plot that was revealed to me in a vivid dream. But I welcomed it, thinking it would send me back to Elohim and the other reality sooner than later, but Yeshua disagreed.

"Lazarus, it's still not your time, my friend," he said, placing his hands on my shoulders.

"What about my sisters? My home?"

"Surely you already know what you must do."

"What about you?" I asked, knowing he'd be in that other realm soon.

"Not in your hands," he said, embracing me. "You must leave Judea."

In the middle of that night, the healer and I headed to the seaside, where fishermen kept their boats. Both of us fled Judea like Yeshi advised, I from the plot, and she from those accusing her of black magic. I knew she was no magician; the properties of the leaves and plants allowed her healing, and it came from Elohim, who breathed life into every grain of sand, every plant and animal. Mary and Martha had given us provisions: bread, olives, lamb left over from Passover, blankets, and clothes. Accustomed to traveling, the healer packed light and brought her bags filled with dried leaves and supplies with the intent on earning her keep through her skills. She brought nothing else. I also carried nothing but some gold coins from my savings to pay for our transit to Cyprus.

The healer—who knew her purpose, who understood her desire to heal others with her teas and poultices, who recognized how the leaves, seeds, and flowers helped us—fell asleep as soon as the boat went underway on that crisp Friday morning at sunrise. Baffled about my own purpose and wondering how I'd discover it, I perched on the deck under the sail and watched her sleep. The barrel of her chest rose and fell, inhaling and exhaling Elohim's breath. Unable to smile, I quietly wept, wondering how long I must wait before I return to Elohim.

On that brisk morning, I didn't know I'd still be waiting thirty years later. On that long-ago Friday morning when my leaking eyes fixed on the horizon as the sun rose, I knew that my dear friend and brother Yeshi would be where I wanted to go by late afternoon. Not to Cyprus. Instead, he expanded into the vast cosmos with Elohim, dancing joyfully on his homecoming and basking in the incredible feeling of unconditional love more powerful than anything experienced on this Earth.

ON BECOMING A PROFESSIONAL PET HAIRSTYLIST

YOU WAKE UP deep in a lousy marriage and decide you are going to get ahold of your life. You know, earn some bucks, gain some independence, and maybe take the first steps to escape into a better life. You look for a job you can do while your kids are in school. You need a closet full of decent-looking clothes to answer phones in most offices, so that eliminates an office job. Plus, you need to have a good phone voice and not the scratchy three-packs-a-day voice you have now. You need a job that gets you home when the kids are home and something you can keep on the down-low from your spouse, who doesn't want you to work at all so you can ask him for every single cent when you need to buy something—like tampons.

The choices are slim for someone with a GED, no good clothes, and no desire to sit in an office chained to a desk all day. The two options left are school bus driver or dog groomer. You only need a driver's license to drive a school bus, but you can't stand the noise, and you want to get away from the kids anyway. You need to have a license and be certified to be a dog groomer, but maybe you can learn the ropes at the vet up the street. See if you like it first. You know you aren't going to make any money finding out if it's your kind of gig, but at least you'd know if it's worth the effort. In the meantime, you fill in your life's history on the back of a 3x5 inch matchbox cover for a brochure from the Maryland School for Professional Dog Groomers just to see what it entails.

You start off small. Wearing nothing fancier than jeans with holes in the knees and a T-shirt that says, "If you can't run with the big dogs" on the front and says, "then stay on the porch" on the back, you walk right into the vet's office up the street and ask in your scratchy three-packs-a-day voice to volunteer a few hours in the morning on school days. You tell them you live nearby and just want to fill up a couple of hours. Since you are not getting paid, you are hired on the spot, and you can set your own hours.

* * *

Butterflies dance in your stomach the next morning, the morning you plan to start your career at the veterinary hospital as a volunteer. You make breakfast for your spouse: eggs over easy with buttered toast. You pack his and the children's lunches.

Your spouse comes downstairs while you prepare the children's breakfast. You place the plate with his eggs on the table. You set out his vitamins. You pour him a cup of tea because he doesn't drink coffee and set that next to the plate. You go back to mixing the pancake batter for the kids' breakfast when you notice your spouse putting his already hot cup of tea in the microwave.

"Why do you insist on giving me warm tea? I like my tea *hot*," you hear him say.

"Thought it *was* hot," you say while whisking the pancake batter.

You hear the microwave bell. You see him pull out the cup with steam rising from the top, and the tea inside is still bubbling from boiling in the microwave. You see him sit down at the table, attack his eggs, and inhale them without chewing. You turn around to retrieve a bottle of vanilla flavoring from the cabinet near the fridge just in time to see him extend his lips around the top of the teacup and suck in the tea, sounding like a cross between a straining vacuum cleaner and a sad teakettle whistle.

"Now *that* is a cup of hot tea," you hear him tell you in between sucks. The tone of his voice sounds superior as if you are not a fully developed human being.

You stare in disbelief. You see and hear him continuing to suck up his too-hot tea in small spurts. You are so annoyed; you grab a cigarette from an ashtray full of yesterday's butts and light up. Even your drags are quieter than his tea drinking, which has increasingly grated your nerves until it is now plucking the last one.

You hear him drop his fork with a loud clank.

"Must you?" you hear him say. You turn around to face him and notice him wearing the same constipated expression as Richard Nixon when he went on TV to resign. "That is just so damn disgusting. How do you expect me to eat my breakfast in peace when you are smoking in the kitchen? Like a fucking chimney. It's the first thing in the morning for Pete's sake. Can't you give it a rest?"

You take your cigarette out to the back porch, where you finish it off and immediately light up a second one. You don't finish the second one because it is too cold outside, and you still have the children's breakfast to finish. You flick it over the side of the porch fence and head back into the kitchen.

Once inside, you call the kids to hurry up, and you start pouring the pancake batter on the griddle.

"What do you plan to do today?" you hear him ask.

"Nothing," you say. You don't want him to know about your volunteer job. You know he will say it is a waste of time, especially since you are not getting paid.

"Nothing?"

"Things. I plan to do things around the house," you tell him.

You watch as he walks toward the cabinet where you just returned the flour and the sugar canisters. He opens the cabinet and pulls out the flour. He dumps it on the floor. He pulls out the sugar and dumps that too.

"What the hell do you think you're doing?" You feel tears well up in your eyes but fight them down. You see your hands shake; you are so angry.

"Thought I would give you a little something to keep your hands busy."

"I'm not cleaning that mess. You made it. You can clean it," you tell him as you bang the spatula down on the stove top.

You watch him grab his lunch box and walk out the door. "And another thing!" you hear him yell through the back door. "Don't throw cigarettes in the yard." You notice he is so overly concerned with the partially smoked cigarette you flicked into the yard that he doesn't even yell "goodbye" to the kids, who are dawdling upstairs.

You ignore the mess on the floor. You'll be damned if you are going to clean up that damned mess. Bastard, you think.

You finish cooking six pancakes, set them evenly on two plates, and call the kids down for breakfast. You are more determined than ever. After you drop the kids off at school, you're going to the animal hospital, and you'll stay as long as they need you. You see the kids finally tear into the kitchen and quickly fall into their pancakes. You pour each of them some juice and set it on the table by their plates.

"What's up with the mess on the floor?" you hear your daughter ask.

You see your son, who hasn't noticed it yet, stand up and peer over the table at it.

"Your father had a little accident is all," you hear yourself tell them.

You see your daughter roll her eyes. She is only ten years old, but you notice she has the eyes of an old soul. She is a mirror image of your mother. For a minute, you wonder if she knows her father is an ass. You wonder how much she heard while getting dressed. You don't utter a word against their father. You see your son shrug and stuff his mouth as if the pancakes are going to get up and run away from his dish.

"Daddy's clumsy," you hear him say through bites of pancake.

"Yep. He sure is very clumsy," you agree. "Eat slower, sweetie, and try not to talk with food in your mouth. You're gonna choke if you put too much in your mouth at once," you tell him as you pat his hair down. You are always amazed at how closely this child resembles his father, as if you spit him out as a perfect clone. You smile to yourself, knowing that although he might look like his father, he has your temperament. When they are finished, they put their dishes in the sink and rush off to get their book bags. You hug them both, squeeze them hard, and tell them you love them before you roll out the door to the car.

* * *

You need to get out of the house to keep your sanity. You don't need any money for extra clothes, and the vet tells you whatever time you can spare is okay by her. She looks skeptical. Her expression says you won't return. Your first task is to clean out the empty but once occupied kennels and line them with clean pages of newspaper. You wear rubber gloves and use a special solution in the water. It stinks. It smells like shit, and you laugh inwardly because you're cleaning dog and cat shit. The kennels where cats stayed are easier to clean than the kennels where the dogs stayed, which has shit inside. You wonder if it would have been easier to stay home and clean up the flour and sugar off the floor, but you press on.

Your second task is to take care of the kennels with animals in them. First, you need to move the cats to the cleaned kennels, one at a time. Before you move the cat, you fill the clean kennel with a litter pan and place bowls of food and water inside. Then you move the card with the animal's name from the front of the kennel and the animal to the new kennel at the same time so that no animals will get mixed up.

You notice that the vet keeps two large, clean trash cans filled with dry dog and cat food. When no one is looking, you sink your hands into the food the way a pirate would finger gold coins. You enjoy the way the dry food feels as it rolls through your fingers.

Once you finish cleaning the kennels and moving the animals, your next job is to sweep the entire floor of the hospital and then mop it with a special solution. After that, you are asked to help the vet techs telephone reminder calls to tomorrow's clients.

The morning's clients start rolling in around ten a.m. The animals and their owners fascinate you. Some of them seem to belong together. Others seem like colossal misfits like the white, hair ball Lhasa Apso belonging to the beefy, muscular guy who looks like a German Shepherd kind of guy. You wonder if he uses the fifteen-pound dog as a weight to exercise his biceps.

By the time you are ready to leave to pick up the kids from school, the veterinary hospital is ready for an afternoon break. The vet and your coworkers tease you about your first day as a volunteer, saying they hoped the kennel duty didn't scare you away. You tell them you will be back tomorrow.

At home, the flour and sugar mess sits on the floor. Somehow, you don't mind cleaning it up anymore. Seems easy after kennel duty. You hear the kids in the living room, jumping on the sofa while the TV blares out the music for cartoon rangers.

"Stop jumping on the sofa in there or no more TV!" you yell into the living room.

Your spouse comes home from work just as you put pasta in a pot of boiling water. You take a quick drag from your cigarette, throw it into the sink, and down the trash compactor. You run water to kill the smell. Your spouse reads the mail and doesn't acknowledge your presence. You notice he looks over at the floor where he dumped the flour and the sugar. Might as well hire a freaking maid, you think to yourself.

During dinner, you barely hear him mutter a muffled apology for the flour and the sugar mess.

You look at him as if he is not a fully developed human being and do not respond. Surprised, you notice he clears the table and loads the dishwasher, so you walk out of the kitchen. "As if," you say to yourself but loud enough for your spouse to hear. You realize you sound like your ten-year-old daughter and do not like it.

* * *

Despite the lack of pay, you gain all sorts of incredibly important skills, such as how to clean out soiled kennels and dog runs, how to mop up bathroom accidents of nervous animals in the waiting room, and how to deal with exceptionally sweet animals whose owners have terrible dispositions. You learn how to properly hold cats and dogs while the vet puts a thermometer in their butts, checks their ears for mites, opens their mouths, peers inside with a little light, and shines the light into their eyes.

You learn you prefer to be around animals more than people and discover that you actually have a knack for bathing, drying, and fluffing dogs. The vet has a professional pet hairstylist come by once a week, and on those days, you assist with the animals and pick up a few cutting techniques. Your heart swells with pride when you learn how to do a Rod Stewart poodle cut.

You go home and practice on your son and daughter, giving them each a Rod Stewart Poodle haircut. They are wild with excitement when they go to school the next day and tell their friends what you have told them: they now have hair like Rod Stewart and Joan Jett. When your spouse asks you about the kids' new dos, you say you read a magazine article and followed directions on how to do it. Just another way to save some dough. You notice his eyes widen just a tad. The corners of his mouth rise almost into a grin, and you see that he is pleased because he appreciates anything that saves some dough.

You learn how to react when animals with behavior problems come in to see the vet. For instance, the best way to deal with angry dogs baring their teeth is to run into the bathroom and lock the door until the animal is safely subdued by someone else and placed in a kennel, preferably not near one you need to work on. You ask to learn how to operate the autoclave machine, in which surgical instruments and plastic needle containers are sterilized. But you are a techno weenie and nearly burn down the veterinary hospital by forgetting to put water into it.

The vet doesn't mind too much as long as none of the animals are injured or perish from smoke inhalation. She says, "No harm done. You are a natural. You have a gift for working with animals." When she says this, you feel as if your heart just sailed over the moon. You find yourself smiling on your way home and feeling lighter than you have felt since the day you found out you passed your GED test. You find yourself joking with the kids when they come home from school.

Because the vet, who is younger than you with a light brown bob, sees your gift that even you don't see, she starts explaining some of the things she is doing. Pretty soon, you are working as a vet tech during your volunteer hours, doing things like cleaning mite dung out of infected ears with long-necked cotton-tipped sticks. One day a week, you still assist the dog groomer.

The vet likes having you around regularly and says she depends on your trustworthy nature, so she starts to pay you eight dollars an hour. You open a bank account under your name and sock away the cash. You don't tell your spouse about your new account.

It is a dog eat dog world after all, and so what's a little pizza when you are helping the vet stitch up a black toy poodle mistaken for an appetizer by his neighbor's yellow chow. You gain confidence in yourself, especially when repeat doggie customers are glad to see you, even though they are actually at the vet. The brochure for the Maryland Professional Dog Groomer School arrives, and you notice that it costs nearly three thousand five hundred dollars for the requisite two hundred and fifty hours of training. You also notice that dog groomers are called professional pet hairstylists. The brochure talks about the potential earnings of a professional pet hairstylist who own their own salon.

A whole week after the brochure arrives, you go to bed dreaming of having the words "professional pet hairstylist" behind your name. PPHS. Sounds as good as PhD. You dream about owning your own shop, Curls for Curs or Automatic Dogomatic. You laugh out loud when you are in bed at night, visualizing yourself as a professional pet hairstylist since you don't even own your own dog because your spouse thinks animals should not live in the house. "This is not a barn; this is a house," he says. "Animals live in a barn."

Your spouse wants to know what you are laughing at, and you say you remembered a joke from a long time ago. He is too interested in going to sleep to ask about the joke. You're glad. You don't mind the alley between your body and his, even though you miss the days when there wasn't even an inch to spare. You are amazed that seven inches can feel like miles.

You notice that you need to get certified and licensed unlike driving a school bus, being a receptionist, or being a cashier. Plus, you can be an artist. With pet hair. You can give a poodle a Rod Stewart do, and you can make the wimpiest German shepherd look macho. You can give an Afghan Hound a permanent wave. You smile at yourself in the bathroom mirror and realize that you are smiling. It doesn't feel weird anymore as if the act of smiling will make your face crack and break into a million pieces. Now you can smile, and it feels as if you have been doing it forever.

You watch yourself smile in the mirror, and your smile grows wider. You realize that your teeth, hidden for so long, could use a good cleaning to remove the cigarette stains. You see your own hair—dull, mousy brown, and limp—needs some highlights and a new cut, and your face could use a spot of color. You wonder when you started to look so drab and remember those long gone days when what you looked like mattered. You notice that your blue eyes look merry for a change. You throw your head back, laugh, and breathe deeply. You make an appointment at a nearby salon, and while you are there, you get a makeover and new makeup. You pay for it out of your own money from your secret bank account. You make an appointment with the dentist for a cleaning. It occurred to you one day, while watching the vet do what she called an oral prophylaxis on a cat, that it had been ages since your own teeth have been cleaned.

During slow moments at work, the vet, the other coworkers—a woman named Molly and a man named Pete—and you discuss health, recipes, and cooking. You are amazed to learn that they are vegetarians who refuse to eat "our animal friends," and you find yourself bringing vegetable sandwiches to work and skipping the twice a day Snickers.

They tease you about your three-packs-a day cigarette habit, and you find yourself sucking on Dum Dums lollipops when you need a smoke. The vet says it is not good to smoke around children and animals because of secondhand smoke, so you tell yourself you are going to quit. Your coworkers notice you're sucking on lollipops without you mentioning your goal, and they start bringing small bags of Dum Dums so you never run out. You notice that they also start sucking on Dum Dums lollipops, and soon it is a joke that everyone who works there is a Dum Dums mouth.

* * *

You start walking to and from the vet's, slowly first and then briskly. After a while, you notice your clothes are getting larger, and your body is getting smaller. You ask your spouse for forty dollars for an electric steamer, so he won't get suspicious when it shows up in the house. Using recipes the vet and Molly have shared with you, you start serving steamed vegetables and fish for dinner. You shrug when your spouse says the food tastes bland; he prefers the usual hamburgers and French fries. You hand him the pepper shaker and half a lemon and suggest he try some of it. He looks at you for a long time as if he is seeing you for the first time.

"What's up with you?" he asks. "Something's different; I can't put my finger on it, but something has changed." You notice he is smiling at you. You notice—*the* smile—his rare, glorious smile where he is showing his upper teeth, and his cheeks push up the crinkles around his eyes. You remember that smile, the one you fell in love with.

Without being able to help it, you smile back at him.

"Nothing has changed," you hear yourself say. For a quick second, when you look at him, you see him as he was fifteen years ago when you first met. His hair was fuller, and his stomach was smaller. You remember the excitement of your first date when he took you to the Twin Kiss for a hot fudge sundae after the first Star Wars movie. The whipped cream from the sundae decorated his mustache. You remember the day he asked you to marry him and how happy you were. It was early May. You remember he was wearing that glorious smile before kissing you under the blossoming pear tree outside the restaurant. He slipped an opal cross around your neck and explained it was a tradition for the men in his family to give their future wives crosses. A ring came later on Mother's Day. You found it in a champagne glass at another dinner with both your parents and his parents there. He slipped it on your finger and handed you a fresh, eggshell-colored gardenia.

You finger the cross now with its smooth opals, still around your neck fifteen years later.

"The kids are both in school now, and I want to do something besides housework all day," you tell him as you place a piece of salmon marinated with olive oil and vinegar in the steamer.

"Like what?" he asks you as he peers into the fridge.

"Like become a dog groomer," you tell him.

You see him shut the fridge without taking anything from it and laugh as if he was amused by a child.

"*Dog* groomer? Absolutely not. You will stink like dogs and bring that smell home. Not to mention the hair. You will drag all that filthy dog hair home, and it will get all over everything," you hear him say.

"I can help pay some of the bills," you offer weakly.

"No wife of mine needs to work to pay bills," you hear him say. As he says this, he runs his thumbs along the inside of his waistband and belt, straightening out his pants. You expect him to say, "I'm a man. I can take care of my family."

Instead, he says, "That's my job. Going to work is my job. Your job is the house and the kids. Plus, I can't imagine dog groomers make that much anyway. It'll be a waste of time."

You can hear the finality in his voice as if he has just announced the cure for cancer. You see him tuck his rare smile away. Usually, you would accept his response without argument or complaint, but now something inside you revolts.

"You know," you hear yourself say, "that may have worked for your parents and my parents, but I am here to tell you that it ain't working for me."

You see the kids' faces peer into the kitchen from the living room where the TV is blaring. You have never spoken to him that way at all, and you can tell they are curious.

"Well, get over it," you hear him say.

"*Beep*! Wrong answer," you tell him. You continue to prepare dinner by washing and placing a bunch of asparagus in the steamer around the marinated fish. "This is a new day," you say calmly. You flash him your own rarely used smile, and you start shaking salt, pepper, and garlic powder onto the fish. You think about how you are going to finally throw away the drawer full of used plastic bags that he makes you save.

You remember how he slowly turned into a workaholic and a penny-pinching miser, saving stupid stuff like plastic food storage bags that he wants you to use repeatedly until they fall apart and Styrofoam plates that meats are wrapped up in. You started smoking to calm your nerves. Then he started calculating the cost of your cigarettes and posting the amount on a large, yellow Post-it Note on the fridge. The calculations always went up, and he started writing the cost in red ink. You see last week's cost was seventy-five dollars. Thanks to the Dum Dums, this week's note has plummeted to a whopping twenty dollars.

Meanwhile, you die inside by degrees. You begin to hate yourself and him. You stop talking to each other. It becomes easier to stay home all the time to avoid questions of where exactly you went, when exactly you were coming home, and how much exactly you spent. You let him do the grocery shopping because it is easier to have him pay than justify why certain things show up on the list. You have watched him every year as his belly grows larger and his hair thins. You realize you don't even know him anymore. Or worse yet, you can't even remember what made you like him in the first place.

You grab four plates from the cupboard, and instead of placing them on the table, you hand them to him. You also hand him the flatware. You expect him to protest, but he sets the plates down on the table and folds the napkins before placing the forks and knives on them. You notice he placed them in the wrong places, but you don't say anything to correct him. You call the children in for dinner.

"Where'd you get the fish?" he asks you.

You shrug. You want to lie and tell him your neighbor brought it over because she didn't want it anymore, so he doesn't ask you how much it cost. "Does it matter?" you ask instead. "I thought it would be a nice change of pace. I don't want you to have a heart attack from eating all that fried food and red meat," you add.

"Something *is* different about you," you hear him say.

The children giggle at the table and say they like the fish better than the same old burgers all the time. They make fishy faces by sucking in their cheeks and protruding their lips. You decide to continue eating, but you see that he stares at you for a long second and shakes his head. He takes the pepper and shakes it on his fish. He squeezes the lemon. He tastes and nods his head.

"Thank you for not smoking. I've noticed that you are trying to quit by sucking on Dum Dums lollipops. The house smells better too," you hear him say.

You just shrug.

"When the catnip tea begins to stir…" you hear him say. He offers a little smile before eating the steamed fish and veggies. He doesn't say another word. You notice he is not inhaling his food without chewing it, as he usually does, but is exercising good manners instead.

"Into each life a little rain…" you say and offer your own little smile.

* * *

You talk to the vet about your dream of becoming a professional pet hairstylist. You show her the brochure and tell her, "Someday."

"There's no time like the present," she says. "You're a good worker."

She makes a deal with you. She will pay for the school if you promise to be the staff animal groomer five days a week at a competitive pay rate. She has extra space where you can set up your own business within the hospital, so you can take nonpatient animals as well. She says that a dog groomer business can attract more clients for her and vice versa. She says you have a gift and her having a professional pet hairstylist on the premises every day is better than having one come to visit only once a week.

You say yes without thinking about how you are going to explain the time away from home to your spouse; you don't care what he thinks anymore. The vet gives you papers to sign, saying that you will remain affiliated with her hospital for the same number of months you need to stay in school. You tell your spouse you are staying at school in the mornings and do not correct him when he says the kids' teachers should be happy to have an extra adult in the room.

While at professional pet hairstylist school, you sign up for morning classes in animal psychology so you can understand better ways of handling angry dogs baring their teeth. Other courses you must take include how to express anal glands, bathing, brushing, fluff drying, nail manicuring, coat conditioning, anatomy and conformation, pattern placement, styling, straight scissoring, and thinning shears techniques. You must also take canine geriatrics, safety and first aid, sanitation, and breeding. It takes seven months to get through all the courses, plus the extra ones on marketing your own business.

While you are in school, you realize you cannot keep up with the housework anymore. Your spouse starts to notice little things like dust balls collecting under the sofa and a layer of dust on the dining room table. You tell him you have been spending more time at school, but you don't say it is professional pet hairstylist school. You hear him complain about the dusty furniture. Irritated, you fish a dust cloth out from under the sink and a can of orange oil and throw them at him. The cloth hits his chest and sails down to his feet. You see him catch the plastic bottle; the orange color of the fluid contrasted with the redness of his face. But your stomach is not twisted into a knot anymore because you don't care.

"Since when are you allergic to furniture polish? If it bothers you so much, you deal with it. I can live with dusty furniture."

"Are you going through menopause?" you hear him ask. "Is that the reason you are acting crazy lately?"

You surprise yourself by laughing out loud. "*Right!*" you say and walk out of the room.

From across the seven-inch divide in the bed, you apologize to your spouse's back for throwing the dust cloth and orange oil at him. You hear him mumble, "Don't worry about it." You see him move an inch and then two inches closer to you. You don't budge but wonder if you should move closer too.

You tell the vet that your house is suffering from neglect. She gives you another brochure—green and navy blue with The Cleaning Genie Solution, Inc. and a number on it. You call the number and arrange a thorough cleaning. They send a four-man crew, and you tell them they have to be done before your husband gets home from work. When they are done, the house looks better than when you first moved in: the windows shine inside and out, the kitchen tile and cabinets have been degreased, the bathroom looks like a hotel bathroom with fixtures so shiny you can see yourself in the faucet, the walls no longer feature fingerprints and black marks, and the rugs look new. The best part is that it cost the same amount as your three-packs-a-day cigarette habit; it's seventy-five dollars for the first cleaning, and fifty dollars for an every other week job. Amazed by the transformation, you pay for it out of your secret bank account and arrange for the Genie crew to come by every other week.

* * *

When your spouse comes home, you notice him looking around, and then you hear him whistle the same way he does when he watches something he considers outrageous on the news. "You worked your butt off today," he says.

You just smile. You notice he looks like a shaggy sheepdog. You remember the lessons about dealing with difficult doggie clients, and you start applying them to your spouse. When he is acting tense and angry, you use soothing and calm words. When he is acting as if he is the alpha male, you challenge him and let him know you are in charge. You are surprised that the lessons work so well on him. Today, he is a friendly, good pup, so you treat him with kindness and care. You see him start to get playful, so you play back.

"House looks damn good," he says as he hugs you from behind while you are chopping eggplants. He kisses the back of your neck. It has been ages since he's done that, you think. You put the knife down, wipe your hands on a nearby dish towel, turn around, and return the kiss on his lips.

"Whoa," you hear him say before you muffle the word with your lips. You feel him kiss you back. It feels new again like the time under the pear tree. You hear the kids whispering in the living room. You can hear your daughter telling your son to look at mommy and daddy kissing in the kitchen.

For dinner, you serve Molly's recipe for curried eggplant over brown rice and baked chicken, and your spouse tells you it tastes as good as at a restaurant. You still can taste his kiss over the spicy eggplant. He clears the table and coaxes the children into doing the dishes, telling them that you worked hard all day cleaning the house. You smile and slink into the living room, where you put your feet up in the La-Z-Boy chair and appreciate the Cleaning Genie view. Later, you discover that he has moved closer in bed. There are only three inches between your bodies now. This time, you decide to close the gap.

You don't care about your lousy marriage anymore because maybe it's not so bad. You changed your mind and changed your life. You stop thinking about your marriage since all your thoughts now focus on doggie hairstyles, doggie behavior, and doggie customers. You are so focused on the doggie world that you are shocked beyond words when your spouse presents you with a pair of gold earrings for no reason one night after he returns from work.

You hold the box open. Your mouth is unable to move.

"They're not for anything. They are just because…" you hear him say as if he could read your mind. "Actually, I am glad that you quit smoking…" you hear him say.

* * *

The day you earn your certificate and license, you start turning the extra space at the vet's into the Pet Palace. You and the vet discuss the marketing techniques you learned at the school. You both make an appointment with a professional graphic designer, and the three of you decide on the logo, the business cards, and the brochures with a coupon for five dollars off the first visit to the Pet Palace. You suggest to the vet that the Pet Palace and the veterinary hospital can send out a joint newsletter to existing and potential customers. You also suggest that the newsletter contain another coupon for five dollars off a doggie bath after a physical at the hospital. The vet is impressed with those two marketing ideas you learned at school. "I love those ideas with a capital L," she says and adds them to the professional graphic designer's list of things to do.

You spend your days arranging the Pet Palace into an attractive groomer's area. You order products. You and the vet meet with an accountant to go over bookkeeping chores. Before you realize it, you find yourself singing with the CD player the vet gives you for the Pet Palace grooming room.

The day before the Pet Palace is open for business, you pick up the kids from school and show them. They help you line up dog shampoo and tick and flea dips on the waiting room shelves. They help you arrange dog brushes, leashes, and doggie and kitty perfume on the shelves hung on the waiting room walls.

You have a ton of things to do before the big day, and you know you are not going to make it home before your husband returns from work. So, you call home and leave a message on the answering machine for him not to worry, that you and the kids are running late, and to go ahead and eat dinner. There are leftovers in the fridge that he can make in the microwave.

Your daughter draws a picture of a yellow cat with a red mouth and nose that you tack up on the waiting room wall. "This is awesome!" you tell her. Your son is inspired to draw a picture of a brown dog with black spots that you hang up next to the cat picture. "This is awesome too. A matching set. Momma will frame them and hang them together just above the cash register," you tell them.

They do their homework in the waiting room chairs, while you put the last minute touches on the brand new Pet Palace. The vet has sent you a bouquet of flowers with a card that reads "Congratulations!" You put it on the new counter in the waiting room. You buy the kids pizza for dinner from your stashed away bank account.

Just once, you allow yourself to think about not being home in time to cook a fresh dinner. The fear that used to grip your stomach at the thought of your spouse growling at you for tiny mistakes is gone.

"He'll get over it," you tell the vet, but you anticipate that things will be tense when you and the kids finally get home well past dinner.

The kids are ecstatic about the Pet Palace. They chatter all the way home, saying this is better than not being able to have pets at home because they will be able to see all kinds of dogs and maybe pet them for a short time at the Pet Palace. The three of you sing along with Bruce Springsteen on the radio, chanting, "Born in the USA."

You can now say you are a PPHS, and that is what you plan to tell your husband when you pull into the driveway. You gather your things out of the car and help the kids with their book bags and coats.

You put your key in the lock of the front door, but before you can turn it, the door swings open. Wild-eyed and pale-faced, your spouse screams at you.

"Where the hell have you been, woman? I have been worried sick about you and the kids! What are you doing running late? With all the crazy animals running around out there, anything could have happened! And now it is so late! What are we going to do for dinner at this hour?"

"In case you forgot, I do have a name. It's Sarah. And you can relax already. As you can see, we're here, safe and sound. Don't worry about dinner. The kids and I already ate. You obviously haven't listened to the answering machine, or you would have eaten dinner already. I told you there are loads of leftovers in the fridge and to go ahead and eat without us."

"Where've you been? I have a right to know where you've been!" your spouse says as he paces up and down the small steps in front of you. A part of you wants to apologize, but you don't because there is nothing to apologize for. You told him you would be late and being late is not a crime. You know apologizing for nothing will open up a stupid can of worms like assuming that you have to ask permission to pee, and you are not going back there again. You know he is going to have to get used to this new you.

"Well, funny you should ask," you say while remaining calm. You even smile because nothing can dampen your spirits. "I have been at work. Yes. At work. I have a job now, thank you very much."

Your spouse stares at you in disbelief. You can see by his expression that he doesn't know what to say.

The kids jump up and down like jumping beans. They both start talking about dog shampoos, colorful leashes, cats and dogs in kennels, and flea and tick medicines at the same time. They describe the Pet Palace.

"I am now a PPHS, and I am a part owner of the soon to be opened Pet Palace," you explain.

Your spouse doesn't say anything at first, but he stares at you as if you are a complete stranger. "And I am the President of the United States!" you hear him bellow like a Great Dane afraid of a little bath water.

You can tell he doesn't believe you. But you feel strong, light, and remade. You smile and laugh out loud. You see that he desperately wants to look like a fierce, snarling like a German Shepherd, but right now, he looks like a standard poodle with a temper tantrum. You offer to demonstrate your newfound skills and think that the old shaggy sheepdog look would be perfect. You continue to smile, and he continues to snarl.

"Hey kids. Let's go show Daddy Pet Palace."

You see them jumping up and down. You can hear them saying, "Pet Palace!"

You place your hand on his shoulder, gripping it. You look directly into his eyes and say, "Calm down, Andy. Come with me."

You step behind him and, with your hand on his shoulder, gently guide him out the door and into the car. The kids follow along and scamper into the backseat.

"Where're we going?" you hear him ask.

"You'll see," you say as you step on the gas and drive past the old Twin Kiss to the Pet Palace. You roll into the parking lot of the veterinary hospital and park in front of the Pet Palace entrance.

You get out of the car and walk around to the passenger side. You put your hands on his shoulder again and lead him to the door. The kids dash out and join you at the front door. Using your key, you open the door and lead him into the waiting room, where you and the kids had arranged all the shelves hours before. You punch your code into the alarm to disarm it.

"Where'd you get that key?" he asks.

"It's mine," you tell him.

You see him notice the kids' drawings and the products they arranged on the shelves. The kids run straight back to the kennel area where the animals are. Dogs have started barking. You direct his attention to your certificate on the wall. You show him the bulletin board with pictures of your favorite doggie clients surrounded by blue and gold lettering that says "Sarah's Friends" in all caps. You show him Polaroid pictures of the vet who owns the hospital and some of your coworkers. Everyone is holding either a cat or a dog except Molly, who is holding a ferret.

"This is where I work, Andy. I am a professional pet hairstylist now."

You see him look around. He studies the certificate. You follow him as he examines the products on the shelves. He fingers the bottles, and you half fear that he will empty them on the floor. You see the curiosity on his face as he tours the kennel area, and you can see him shrink away slightly from the barking dogs. Surprised, you see him extend his finger to touch the nose of the little white beagle asleep in the topmost kennel. And you realize that all these years, you never knew that he is afraid of dogs.

"He's in for a bath and a dip," you tell him as he tentatively rubs his finger across the dog's nose.

You see him remove the lids of the garbage cans filled with dog and cat food and take a deep sniff. You see him dip his hands into the food, running his fingers through the pellets and lifting a handful to his nose.

"Smells good enough to eat," you tell him.

He smiles only slightly at the joke.

You see the kids lead him around the salon, showing off their handiwork from earlier.

They both jabber at the same time, and all the dogs are now barking loudly because they are running in and out of the kennel area. He stares at the bulletin board and sees your smiling face peering out from the dozen Polaroid snapshots; in each one, you are posed with a different dog.

You follow him back out to the waiting room, where he plops into a chair and looks around as if he has been dropped onto an alien planet. For a moment, no one speaks. You expect him to tell you he's leaving or you're leaving. You both look at each other, waiting to see who will cross the divide this time.

"I am not sure I can be married to a PPHS," he says. "I don't know. Doggie hair and doggie breath. Ticks and fleas. I don't know about this at all. But I'll try." He stands up, puts his hands inside his pockets, and takes another look around. Then you see it; he breaks out with that rare smile.

"Peter! Becky! Come quick!" he calls the kids into the waiting room.

Eyes dancing with excitement and faces smiling, they appear in the doorway. "Oh Daddy! Those dogs and cats are just so cute," your daughter says.

"Yep, they are. And it looks like your ma is going to help them stay that way. Come on, kids. And come on Sarah, you PPHS you. Let's stop by Twin Kiss on the way home and get us some hot fudge sundaes."

The kids run out to the car and scramble in. You remember to set the alarm and lock up.

You admire the sign in the window that says, "Sarah Winkler, proprietor" and can't believe it's your name right there in black and white.

"Tomorrow is the grand opening, and I already got a full day scheduled," you tell him.

He grabs your hand, and you both walk to the car together, looking like a couple of teens.

FINGERPRINTS ON THE FLOWERS

THE MAN TALKING on television says that King is dead, a bullet shot straight into his neck when he was standing outside on a hotel balcony in Tennessee. Later, the television man says a white man shot the black King. The next morning, on a Friday, we go to a school attended by both black and white students, a school where parents worry about tuition payments. On Saturday, we cannot play outside in front of our houses, and the adults shush us because the television man says riots broke out downtown. On Monday, the nuns call saying that school is closed because of the riots. We laugh and giggle, happy about the unexpected vacation days from school. We wonder if we will break out in riots too since we already suffered from breakouts of chicken pox, measles, and mumps, which also brought us unexpected days off from school.

On Tuesday, the television man says the mayor who grew up in our neighborhood had prohibited anyone from going outside after dark, and everyone had to be inside by a certain time to avoid riots, but the adults went outside anyway. When it is dark, we peek through the curtains of our second-story windows to see soldiers riding around in green jeeps with guns pointed at our houses. Adults return later with riot stories, saying it's contained at the borders of our neighborhood by immigrant men standing on roofs with their own guns, unafraid to shoot.

In our side by side backyards, we cousins travel to and from our grandmother's house next door, where Auntie, Uncle, and our cousins live with Grandmother. We jump the little fence—a cinder block structure with red, white, and green tiles laid across the top that joins the second-story porches—and play with our cousins in both of our yards, flying back and forth over the fence, like a murder of crows, after a dodge ball we toss up and down.

In both yards, fig trees rise up from the gardens that outline the yards, two in my grandmother's yard and one in ours. Their limbs reach out of the dirt like thin gray fingers, heavy with rounded three-pronged leaves, with purple and white figs that our mothers turn into Christmas cookies, and with our bodies trying to swing from the lowest branches until our grandmother screams, "Eh, Stronzino! Mafalda! Iolanda! Get out of my tree!" in a different language.

Mint leaves overcome large sections of the gardens. The fragrance of the almond-shaped leaves mix with the aroma of large leaf basil grown from seeds Grandmother brought from Italy. Oregano and rosemary grow in abundance next to Grandmother's violets and irises in her yard. They fight for the sun in our garden under the shade of a seven sisters rose bush, with its miraculous seven buds blooming on each stem.

Attracted to the overripe figs and Grandfather's purple grape arbor, starlings, pigeons, giant horseflies, and gnats invade both yards. Orange and black butterflies alight on Grandmother's pink and white fan-shaped zinnias before floating over the fence to Mother's red buddleia. Its fragrance overpowers the mint and basil like the queen of the garden.

The sun rolls across the smoky sky like a bloodshot eyeball, flashing a startling luminosity in the city's streets, over row homes, and in parking lots and church buildings. It paints streaks of red as it arcs above us. The blackened embers from burning stores rain down on us, leaving fingerprints on the flowers, figs, and herbs. The stench of the afternoon's melting rubber and charred wood mingles with the fragrance of mint, basil, and buddleia, while sirens wail all day and deep into the night, harmonizing with the deep-rumbling jeeps carrying soldiers with guns. They are ready to aim, ready to fire as they echo along the streets, and the *thwap-thwap-thwap* of police helicopters, sky bound eggbeaters, reverberate the sounds of war above us and drown out the shrieks of children's games and wails of adults' despair.

It's Easter week, but we skip all those endless church services. Our parents and grandparents shush us, telling us to stay out of the way and to be quiet. We follow Grandpop into the basement, where he works on his sewing machine. He turns on the radio and twists the dial until he hears the Orioles. He cheers when they win. "*Tree to wun!*" he shouts up the stairs to Grandmother. Giant, solid chocolate bunnies greet us when we wake up on Sunday. Large baskets filled with chocolates eggs and beach toys occupy the entire dining room table, and we sneak handfuls of chocolate treats from the baskets, hiding them in our pockets for when we go to school on Monday. The helicopters and jeeps with soldiers and guns continue patrolling in the now quiet city.

A week later, the nuns say, "Good morning" when we return to school. They line us up by height two by two, shortest to tallest. Their faces do not smile beneath stiff white muslin wimples starched to stand tall on their own for days. The nuns herd us into classrooms, Black and white students, like usual, quaking about undone homework and unmemorized lessons. Our school shoes squeeze and trap our feet. Our freshly cleaned and pressed uniforms itch and pinch. We wave our arms and yell, "Present!" during roll call, except for Clio, a Black boy with deep dimples, root beer colored eyes, and a smile that stretches as wide and long. He is absent because the riots killed his daddy.

WITH GRATITUDE

For their inspiration and insights, for being group of peers with incomparable talent and generosity, I'd like to thank members of my writers group who have read multiple versions of these stories over time: Susan Mauddi Darraj, Carla du Pree, Lalita Noronha, Patricia Schultheis, Jen Michalski, Andria Nacina Cole, Lauren Francis Sharman, Barbara Westwood Diehl, Todd Whaley and James Magruder.

For proofreading, website management, and much more, I'd like to thank everyone at Writer's Relief, whose deadlines to submit new work motivated me to keep writing. I'm grateful to everyone at The Writer's Studio in New York City, and to Tom Jenks, editor of Narrative Magazine (online) for teaching me to improve my writing craft, a lifelong endeavor; thank you to all the writing instructors and teachers along the way for emphasizing the power of sentences and the art of storytelling.

For keeping me young at heart and aligned with all that's fresh and new, I'd like to thank my family: kiddos—Richard, Erin and Antoinette—and their families. I thank my parents without whom I never would have been able to write anything more than a grocery list.

Finally, for taking a chance on me, for editorial guidance, exceptional talents, precision, and patience for getting this book made at the height of unrest in Portland, Oregon, and through the challenges of a pandemic, I'd like to thank the Unsolicited Press team: Esme, Summer, A.Cervantes; Robin Ann Lee, and Kathryn Gerhardt.

ABOUT THE AUTHOR

Rosalia Scalia's fiction has appeared or is forthcoming in *The Oklahoma Review, North Atlantic Review, Notre Dame Review, The Portland Review,* and *Quercus Review,* among many others. She holds an MA in writing from Johns Hopkins University and is a Maryland State Arts Council Independent Artist's Award recipient. She won the Editor's Select award from *Willow Review* and her short story in *Pebble Lake* was nominated for a Pushcart Prize. She lives in Baltimore with her family.

ABOUT THE PRESS

Unsolicited Press was founded in 2012 and is based in Portland, Oregon. The small press publishes fiction, poetry, and creative nonfiction written by award-winning and emerging authors. Some of its authors include John W. Bateman, Anne Leigh Parrish, Adrian Ernesto Cepeda, and Raki Kopernik.

Learn more at www.unsolicitedpress.com

CPSIA information can be obtained
at www.ICGtesting.com
Printed in the USA
FSHW020713021121
85796FS